All Mortal Greatness

THE SESSIONS UNIVERSITY SERIES

BOOK III

ALL MORTAL GREATNESS

A NOVEL

NELSON COVER

Epigraph Books
Rhinebeck, New York

Hardcover ISBN 978-1-960090-70-6
Paperback ISBN 978-1-960090-68-3
eBook ISBN 978-1-960090-69-0

Contact the publisher for Library of Congress control number

Book and cover design by Colin Rolfe

Epigraph Books
22 East Market Street, Suite 304
Rhinebeck, New York 12572
(845) 876-4861
monkfishpublishing.com

To Gretchen Chell Cover and Nelson Cover III

"Be sure of this, O young ambition,
all mortal greatness is but disease."

HERMAN MELVILLE, *Moby Dick*

I

A New Foundation

WAITING PATIENTLY HAS never been my strong suit. But I had no choice.

Tuesday the first week of October at the new headquarters of The Mark Berger Foundation in the penthouse of the downtown Intercontinental Hotel I watched the elevator doors from my office chair, waiting for the multi-billionaire himself, my good friend and now my new boss, to appear.

Well, hell, he was often late.

My cell phone rang, as it always seemed to at an irritatingly inconvenient moment.

I looked at its screen, intending not to answer.

Alicia. A delightful tall, blond, wonder woman, law degree from Georgetown, former private detective with The Blaylock Agency, Aikido black belt, newly appointed executive director of her family's foundation in Chicago. Over the last two years of turmoil a major ally. What she saw in me was a bit of a mystery, but there certainly was a mutual attraction.

I answered the call.

We talked for a moment, catching up, before she asked, "Thomas, so when are you planning a trip to the Windy City?"

"I wish I knew. Things are a bit crazy right now. Mark's due here at any moment. Let me give you a call later."

"I'm sure you'll find a way."

"Thanks."

"Be inventive."

"Good thought. I'll work on it."

"Well, take care. I'll be thinking of you."

"Same," I heard myself say distractedly.

We ended our call.

Tempted to check email, I glanced at my computer only to have the screen saver distract my attention with its picture of our family on a brief vacation last summer in Washington, DC, by all appearances a happy scene.

Beneath the surface I saw different realities.

Janet, my brown eyed, honey blond winsome wife, a psychologist, was increasingly adrift and rudderless, beset with the growing absence of children, a career where real accomplishments were difficult to measure and a husband distracted by his work and other relationships, like Alicia.

Our eldest perfect child, Sarah, who had been admitted to our local Sessions University's Center for Gifted and Talented Youth last year, had skipped her last two years of high school and was a rapidly maturing young lady, a sweetheart, whom we feared with quiet anxiety would soon be finding reasons to leave our home.

And then there was our son, Tommie, an Asperger's Syndrome obsessive who had in earlier years been monomaniacally immersed in everything related to fire engines to the point where I had constructed a Tommie Town village in our basement for him to act out various fire engine scenarios.

Because of his very difficult, underachieving school experience we had become convinced that he was limited as well as an open threat to burn down our house.

Then last year his interest had shifted as he entered a new school to a mania for computers and technology. Tommie Town suddenly became a thing of the past. The Schossler Academy, which specialized in children like Tommie, had through testing discovered that he was in fact not just gifted but a budding genius, nevertheless one whose sense of others and right or wrong was highly undeveloped. So, now Tommie took weekly counseling and technology classes at the Center for Gifted and Talented Youth with Sarah and I providing his transportation. What would be the next surprise from Tommie?

And who was that good-looking fellow in the picture who seemed so happy, caught up in a moment of family togetherness? I had to admit I was not fully sure. Meet Thomas Simpson the chameleon, a walking mirror who presented himself to everyone as their own reflection. Unerringly politic, possessed of a perceptive ability to size up others and complex situations and know how best to proceed, he stood in personal introspective quicksand, relatively clueless about himself and his relationships, perceiving his limitations and troubled by them, continually wrestling with their meaning and impact, complicated by the unfortunate fact that certain women found him attractive and pursued him. Risk at every turn.

I found myself shaking my head.

Rotating my chair, I raised the footrest, assumed my already well practiced hands-behind-my-head position for contemplation and stared out the floor to ceiling window of my office at the remarkable view of the city spread out before me in the bright afternoon sun, trailing away to the harbor on a crystal-clear early October afternoon.

Two years ago, I had been a nobody associate professor of communications at Sessions, dealing only with my courses to ever more ill-prepared and clueless undergraduates, enjoying pleasant exchanges with my department head and hanging out at the university club with Zoltan.

Zoltan was my best friend, a leading cancer researcher at Sessions' downtown medical center, a second-generation Hungarian, a giant whose on-the-edge-of-going-berserk countenance scared off anyone who did not know him and belied his true character.

Zoltan, while being utterly and often hilariously politically incorrect, was a rapscallion truth teller, a passionate lover of opera, a virtual uncle to our children and as faithful and loyal a friend as one could find.

Our misadventures had begun in those early days quite by accident when we ran into alumnus, billionaire board member, Mark Berger at a university reception. We had taken an immediate liking to one another and again by circumstance we had been brought together, working as a team to remedy an international espionage scheme that threatened the university, our lives and our family's lives.

Noises from behind the elevator doors made me lower the footrest, turn around and walk quickly out to the reception area.

The doors opened and ...

Zoltan emerged, dressed as usual in his triple extra-large worn-out herringbone sport coat, black mock turtleneck and black Levi's, his unshaven, mustached, Hungarian ax-murderer face scowling, curls of black-grey hair springing from his head as if electroshocked.

"What the hell ... What the hell are *you* doing here?"

"Why I spend good money for dirty, infected cab ride to university when I can ride there with you in nice Bimmer? We anyway both got to meet with Nowhere Man and Cheapskate Doctor God," he told me, referring to the acting president of Sessions University, provost Don Powers, and to Dr. Harold Ramis, the director of the medical center, Zoltan's direct superior. "So, I walk over here from medical center. Beautiful day."

"Walked here? That's like twenty blocks."

"Twenty-four. Yes, I am fit. They should have this city walking in Olympics. I probably enter."

"They'd have to have a special 'disreputable' category for you."

"Ah, yes, I like that. As long as medal real gold, I be faster disreputable walker ever was."

"Don't you have enough to do already trying to cure cancer?"

"Yes, that true. But one must take in beautiful day when they here."

"Yeah. Okay. But how did you know to be here now?"

"You tell me yesterday at university club. Berger coming here at 2."

"Oh ... yeah. Now I remember." I also remembered that sometime in the last week or two I had emailed Zoltan the foundation's address, phone number and the elevator code. Stupid.

Well, three would be a crowd. I had hoped to have Mark to myself for a bit. But I could roll with Zoltan as our sidekick. Seemed like old times even.

"Thomas," Zoltan said, looking around, noticing the penthouse for the first time, "These your offices for the foundation? You in fucking paradise now! Office here for me?"

"Of course not."

"But I can come visit, yes?"

"Yeah, I guess so."

"Bring Kristina or dates even?" he added, looking toward the living quarters. Kristina was Zoltan's significant other, an attractive Belarusian scholar working at Sessions' School of Foreign Service in Washington, DC.

"Hell no. You're joking, right?"

"Of course," he told me dubiously. I made a mental note to change the elevator code.

Noises came from behind the elevator doors again.

As we turned, the doors opened and Mark stepped out looking, not surprisingly, like a derelict, inappropriately dressed in his boat clothes, having just arrived and spent the evening aboard his ocean-going trimaran sailboat, *Calypso Too*, fresh from the Med with a stopover in Miami.

Berger's large, frizzy 1800's style orange sideburns were connected to an equally frizzy orange mustache and he had also not shaved for several days. He was wearing worn out blue jeans with varnish and paint stains on them. They were held up on his skinny hips by a figure eight knotted sun-bleached red sail tie. A faded blue knit shirt with *Calypso Too* stenciled on its left pocket graced his torso and scuffed and dirty deck shoes covered his bare feet. An ocean-going Jewish Yosemite Sam vagrant.

For a moment it amazed me that he had made it past hotel security. Then it occurred to me that, of course, given that he owned the place there had been some advanced warning to the hotel's personnel.

As we shook hands all around, Berger checked out the penthouse, moving his eyebrows up and down over his ovular, center hinged, thick lensed black framed glasses while running his other hand over his close-cut greying black hair that faded into his sideburns.

"Fuckin' A, my friend, fahrst class," he told me with his Boston accent, "Thanks to some genius who figured out this would be a perfect setting for the foundation."

"That some genius being?..." I responded with a smile.

Berger smirked. Housing our offices at the Intercontinental had numerous tax and financial advantages that his teams of rodent attorneys could use to his advantage.

He held my hand for a lingering moment then placed his other hand on the back of mine, signaling brotherhood. "An' you, Thomas, bein' here as the fahrst executive director of the foundation, is just right too."

"Thanks," I told him, hearing in my voice a mix of sincere enthusiasm and affection.

"I think I maybe going to cry," Zoltan remarked, straight-faced.

II

Transformation

WHILE BERGER'S LAWYERS had applied for and structured the legal existence of the foundation, it had fallen to me over the past summer to bring it to life.

Although established in Boston, Massachusetts at the headquarters of The Mark Berger Companies, Berger had decided that it should have its primary offices near the university given that much of its philanthropy would be directed to it and the medical center. As well, its location was an inducement for me to accept the executive director position. That and doubling my compensation had its intended effect, although the truth was, given the political situation at Sessions, I might have damn well volunteered.

Over the summer, while working from home, I had made the foundation an operational reality with the exception that a board had yet to be named and an executive assistant had yet to be hired. Topics to be covered during Berger's visit.

At the same time I worked on the foundation, a team from Berger's hotel renovation division had built out the penthouse with little input from me. Our offices were off to the left side. A residential area was off to the right, better to take advantage of the sweeping views of the city and harbor. The renovation had turned out looking and feeling hotel-like, top quality, impersonal and sterile. I had shrugged. As long as Mark was happy, so was I.

"So," Berger said, turning to Zoltan, "On a more serious note, how things going with your work?"

"Ah," Zoltan clasped his hands together, his expression suddenly changing, focusing. In a nanosecond he became a bona fide research scientist. "As we discuss last spring, although we had found very successful cancer treatment, we also discover there no such thing as universal vaccine. It fantasy. What we now know is using each patient genotype, we need to develop a vaccine for each patient. Much greater challenge. Need worldwide database of successful treatments of different genotypes to help with artificial intelligence design success for each patient. So, we now formed and have access to an international consortium of research institutions, building this database. You come to lab. I show you several patients with cancer. Show you how we work to design treatments, find right one, maybe even cure cancer for that person."

"God damn, Zoltan," Berger remarked, his eyes widened, "That's remarkable. Good man. I'll look forward that."

He turned to me. "So, show me around."

I showed them Mark's personal suite which had been fully furnished, decorated and outfitted as well as stocked with clothes and some personal items. Interestingly, an ancient Menorah had been placed on his low fake rosewood bureau.

"It was my parents'," Berger told us when he saw us looking at it, "Bless their souls. True believahs. It reminds me of them, our tenement in Bahston, the gahrment district, all the shit we went through. Never enough money. Wish they could see me now."

"Yeah. They'd be proud, I'm sure."

Berger gave me a perfunctory nod and an indulgent half-smile, acknowledging his cynical appreciation that my lot in life was to always say the politically correct thing.

I showed them the guest suite, the kitchen and laundry closet, the bar and lounge area with its big screen TV, then the spacious conference room and his office, large and grand, behind his desk a giant giclee taken from a photo of *Calypso Too* underway in a stiff breeze, wild ocean all around her, her port pontoon lifted, Berger at the helm, his face an heroic visage of concentration, his mustache askew in the wind, crew members working at key stations.

"Hey, when I'm not around," he told me, "Which will be most of the time, should anybody be calling on us, feel free to use this office. Okay?"

"Sure."

My office was to the side of his and modest, all of which met with his approval.

"Okay, so let me change," he told us. "Agenda for this afternoon, Thomas and I call on interim president Powers and congratulate him on his service, see what he has to tell us about the search for a new president, which knowing him will be as little as possible. What he doesn't know is that the unctuous managing partner of the search firm, who is also a fellow alum, already gave me an update given that I'm incoming board chair. I'm sure he's hoping that my companies might give him other business. Fill you in latah on the search. Anyway, with Powers we go over how Sessions and the foundation can work with one another this year and beyond.

"Once we've finished with Powers, that butthead, Ramis, and Zoltan will join us. We'll have an overview conversation with them about the foundation's interests and priorities for the potential funding of Zoltan's cancer research over the next year. Then you and I and Zoltan go to the university club for what will be a much-needed drink. Right?"

"You got it."

I went into my office again, while Zoltan went to the kitchen to commune with the espresso machine. After a few minutes of sitting at my desk resisting again the urge to check emails, I rotated in my chair and raised the footrest, gazed out the window, my mind drifting as I took in the scenery. As always, my thoughts turned for the thousandth time to how I had been lucky enough to escape the tumult and danger of the last two years at Sessions and had landed this new position as executive director of Mark's foundation.

Bryan Q. Fitz-Hugh was our superstar president two years ago when the provost at that time, Samuel Kravitz, purportedly committed suicide. Fitz-Hugh had arrived at Sessions three years before, with his Hollywood good looks, and was a breath of transformational fresh air.

His first priority was to make Sessions as much as possible a green campus.

With his charismatic charm and forceful brilliance, he had built a consensus for this project among the board, the faculty, staff and even the student government. The team effort results had been dramatic for their success and for morale. He had been the key force in raising the funds for energy conservation, especially for outdated facilities, solar power, the greening of the campus, recycling and the conversion of university vehicles and equipment to electric.

With the momentum from the success of his green initiatives, he then turned his attention to making Sessions The Global University, working to change the focus of its admissions and curriculum and to establish Sessions University centers abroad, beginning with Beijing, with plans for Brussels.

By then however, behind the scenes, those of us in the know began to worry about his behavior, particularly his philandering with, it seemed, anyone and everyone, including a board member's wife. He had chosen not to live with his wife and two children in the President's Mansion on campus, wanting to avoid them being in a fishbowl, which was understandable. But then with his travel across the country and in other countries he frequently strayed. As well, he began to short cut his consensus building in favor of simply powering his way forward. A feeling of uneasiness began to build in some quarters.

The death of provost Kravitz was the first indication that something was very wrong at the university. Kravitz deeply disliked Fitz-Hugh for having been chosen president over him. He also saw Fitz-Hugh's ambition for Sessions to become The Global University as an attack on the humanities. No fool, he could see clearly that the funding for the university's new Beijing Center did not add up. He secured a vote from the Faculty Senate for an independent audit of Session's finances.

Days later he was found in his car in the park bordering the university having apparently shot himself to death. His death not only shocked the university community and devastated his family but in truth was so out of character that questions were raised about whether it was in fact a suicide.

During this time Fitz-Hugh became unhappy with the university's existing public relations, marketing and communications. He persuaded the university's capital campaign consultant, Frank Lusby, to begin bringing me and Zoltan as my closest friend into influential meetings to test our capabilities.

We had passed tests that we sensed might be occurring but were unsure of their purpose. Then Fitz-Hugh had appointed me director of university and campaign communications. Along with this promotion came a rather awkward, but extremely intense dalliance with his assistant, Ursula Mueller. Ursula was a Germanic life force, her beautiful face complementing a physique that was impossible to ignore, charming when she wanted something and that something happened to be me.

Zoltan, as my ally, was awarded with his own cancer research lab.

The intent of our promotions and my seduction we now realized was to have us as key loyalists at the university and the medical center.

It took a good part of the year before Lusby, who had become our friend, revealed to me fiscal malfeasance of substantial proportions where secret, anonymous, international wire transfer gifts were being made to Sessions' capital campaign to help Fitz-Hugh build the international centers in exchange for U.S spies being placed by U.S. Special Operations in those centers, a situation brought on by his overweening ambition and his amorous relationship with the Secretary of State, Greta Hauser, with whom he had attended the

Harvard Kennedy School. And who was running the Special Ops project? I learned much later, Ursula.

The end result of the discovery of the illicit wire transfers, negotiated in secret with the department of State by the board chair at that time, Fritz Johnson, a big as life Texas attorney, was a slick coverup where Fitz-Hugh made an exit to become the undersecretary of state for the European Union, an appointment of such repute and importance that it seemed a natural progression to his career. He left Sessions as an apparent hero, while Berger brought in a team of auditors to clean up the books and return the clandestine contributions, which he then made up through his own gift of $25 million.

With the exception of myself, Lusby, Zoltan, Berger and Johnson, no one knew that Fitz-Hugh's promotion had been negotiated with the State Department in exchange for silence about the failed U.S. Special Ops mission.

The stakes for our continuing silence were high. We discovered during the following year that our professional and personal communications were being monitored. Lusby, who suffered from alcoholism, went on a bender where he cluelessly blabbed about the covert mission to agents who had been following him. Like Kravitz, he was executed the next evening. For Lusby, his assassin made it look like an overdose of alcohol mixed with fentanyl. This was enough to cause Fritz Johnson to resign.

That Mark agreed to replace him demonstrated his loyalty to Sessions, but his acceptance did not come without some distrust of the next administration. A distrust that was validated all too well when Fitz-Hugh's ally, the Dean of the School of Continuing Studies, a very talented administrator but also an obese common operator, Dr. Jack Wentz, was selected to succeed him, the board of trustees in their ignorance deciding it was best to appoint someone who could seamlessly succeed the outgoing president.

"Hey, let's go," Berger said from the doorway.

Zoltan on hearing him walked out of the kitchen to join us and with one look stopped abruptly, "Good God," he exclaimed, "Look at you. You now what ... ? Like *Commendatore* in *Don Giovanni*, a superior being."

It was true. Berger had transformed himself. Now a shaven, idiosyncratic looking but commanding figure stood there in a white-on-white dress shirt, blue pin stripe, three-piece suit, black dress shoes and, nice touch, wearing a Sessions University tie.

"Hah!" Berger acknowledged Zoltan's compliment, then turning to me asked, "How we gettin' there?"

"How about we take my car? I can drop you back off at *Calypso* after the club."

"Sure, no problem."

I grabbed my briefcase and shoved my iPad and portfolio into it.

My 2005 BMW M3 E46 mystic blue metallic convertible with its tan leather interior was parked in its assigned place in the hotel basement.

"Holy shit, a little Bimmer," Berger said enthusiastically when he saw the car. "Six speed manual?"

"Yeah."

There was a pause while I watched Berger admire the car, looking at it with both appreciation and, yes, desire.

"You look like you wouldn't mind driving it up the university with the top down."

"You'd let me do that?"

This is hilarious, I thought. *He could buy ten of these anytime he wanted.*

"Uh, sure."

"Thomas, you didn't say that with total conviction."

"Uh, well ... uh ... Go ahead," I said, handing him the keys.

III

They Love Us!

"HEY WATCH THE redline!"

Berger shifted in time, barely, into third, as we rocketed top down, foot to the floor toward the university. Crisp air filled with the dusky, leaf burning scents of fall was flowing around us, a canopy of yellow and russet leaves overhead, Berger's mustache fluttering randomly in the air rushing through the car, revealing a large smile.

I had given Zoltan the front passenger seat and scrunched up in the back seat behind Mark. Comically, Zoltan's head was six inches higher than the windshield, his coils of hair blowing around like miniature Slinkys. His breadth took up two-thirds of the front seat, barely allowing Berger room to drive.

Berger shifted gears and drove the car with more verve and expertise than I would have expected from someone who was driven everywhere, heel and toe downshifting to synchronize the flywheel and clutch revs as we moved through traffic.

"Hey," Zoltan said, turning to him, "How come you drive so good?"

"Ah, driving school at Sebring a couple years ago. Had a blast."

As we raced toward the university, I began feeling some anxious curiosity about how we would be received at our upcoming meeting with my former employer, especially now that I was with Mark.

For years the university had been after him for an endowment gift of hundreds of millions of dollars that could help transform Sessions into a far more accomplished and significant enterprise, especially compared to its competitors, the endgame of any university being a superior academic reputation via an enhanced faculty and admissions. The figure of a billion dollars had even been tossed about, and the facts were that such a gift was within his capability.

The problem was that as Mark learned the intricacies of the board of trustees' and university's culture, its investment policies, bylaws and leadership, he had come to three conclusions:

First, the performance of its investment companies guaranteed much lower yearly returns than the hedge fund he owned, a hedge fund that had focused initially on currency trading where he had made his first fortune, then expanded into commodities and equities trading, then finally into the outright purchase of part or all of different companies specializing in commercial real estate, energy, insurance, transportation, technology and beyond.

Second, that the endowment, which board bylaws limited to an annual five percent expenditure of its corpus, guaranteed a lack of immediate impact of any new funds committed to it. As an entrepreneur, he would much rather invest cash directly to support traditional programs in the humanities that needed strengthening or new programs in business, the sciences or technology that might achieve sustainable, even income-producing results.

Third, regrettably, as demonstrated by unethical manipulations over the last two years, different administrations' fiscal management over time could not be trusted and therefore their honoring the terms of one's gift was questionable.

Beyond Fitz-Hugh's chicanery, newly inaugurated President Wentz had then followed up with his own.

Last year, Zoltan's lab had made significant advances in cancer immunology research. Pharmaceutical companies had jumped all over his success, wanting to partner with the medical center to take such a discovery from lab bench to bedside.

Because of the companies' eagerness, former president Wentz

with the medical center's Dr. Ramis had cleverly approached them on behalf of the ongoing capital campaign, asking for their consideration of a long-term gift to medical center endowment. Officially these requests were unrelated to Zoltan's work but were sought as an expression of confidence in the medical center's overall work. Of course, the less than subtle implication was that such an endowment gift might help any particular pharmaceutical firm receive preferential selection to help partner with future discoveries. This was perhaps not the most ethical tactic but it was nevertheless not so unusual; could be thought to be clever or slippery depending upon the viewer.

But then came the clincher. Wentz and Ramis also extolled the services of an attorney specializing in structuring corporate/university partnerships as someone who wink, wink might also help assist the companies developing a productive, read preferential, relationship with Sessions.

Their attorney had been hired by several of the companies for very healthy retainers that were split between her, Wentz and Ramis via transfer to the Cayman Islands.

Lusby, shortly before his untimely death, became suspicious and had discovered their scheme through tapping into Wentz's private line. Again, Mark Berger was called to the rescue. He had engineered Wentz's termination, given that he was the instigator, put Ramis on notice and put their lawyer out of business, returning the retainers, noting to the companies that her services were not endorsed by the university.

The ultimate outcome of these untrustworthy transgressions was that last spring Mark had held a meeting with Zoltan and me to tell us that Wentz had resigned for health reasons, another cover-up only partially true fabrication. Then he had blown us away by revealing his intent to establish The Mark Berger Foundation with an initial contribution of $650 million. He wanted me as its executive director and Zoltan's cancer research to receive a major annual operating grant.

Needless to say, the university administration and the board of trustees, upon learning of the creation of the foundation and realizing they had missed out on a potential $650 million gift were just a bit miffed. But what could they do? Berger was now incoming chair of the board. Much of the foundation's giving would be oriented to Sessions. Plus, in the interim, and I found myself grinning at this, given the run up in Mark's hedge fund investments over the summer, the $650 million was now worth over $750 million.

As we drove over a hill on University Boulevard toward the main gate entrance, the east side of the Sessions campus came into view and it looked splendid, a lovely Georgian vision of the upper quadrangle anchored by the white steepled McFarland Hall. As a former Sessions professor and director of university and campaign communications, its beauty both tugged at my heartstrings and brought home my many experiences with its always ongoing academic and administrative turmoil.

Woven into the fabric of all that had transpired during the Wentz administration was a relationship that was developing between me and Alicia McDonald.

We had first met when, as a private detective working for The Blaylock Agency, hired by the Kravitz family to independently investigate the provost's death, she interviewed me. Something clicked, although neither of us would acknowledge it at the time.

Then she had appeared out of nowhere at our neighborhood's village center as I fetched a pizza, quizzing me about what I actually knew about goings-on at Sessions and I had warned her off her inquiry, told her the smartest thing she could do would be to quit not only the investigation, but also Blaylock. Mark, Zoltan and I were under the watch of Special Ops at that point, the same team that had killed Kravitz, and legitimately feared for our lives. I did not want her endangering herself.

Later she shocked me by following my advice, asked whether she might take me to lunch as thanks for my helping her with her career decision. There it became apparent as we began to know one another that there was a mutual attraction. She became an ally and a friend, while all the time we both sensed that there was some kind of undefined future ahead of us.

Then there was our final conversation in Washington, DC where in the strangest turn of events I told her I was being hired to run Mark's foundation and she informed me that she was moving to Chicago to do the same for her father and their newly formed family foundation, circumstances that left us hoping that our new professional roles might allow us to stay connected. I was both relieved that my life with our family would in no way be compromised, at least in the short term and in my heart of hearts also disappointed.

Berger turned into the university's main drive, and we worked our way around until we came to the back of the campus and the administration building, a dated faux Georgian bastardization that Berger and everyone else on campus wanted to see replaced.

We pulled into the Chairman of the Board parking space at the side of the building and as we raised the top and windows, Berger told me, "I haven't had this much fun since Sebring. Thanks!"

As we exited the car, a campus cop came half-running up to us, his equipment flopping around him, "Hey, you can't park there, that's for the ... Oh, Mr. Berger! I'm so sorry, sir. I didn't recognize you for a moment there. I'll go get a parking pass for you and place it on the windshield."

"Ah, no problem my friend. Sorry we couldn't give some advanced notice about the car we're using. You'll remember my colleague, Dr. Simpson, who used to work here, and Dr. Vastag from the medical center. Thomas nicely offered to let me drive his beautiful car up here from downtown."

"Well, it certainly is the day for it, sir. Good to see you, Dr. Simpson, Dr. Vastag. It's been a while."

"Yeah, it has. Good to see you too." I remembered this fellow. On the several occasions this same guard had become threatened by Zoltan's appearance when he had met me at the front atrium of the administration building. I pictured him then, hand on his nightstick, other hand ready to call for backup.

As we walked into the building, Berger turned to me and whispered, "They love us!"

"Yeah, today."

"Hah!"

IV

Nowhere Man

W E PASSED THROUGH the double security doors leaving the luscious fall air outside and entered the overheated dust and urethane-smelling atrium. The building's failing HVAC system's noxious atmosphere brought back all the memories of my tenure there, living in that stale air, listening to the buzz of fluorescent lights and feeling as if I was incarcerated in a polluted prison.

The elevator to the third floor opened to a maze of hallways leading to the president's office, where we discovered that its gatekeeper, the redoubtable Ms. Bemis, was gone. Sitting at her desk was an officious looking young man, unshaven, casually dressed, his persona shrieking Graduate Student.

"Can I help you?" he asked cluelessly. Clearly our presence was interrupting his hourly wage séance. I thought, *You dumb ass. Look at your calendar.*

"What happened to Ms. Bemis?" I asked in response as Zoltan squeezed into one of the rock-hard university seal chairs and pulled out his cell phone to check in on his lab, while Berger stood to the side patiently.

"She'll be here in a minute."

"Okay," I acknowledged. I thought, *Wow, this is interesting.* For many years as the baleful protector of the president, Ms. Bemis, had terrified and intimidated me and anyone else who dared trespass on her turf. Then last year, thanks to Alicia, I had discovered the other side of her personality, and she became Jo Ann, a major ally in our effort to discover and deal with Wentz and Ramis's scheme.

Now she was being replaced or was she just training this twit?

The hallway door opened, and Ms. Bemis walked in dressed in a voluminous red pants suit, red spangled gloss plastic earrings hanging in hexagon pieces from her pendulous ear lobes in stark contrast to her shaved head. With her inch long bright red nails, red spike heels, red silk blouse and ornate gold cross hanging from her neck on a red lanyard she had done herself proud today.

"Gentlemen," she acknowledged in her most distant, hostile and off-putting manner, a slight nod of her head. "Dr. Simpson, could I see you in the hallway, please?"

Even though I now knew her game, I felt as if I was about to be reprimanded by a school principal for some major cherry-bomb-in-the-toilet travesty.

"Sure."

We stepped out in the hallway.

Instantly the professional patois vanished. "You know what that muthafucker did to me this mornin', Thomas?" she told me in a hissing whisper, as she glanced down the hallway in each direction.

"I'm guessing it isn't good."

"After all these years! And with what I know. I could ruin this place! But that's not my style."

Tears formed in her heavily mascara-ed eyes. I found a Kleenex in my suit pocket and gave it to her.

"That fuckin' bas-turd FIRED me!"

"No problem," I told her.

"Ain't you that been fired!"

"Cause you jus' got hired. New job."

"What?" she froze mid-dab and stared at me.

"To be my right hand – we'll figure out a title – at The Mark Berger Foundation."

"Oh, honey. You kiddin' me?"

"Hell, no."

"Oh, I accept, I accept, I accept your kind offer! Of course, you're going to pay me way more than I'm worth. Right?"

"Oh, I'm sure."

"Jus' pulling your leg. I don't care. Oh, honey. We can have so much fun!"

"Christ, let's hope. We better get back in there."

"Who cares about there," she laughed.

"Mark cares."

"Yeah, good point."

Instantaneously she again became the baleful goddess of uncaring rejection. She turned and very formally opened the door for me.

Berger, seeing us, said to the graduate student, "Please let Dr. Powers know that Mr. Berger and Drs. Simpson and Vastag are here to see him."

Moments later the door to the president's office opened and we were greeted by tall, immaculately dressed, blow-dried black haired Don Powers, the former interim provost, now interim president, a self-confident cipher if there ever was one.

"Good afternoon, gentlemen. Please come in."

The office was as I had remembered it, beautiful mahogany walls hung with large oil paintings of the campus, surrounding a superb vista of the lower quadrangle, students on the walkways under elm trees, the floor graced by a massive intricate Persian rug that covered up a deteriorating parquet and underlayment, to the left a large mahogany conference table and chairs, display shelves along the wall.

In Fitz-Hugh's time the shelves had been filled with awards and grip and grin photos of him with the rich and famous. During Wentz's brief tenure they had been empty and now more of the same, quietly shouting Vacancy.

Whereas intellectually I understood the utility of Powers, a man who absorbed all but committed to nothing, in my heart of hearts I had always disliked his sage, detached superiority. Some people succeed in life by simple inertia and Powers was one of them, a former mathematician, a harmless place card with no agenda. Where his self-assured arrogance came from was anybody's guess but it was effectively off-putting. Why challenge feckless authority?

"What happened to Ms. Bemis?" I asked as we sat across from one another at the conference table, wanting to see what his response would be.

"Ah, yes. Preferred to have my own assistant. Had to let Ms. Bemis go, unfortunately. We're hiring now should you know anyone. Using temps from HR. Not ideal."

"Too bad," I said perfunctorily, "I'll give it some thought."

We took our seats and I let Berger take over our meeting. My role was to listen and take notes.

He and Powers exchanged congratulations on his appointment as board chair and Powers as interim president and then Mark began, "Hey, so Don, I take it you've reviewed the email Thomas sent about two weeks ago outlining the programmatic interests of the foundation?"

"Yes, Mark," Powers said, placing the fingertips of his hands together. "A first-year demonstration grant of $1 million funding undergraduate merit scholarships with a before and after review of the attainment of the anonymous students funded, and at end of the academic year testimonials from them of how the scholarship enabled and impacted them."

"Right. Very good."

"Then another grant for $250,000 funding student innovation awards with the students submitting competitive applications, an awards committee of faculty chosen from my recommendations and with your approval making the final judgements for awards."

"Excellent."

"Finally, continuing conversations with Thomas and you on structuring a perhaps five-year $5 million gift to strengthen the humanities.

"Yeah, despite my advanced degrees, I remember fondly my

days here at Sessions, clueless undergraduate that I was. But I really did enjoy and remember well my professors and my courses in the humanities, and frankly I feel they gave me a very good foundation for understanding civilization and the world at large. Comes in handy at times.

"So, on another subject, how is the search going?"

"Some progress being made from what I've been told by the search firm's partner. Credentials of the top dozen candidates should be forwarded to the search committee shortly. Of course, I'll send you a copy. That's about as much as I know."

"Ok, Don. Thanks." Berger said with a small side glance and hint of a smirk to me.

"Now let's get onto the big stuff. Whatyasay we work together with my new foundation to build a new university administration building? Get rid of this piece of crap we're sittin' in. You think the board would go for that?"

Powers nodded noncommittally. "Mark, that's a remarkably generous initiative on your part. I've had preliminary discussions with the board's building and grounds committee as well as with key alums and friends in the construction industry. Further I've talked with several other university presidents who've recently constructed new administration buildings."

"Yeah? So, what's the consensus?"

"Very interesting. First, universal agreement that this current building has lived its useful life and is already a bit of a maintenance dinosaur."

"Plus, it's butt ugly. Friggin' 70's modernist architecture. Never should have been built. A travesty. Blight on the campus."

Powers smiled. "You'll get no argument with me there. It's also been suggested, since any administration is these days viewed negatively by students, a majority of faculty and by many graduates, that we combine any new structure with programs and departments where there is an equal need for new space and which would have great appeal to our local, regional and even national communities."

"Yeah, and say increase the price fifty to a hundred percent, but let's go with that for now. What's your thought?"

"Our visual arts programs and other departments are in great need of expansion and emphasis, link into everything from art history to architecture to engineering. Such a combination of cross disciplinary space devoted to arts, architecture, and engineering with the upper levels of the building housing administration might very well be a beneficial partnership."

Berger thought for a moment, "Yeah, you know, I like that idea. Might even be a nice naming opportunity in honah of my parents."

Powers continued, "In terms of construction, we have plenty of space to the south and even the east parking lot for the new building and can operate this existing structure during its construction, then raze this upon its completion."

"I like the concept," Berger told him. "I'm figurin' this is a $25 to $35 million project as an administration building. Add your cross disciplinary concept and figure that'll double the amount just to be on the safe side. Usual costs for architectural and site design are 9 to 15 percent. Highway robbery but we'll leave it at that."

"Yes."

"So, Don, here's the deal. The foundation will consider pledging up to an initial $3 million toward the site planning and preliminary architectural concept designs.

"For now, let's keep the foundation's possible involvement under wraps. Let's let the building and grounds committee and the board form independent assessments, get their straight shot yea or nay input on this proposed project without them thinking I'm Santi Claws. If they support the idea, then we can solicit and have a formal presentation of proposals, select a winnah. And only then do we want to bring up the foundation's participation. Of course, I'll recuse my firms from any involvement with this project. Total conflict of interest. But you should feel free to consult them about recommendations for possible bids. They know who's who and what's what."

"Do I take it," Powers asked, "that your foundation, after a site plan is fully developed and approved, would consider a lead naming gift for the building?"

Berger smiled at him, "Yep. The foundation or me personally."

"Excellent."

Mark turned to me, "Hey, I have an idea. I wonder whether we might get the Kravitz family to join us in funding for the humanities space for this new building in honor and memory of our former provost."

Powers looked a bit puzzled.

"You know Jeremiah Blank and Sons, the clothing store with outlets all over the country and a big online presence?" I asked him.

"Of course. Have even shopped there occasionally."

"So have I. Well, Joan Kravitz is Jeremiah Blank's only child. There were no sons. He sold the company way back and then turned those proceeds into a commercial real estate fortune. Upon his death, Joan had all the real estate liquidated. As a result, she, though you'd never think it given her grandmotherly, PhD persona, is a very wealthy widow."

"Ah ..."

Berger turned to Powers. "Thomas could bring this up with Joan and Natalie, their concert pianist daughter. They seem to favor him, which doesn't hurt."

I could feel my stomach seize.

For some reason, the Kravitz family had decided that I was a close colleague of the former provost. Nothing could have been further from the truth. Fact was, he held me in complete contempt. But through my own inability to say no, plus the favorable impression left on them from Sarah's babysitting Natalie's children, I had been sucked into a relationship with them after Kravitz's death. In fact, I had visited with them last Christmas season, the reward for which was getting cold-cocked by their hot head son, Sammie, who was convinced his father had been murdered and saw me for what I was, part of a cover-up. Fortunately, his mother and sister were not of the same opinion and had been horrified by Sammie's aggression.

Then it was time for Ramis, who arrived with a very different mien and attitude than last year. Last year he had been the Master Clinician, a confident figure. With his close-cut grey hair and titanium rimmed glasses, he had exuded scientific rigor. Now, despite his expensive glen plaid suit, white button-down dress shirt and bright red bow tie, he was a chastened entity.

As he shook hands with us, there was a momentary diminishing of light as Zoltan stepped through the doorway, the graduate assistant holding the door looking at him with stark amazement and the dawning of fear.

He reached out to shake hands with Powers and I watched as Powers' manicured hand disappeared into Zoltan's massive paw.

"Greetings Provost Powers," Zoltan said with just a hint of disrespect. "Glad to see you. Glad you here. Make sure nothing more happens to Mother University," he added, smiling his most horrible rictus grin.

Powers had no reaction, simply continued to look at Zoltan benignly with a slight, uncertain glance down to his hand to make sure Zoltan released rather than crushed it.

We took our seats around the conference table.

Berger continued to run the meeting.

"Okay, fellas, as you know Zoltan has been meeting with my main numbers guy, Neil Wexler, over the summer to develop a complete and detailed, realistic budget of his fiscal needs for this coming year. You may remember Neil, Dr. Ramis, from his work at the university straightening out Sessions finances which had been left in disarray by the former comptroller."

I felt myself suppressing a smile at this additional fabrication.

"Yes," Ramis acknowledged, his color heightening. It occurred to me that this was the first meeting between Ramis and Berger since Berger had reamed him for his scheme with Wentz. Obviously, the remembrance was playing in the background of Ramis's mind.

"So, we're talkin' to the dollar almost a half million this year of restricted funds being contributed by The Mark Berger Foundation to the medical center on behalf of Zoltan's work. The money is to be deposited directly into a separate holding account for his research expenditures. We are to receive a monthly report of expenditures. No overhead or other administrative fees shall apply. Do we understand one another?"

"Yes sir," Ramis said obsequiously. "And let me express our extreme thanks and gratitude for such a generous contribution."

Zoltan gave me a look, his face consumed by his normal, menacing scowl, his eyes dancing with joyous vindictive triumph.

Berger waved a hand, "No problem."

We all looked around at one another. There was no more to say. As we were standing to leave, a faint cell phone ring came from the massive partner's desk that had once been Fitz-Hugh's. Powers strolled over and picked up the phone.

"Yes?" he answered, then listened while his expression became pinched and focused. As he continued to listen, his face whitened. "Oh, my God," he said finally.

The rest of us glanced at one another with concern. I thought back to sitting at that same desk with Wentz when he had received the call from Lusby's consulting firm president that Lusby had been found dead in his apartment.

Powers hung up and looked at us blankly.

"That was our head of university IT. We've been hacked," he told us. "Ransomware. They want one and a half million dollars."

V

A Good Life

D ON POWERS SAT back in his chair behind the partner's desk in the president's office, watched as Mark Berger shut the door behind him and thought, *If there was ever a time that demonstrated vividly why I was wise not to pursue the opportunity to be president of Sessions University, this is it.*

He and Berger had just finished an emergency Zoom conference call with the executive committee of the board of trustees and the university's IT director to discuss the ransomware attack, which they had learned had encrypted the admission's office student and parent files.

Frozen out of these files, which contained biographical, academic and extensive, sensitive personal and financial information, it would only be a matter of time before such a breach was discovered by or leaked to the outside world creating a crisis of negative publicity, a public call for accountability and lawsuits galore.

After a long debate, the committee members in a close majority reached the same conclusion Mark Berger had initially expressed, that "We're at these fuckers' mercy. Back against the wall." Given this realization, they had made several decisions:

First, to pay the ransom, despite their awareness that the FBI publicly recommended against such a practice. The FBI's reasoning was that those seeking the ransom once paid, or even partially paid, could either escalate their demands or simply not provide the proper information to unencrypt the files. There was a further concern that paying the ransom could very well encourage similar attacks on more sensitive and vital information.

Berger's and Powers' hope, along with the executive committee, was that this attack was on the technologically low hanging fruit of the admissions office programming which they had learned ran on antiquated, not properly secure technology with no back-up. Accordingly, they were willing to take a risk that other systems within the university and medical center were more current in their protection and not as vulnerable.

Their second decision was to have an audit conducted of the university and medical center's technology protections and have recommendations made on their better coordination and protection as well as try to determine the origin of the attack.

Powers noted that he had recently met with The Blaylock Agency about their new technology division which was expanding their investigative services into cybercrime and suggested that perhaps they should be contacted about conducting the audit.

Blaylock's findings on behalf of the Kravitz family's investigation of his death had been well informed but in no way conclusive, leaving the family dissatisfied and the university secretly grateful.

There had been a bit of a pause when Berger revealed that one of his holding companies had bought Blaylock that previous fall. But then the group's discussion drifting to Sessions being a known entity and Berger being able to extract a discount for their fees. They asked Berger to contact the agency.

Powers closed his eyes and rubbed his temples, wondering whether Berger's purchase had influenced Blaylock's inconclusive findings. He shrugged. No one would ever know.

He gave himself credit for not letting his dealing with Mark Berger's overt Jewishness rankled him. Who the hell did this man think he was anyway? This thought caused him to smile a rarely seen rueful smile. Well, one of the wealthiest men in the universe. Powers was all too aware that wealth, unlike knowledge, had its way with the world, a perfect example being the executive committee's behavior earlier.

He stood, pulled the vest of his three-piece suit down into place. Walking to the door, he took from the coat stand his jaunty and somewhat incongruous pork pie hat that his wife, Claire, had given him and continued into the waiting area. Ms. Bemis remained, packing up her desk. She pointedly ignored him.

He proceeded down the empty maze of hallways now quiet save for the eerie noise of the fluorescent lights and made his way out of the dry and stuffy indoor air pollution into the pleasant cooling autumn air and the afternoon's dusk.

He and Claire had been visionary and lucky enough over a decade ago when they had purchased a top floor condo in the University Boulevard building across from the campus, so daily he had the pleasure of walking its narrow, winding roads to and from work. Now he looked forward to seeing Claire and their dachshund, Alfie, and sampling a new Cabernet he had ordered online the week before last.

He walked past the wrought iron gates of the Farr Botanical Garden, its entry lined now with a multi-colored shout out of mums. Yellow, crimson and mauve leaves from tall trees drifting down kaleidoscopically. The temperature descending from the heat of the day had become almost brisk.

Powers reflected on his good fortune in life, a daily thought which brought a self-satisfied smile.

His father had been a Presbyterian minister, his mother a high school mathematics teacher. His childhood had been pleasant yet disciplined, his education rigorous, with his mother serving as a beneficent tutor. The fact was he had always been the brightest child in his classes, straight A's all the way through grade school, skipped sixth grade, an emphasis at home being placed on excellence, humility, morality and bringing no offense.

Always the best behaved and brightest child, he advanced rapidly. Fortunately, he was reasonably tall and athletic, which helped assure that he was not bullied. He sailed through high school as class valedictorian and as the basketball team's forward, was accepted through early admission to MIT. His brilliance was soon recognized, and his courses accelerated so that he could achieve his PhD in mathematics in five years, during which he tutored those not as proficient, which led to his being offered a fellowship and teaching position.

Eventually his excellence propelled him up the ranks of academia where he was recruited to head the department of mathematics at Sessions and then to interim provost following the most unfortunate suicide of Samuel Kravitz and now, with the welcome departure of reprobate president Wentz, interim president, creating the possibility in his mind of a presidency somewhere other than his present seemingly jinxed employer. His father would have commented, 'Sometimes the Lord works in strange ways.'

Joggers made their way along the sidewalks, weaving between continuing education students hustling to classes and local residents out for a stroll. These sidewalks and roads, now serving an excess of people and traffic, were too often crowded, pedestrian injuries and even a fatality or two taking place annually.

Apart from the endowment emphasis of the current capital campaign, was a proposed master plan to make the university a pedestrian campus through moving all vehicular traffic and parking underground. At present the administration had no clue where the money for this project might come from but had been encouraged by their fund raisers to launch a comprehensive campaign with the hope that the campus redevelopment project's vision might inspire as yet unidentified contributors.

Powers found himself wondering whether they might get Mark Berger to develop an interest. He found himself shaking his head. It did not seem likely. Yet it also seemed as if every several months or so when he read the Wall Street Journal there was one of Berger's entities buying up another company for multi-billions of dollars. So, the wherewithal, the potential was certainly there. All the more reason to tread very positively and carefully when dealing with Berger's erstwhile and unpredictable personality.

As he walked past the drive toward the university club, he was aware suddenly of a faint buzzing, as if from a thousand mad bees, growing rapidly louder. Looking up he saw to his surprise a four-engine drone. *God,* he thought, *what will mankind think of next to destroy the peace and tranquility of the world, one of the few vestiges left to enjoy on a daily routine.*

He was further surprised to see the drone descend toward him with a surprisingly supple motion.

He stopped abruptly, a bit puzzled, a bit amazed at this technological marvel.

The drone moved further downward and toward him and momentarily came to face him, hovering directly in front.

Powers was transfixed, caught between a sense of invaded privacy, yet taking in and marveling at the whirling four-armed, propeller driven machine, at the gimbaled camera at its center and below that, what? There seemed to be a plastic toy pistol attached by a set of three claws on further gimbaling.

At the very moment he began to dawn on him to be alarmed, the 'toy' pistol fired a loud, percussive shot and its 9mm hollow point round passed into Powers' chest and obliterated his heart. There were screams and shouts of horror from fellow walkers and joggers, several of whom came running toward him.

In a quick motion the drone's three claws simultaneously released the plastic pistol, which fell to the sidewalk with a mild clatter. The drone instantaneously rose sky high, its buzz diminishing rapidly, and sped off to the west, leaving Powers crumpled body lying in a growing pool of blood.

VI

Aftermath

ZOLTAN AND I had chosen a table in an isolated corner of the university club bar.

Our drinks stood between us, Berger's first scotch, Zoltan's second vodka and my second beer sweating onto university seal napkins while small bowls of mini-pretzels, potato chips and party mix were scattered around randomly from Zoltan and my nervous grazing.

As other members entered and surveyed the room, one glance at Zoltan was all they needed to persuade them to sit elsewhere. Very helpful for our privacy.

Zoltan took a slug of his vodka, set it down. "So," he asked Berger, "What you and Nowhere Man talk about after Thomas, me and Cheapskate Doctor God leave?"

With Powers' news about the ransomware attack, Berger had asked to speak with him in private. Ramis had headed back to the medical center, already on his cell phone talking with the IT head there. Apparently, all was well, and they were already discussing how to beef up system security.

"Powers was totally flummoxed," Berger told us. "He might have to take a stand, you know. Make a decision."

Zoltan laughed, a demonic cackle.

"Luckily, Ms. Bemis was still around. She adroitly set up a Zoom meeting of the majority of the board's executive committee. Lucky as hell to find that many around this time of day."

Berger paused and took an appreciative sip of his scotch. He turned to me. "Thomas, remember The Blaylock Agency, who the Kravitz's hired to investigate the provost's death after the university gave them nothing but lip service?"

"Sure," I responded as neutrally as possible.

"As it happens, Blaylock has recently formed an investigative unit for cybercrime. Powers actually brought up using them to help us. I noted that one of my holding companies now owned them. A bit of a pause, and then some discussion which trended favorably toward Blaylock making us a priority and my being able to strike a discount for their services. Funny, you never know how that kind of conversation's going to play out. They asked me to get in touch with them. Powers seemed quite relieved, although the fact is, for this particular situation he and Sessions are likely pretty well screwed.

"What got hacked was all the student and parent records, including social security numbers, confidential evaluations, financial info, the works. Very sensitive shit. The hackers have frozen it in place with encryption and they want $1.5 million in Bitcoin to unencrypt. Can you believe this, the admissions office had no backup for these files, ran the data with an antiquated program. Dumb schmucks trying to save money."

"That be our beloved university," I commented.

"Plus, I had to explain to Powers about how Bitcoin works. I mean, okay, he's an academic. But it just goes to show that whomever we get as our next president has to have a diverse background as well as skill set. Today's president has to be conversant in management, finance, investing, and academics."

"Yeah, couldn't agree more. What happens if Sessions refuses?"

Berger shrugged, "Well, the perpahtraitors for now will just continue to wait. Sessions is in effect locked out of all that information. Fuck, and you know that can't last long before this disaster is leaked to the media and all hell breaks loose. This kinda extortion is happening everywhere. In some respects, we're lucky. These assholes could be willing to make all the info they hacked public, or they could have hacked much more sensitive research files. Can you imagine what would happen then?"

"Those systems much more robust, much better protected," Zoltan said, taking another slug of vodka.

Berger raised his eyebrows, "Yeah, Zoltan, that's exactly what we figured and why the executive committee advised Powers to pay the fuckers, despite all the warnings the FBI has against that. Actually, guess who's gonna make the payment? My hedge fund can do a Bitcoin transfer at my direction in a couple seconds. The university would probably just mess it up. Anyway, these hackers are just going after the low-hanging fruit."

"I already think of this," Zoltan told us with a touch of pride. "You think I trust medical center, where all departments cluster fucking, fighting over everything, computer system a mess? Many departments have different systems and programs than medical center system. I have own encrypted and backed up systems, on separate hard drives, for all our research. I only person who have access. I enter all information on my own."

"That's a lotta work."

"Yes."

"What happens if something happens to you?"

"Ah. I learn from Lusby. Keep backup in safe deposit box across street from university. Update weekly. Take old and erase it. Something happen to me, Kristina authorized to retrieve."

"Hmmm ... Where's the original?"

Zoltan grinned, reached into his breast pocket and produced it, a small external hard drive residing in a Ziploc bag.

"I hope you're as smart as you think you are."

"Yes. I do too ... So, what happen now with ransomware?"

"Fuck, so we pay 'em. We got no choice, pay 'em, then investigate while we bring in folks to strengthen our system security.

Maybe joining forces with other universities. Work with the FBI and Blaylock to see whether we can figure out who's done this to us. I did tell Powers that I would make some behind the scenes calls to see whether these hackers might be foreign agents. The word is that the Russians are taking the lead in this crap, but it could be anyone, say Middle East, say Iran , China or North Korea or even some disgruntled professor, parent or student extorting money to pay for further attacks on us."

"Who are you calling?" I asked.

"Ah, as you know, I still talk here and there with our former president Fitz-Hugh. I want to get his perspective on this."

"You mean, have him find out through Madam Secretary and the State Department what the government knows about this?"

"Exactly. Which reminds me. The presidential search. As you know, this year's national presidential election looks pretty certain that it's going to the other party, which would mean there would be a whole cast of characters out of jobs, former U.S. government dignitaries, including Fitz-Hugh and in all likelihood, Madam Secretary, trying to figure out what their next move is going to be now that they have been disenfranchised."

"Oh, God," I heard myself say.

"I don't think he has much to do with it."

"Don't tell me that Fitz-Hugh would consider returning to Sessions as an interim replacement for Powers or for a second time as president?" *With Ursula!* I thought, feeling a rising pang of anxiety. I thought about Ursula and my last exchange at the board of directors meeting at Berger's Tribone Hotel in Washington, DC. She had come to my room, and I had confronted her by demanding confirmation about Kravitz's death and Lusby's. She had readily admitted her involvement and being point person for Special Ops work at Sessions. However, she told me that Kravitz's death was a complete accident, her team screwed up and that she had no idea about Lusby being killed until she learned it the day after. She had then countered with a demand about what had happened to their agent who, through Zoltan's intervention, had disappeared. I had straight faced lied that I knew nothing and for once she could not tell whether I was being truthful. A very unpleasant and stressful exchange.

"Thomas," Berger remarked, "You are one smart fucker. The idea for interim has been broached. Further there are other ideas broached that are even bigger doozies."

"Yeah?"

"Greta Hauser as our next president."

"Oh, shit. The outgoing Secretary of State? Fitz-Hugh's lover? The key partner, ten times removed of course, in the scheme to put U.S agents in our international centers? Mark, Mark, these people are all friggin' parasites. No real interest or loyalty to Sessions, just using it for other ambitions and purposes."

Berger shook his head, a sage and sad look upon his features, "Yeah, but the board is clueless obviously about these folks' past reprehensible behavyah. To the board, they would bring nothing but prestige and powerful contacts. So, even if Fitz-Hugh and Hauser don't emerge as presidential candidates, the board might want them as fellow board members."

"Aw, Christ," I said, shaking my head and reaching for my beer. I needed a long draught.

"You got very great job, Berger," Zoltan told him.

"Yeah," Berger agreed, reaching for his scotch, "Fucking bed of roses."

Out of my peripheral vision, I noticed movement at the doorway of the bar. The club receptionist, a pleasant, long-serving woman dressed in a university club uniform whom I knew only as Alice, had just crossed the threshold. She came directly to our table.

"Mr. Berger," she addressed Mark and leaning over whispered in his ear.

Berger blanched at whatever it was she was telling him, turned to her and thanked her, then turned to us.

"Big trouble," he told us. "We gotta go." He stood.

Zoltan and I looked at one another, mystified.

"What's going on?" I asked as we stood and followed him out to the reception area, the other patrons in the bar looking at us with curiosity.

"We'll know better in a minute."

Standing in the reception area, tears streaming down her mascara-marked face, was Jo Ann. She looked at us as we approached, bereft.

"Hey," Berger said, taking her by the arm gently, "Let's go outside."

We walked out the front door, down the few stairs to the flagstone walkway.

"What's happened?" Mark asked her.

"Dr. Powers," she blubbered. "He's DEAD!"

"WHAT?" all three of us said almost in harmony.

"I be still in the office packin' up my things and all of a sudden all the phone lines went off, like almost exploded. I pick it up the phone and its campus po-lice. They tell me Dr. Powers been shot dead right on the sidewalk 'bout a hundred feet from here. He was jus' walkin' home! So, I know you at the club, so I come over to tell you. Po-lice everywhere, area marked off with yellow tape. Am-bulance remove Powers. I don't know where they take him. Someone gotta call his wife."

"Okay," Berger said, evenly, grimly. "You did the right thing. Thanks so much, Jo Ann. Looks like I'm interim president again for a couple weeks, like last spring. You go home. We'll go check out the scene. I'll call Mrs. Powers and go see her. I'll really need your help over the next couple weeks. Consider yourself rehired."

"Yes sir." Jo Ann looked at me.

I shrugged, nodded at her, acknowledging the far more important need for her to help Mark. We would work things out about her working for the foundation somewhere down the road, whenever the hell that might be.

Jo Ann turned and walked away toward the administration building.

Berger turned to us. "Let's go check out what's happening on the campus drive."

"Wait a minute. You guys go ahead. I need to talk to Jo Ann for a minute. I'll catch up with you."

"Sure."

I caught up with Jo Ann at the botanical garden.

"Hey," I called to her.

She turned.

"You're going back to the office, aren't you?"

"Yeah, Thomas. Might as well unpack all of what I packed. Going to be all hell breakin' loose tomorrow."

"But you haven't had any dinner, right?"

"Nope."

"Follow me."

I led her back into the reception area of the club where Alice was greeting people.

"Alice, this is Ms. Bemis, the president's assistant. Could you please arrange to have a quick carryout dinner prepared for her. Put it on my account."

"Of course, Dr. Simpson." She looked sympathetically at Jo Ann. "You jus' sit right here, honey," she said motioning to one of the chairs beside a credenza. "I'll be right back."

"Thank you," Jo Ann told me, clasping my hand in hers.

Out of the corner of my eyes I sensed club patrons watching this scene and could only imagine what they were thinking – something along the lines of how dare I bring this outlandishly dressed hooker into the club for a free meal. I could not have cared less.

I hustled back to join Berger and Zoltan.

The scene was just like the movies. Yellow tape cordoning off the whole area. Flashing lights everywhere from police cars from different jurisdictions, even highway patrol.

Berger introduced himself to a young detective with an iPad. Showed him his university ID. They began talking, the detective taking notes on his iPad and pausing to provide Berger with information.

Zoltan and I took in the crime scene. *Why?* I kept asking myself.

Another senseless death to deal with. Who could have done such a thing? Powers' killing just did not fit into any realm of possibility. Certainly not Special Ops. For all we knew they were gone. Doubtful that it would be ransomware related. What possible motive could there be?

Berger finished talking with the detective and walked back to us.

"This whole thing is fucking insane," he told us.

"He was murdered by a God damned drone of all things, shot point blank with a 3D-printed pistol that the drone then dropped at his feet. Totally untraceable. Almost like whoever did this is rubbing it in our face as the perfect crime. In essence it was an assassination."

"Why would anyone do that?" I asked, shaking my head, "Powers was a non-entity of no threat to anyone."

Berger shook his head. "There has to be a symbolic meaning to this somewhere. Just what it might be, I have no idea. The cops suspect there may be follow-up communication. Want us to be on the lookout for it."

He paused to take a deep, stressed-out breath, "Okay, so I gotta call on Mrs. Powers, Claire. I've met her in passing once or twice and I gotta go over to their place and comfort her and see whether she has some support, family or whomever. I'm guessing that I may have to go down the morgue with her to identify the body. You guys should go home. I'll give Jean Claude on *Calypso* a call and give him a heads up. Thomas, you should show up at the administration building tomorrow morning after you've checked in at the foundation and gotten whatever you need from there. We'll find an office for you. Zoltan, you just be available. Let me know how this is going down at the medical center."

"Okay, Berger. I do whatever you need."

"Ohhh shit," I heard myself exclaim.

"What?"

"Look who's here."

Emily Sayzak, for the last three years my nemesis, a reporter for our daily paper, a woman of keen instincts who at times had been of significant assistance to me was making her way around the crime scene toward us. Emily knew in her heart-of-hearts that I was the keeper of all secrets regarding Sessions, and she was determined to pry them from me.

Her primary inducement was the offer of in-depth carnal knowledge, and she was in fact an attractive, permed blonde, with a nice figure, an idiosyncratic small, canted mouth and a funny way of pronouncing her words. Thankfully, she managed to cancel out this nice package with too tight clothes that were too revealing, cheap perfume, heavy red lipstick and makeup, overdone mascara and an aggressive approach that made me want to run in the other direction. On the other hand, I realized that maintaining a flirtation with her seemed to keep her in check, had even caused her to be an ally here and there. A dangerous pastime.

Tonight she was dressed in tight, royal blue, stretch slacks that left little to the imagination, braless in a thin silk crème-colored blouse, her imitation leather satchel on her opposite shoulder, glancing at me as she stepped over the curb.

"You guys vamoose. I'll stall her."

"That shouldn't be too hard," Berger smirked.

I was glad to see he had retained his sense of humor.

"Trying not to be hard is definitely part of the problem."

"Hah!"

He and Zoltan gave one another knowing looks and hustled away in opposite directions.

"Hey, handsome," Emily greeted me, hugging me, pressing her right breast into my chest, her *Eau de Drugstore Parfum* overwhelming me while her hand snaked into my suit coat, ran down my side and softly grabbed a love handle, "What are you doing here? I thought you worked downtown now."

"Jesus, Emily, is this any way to behave at a murder scene?" I asked, hearing a slightly squeamish whine in the voice.

"Happens every day, Thomas," she said with a matter-of-fact shrug. "Except this one is really wild, will be national news. Not your normal black on black or crime of passion killing. This sucker will have legs. Academic assassination."

Of course, she was right. I could see the headlines now. I found myself shaking my head at the oncoming tsunami of inquiry and attention. It was going be a chaotic disaster for Sessions' communications and PR, not to mention marketing. Right in the middle of our peak admissions visits.

"So, what are you doing here?"

"Had a meeting with former colleagues and then went to the club for a drink. God, this is just awful. Beyond senseless," I said as I took in the crime scene again in the growing darkness, the outline of Powers on the sidewalk.

"Who were those two guys you were with?"

"Oh, a professor from the medical center and another professor here at the university, an astronomer," I told her, figuring what the hell, any lie to forestall a thousand questions.

"I've seen that big mean, monster-looking guy before. He's a friend of yours, right?"

"Yeah."

"But the little, funny looking Jewish guy ... An astronomer?" she laughed. "I don't think so. How many astronomers walk around in thousand-dollar suits? I think I've seen his picture somewhere, haven't I?"

"I know you're an avid reader of National Geographic, so maybe."

Before the evening was over I knew she would have figured out Berger's identity. All she had to do was take a look online at the university's annual report.

Emily laughed, "You kidder ... So, why do your key people around here keep getting murdered?"

"You mean like Kravitz? It's never been proven that it wasn't a suicide." I knew she was trying to trap me. Wasn't going to happen.

"What do think happened here?"

"I'm completely damned mystified."

"He was your acting president. You think this'll complicate the search?"

I smiled at her. "No comment."

"Thomas, now that you're downtown, how about I stop by your office sometime. We can have lunch."

Oh, I thought, *And what a lunch it would be.*

"Office is off limits. No guests allowed. We can meet somewhere though. Just like old times."

The last time we had met, which happened to be at the Intercontinental, she had dumped an envelope of 8x10 black and white glossies of Jack Wentz and Frank Lusby naked in a bathhouse full of boys. The pictures had become exhibit A in Berger's meeting with Wentz to get him to resign the presidency.

"That'd be fun," Emily told me, her red lipstick mouth moving coquettishly, her tongue moving across her teeth.

"Well, I gotta go home to the wife and kids. See you later."

"Bye for now. Call me, Thomas, even just to say hello."

"Sure" I said, turning, saying to myself, *Never!* And breathing a sigh of relief.

I walked back across campus to my car which had a parking pass under its wiper as the guard we had met promised and then two parking tickets on top of the pass from what I presumed was the next shift. Any other day, I might have thought it was funny. Tonight, all I could do was shake my head.

VII

Home

I TOOK OFF my suit coat before entering the car, then once in set it on the passenger's seat, loosened my tie, unbuttoned my shirt collar and sat for a few minutes, collecting myself, trying to shake off the vision of the Powers' murder scene, my mind leaping randomly through the day's events while I opened the windows to rid myself of the redolent smell of Emily Sayzak's perfume.

A stray thought hit, *Damn, I needed to call home. How could that have escaped me?*

Janet answered her cell on the second ring. "Hey, honey, you okay? I was beginning to worry."

I let out a loud and long exhalation.

"God, Janet, I don't even know where to begin." I let out another exhalation. "Don Powers. You know, the provost serving as acting president, was murdered on his walk home through the campus."

"Oh, my God, Thomas."

"Mark Berger, Zoltan and I had just finished meeting with him about an hour before to discuss the foundation's giving to Sessions this year. Very strange circumstances. A drone came down from the skies and shot him point blank then dropped a 3D-printed pistol at his feet. They're untraceable you know. They call them 'ghost guns.' It was like an assassination. Everyone's mystified. I mean, Powers is the last person you would think would have something like this happen to him."

"Lord, Thomas."

I could read her mind. "Yeah, too many damn deaths of key administrators. Looks very odd, very suspicious, like something's really, really wrong at the university."

"Yes ... Is there?"

"Oh, come on. Not that I know of. *Lie.* Anyway, I'm just leaving now. Just heat up some leftovers."

"Sure."

"Everything okay there?"

"I'll fill you in when you get here. Sarah has a friend here. He may still be around when you arrive."

"Friend? He?"

"Yes. Jacque."

"Jacque?"

"Yes. He's French obviously, a graduate student in computer science, one of Tommie's tutors. That's how they met. Tommie thinks he's wonderful."

"Christ." Jean Claude, Berger's French first mate of *Calypso Too,* flashed into my consciousness, suave, urbane, charming, duplicitous. NOT for my little girl.

"He's a nice guy. You'll see. See you, honey."

"Okay."

I hung up.

I hated change in our family, the one place I counted on for some permanency. Yet, like everything else, change happened every day. I realized how unrealistic my desire to have Sarah and Tommie never grow up was, but it still rankled me.

I drove home with an even more than usual sense of foreboding. Called Alicia and got her voicemail. Left a message that the provost had been murdered and not to expect to hear from me for a while. Best I could do.

A worn-out Hyundai was parked against the curb in front of our house, your typical graduate student first car beater.

Entering the laundry room from the garage, our Dalmatian,

Sparky, named by Tommie in his fire engine days, offered her usual excited greeting, barking joyfully and circling me until I stopped, petted her and dutifully told her goofy doggie endearments. Looking up I saw Janet, Tommie, Sarah and a tall, pale young man staring at me like I was the village idiot, probably not too far of the mark, but nevertheless embarrassing.

"Dad, this is my friend, Jacque. He's Tommie's tutor and, uh ... a good guy," Sarah told me, smiling awkwardly.

We all stood looking at one another, semi-paralyzed.

My mind immediately began finishing Sarah's sentence, *and, uh ... yeah, Dad, he's fucking my brains out!*

I shook my head involuntarily to rid it of any further grotesques, took a step forward.

"Welcome to our home." *No, no, please go away! I can't deal with this and a damn murder.*

We shook hands. His grip was firm, his manner polite and deferential.

I looked him over, more carefully. He was slim, plainly dressed, an abundance of brown hair as with any impoverished graduate student who would have no time, interest or money for a haircut, plain features, white complexion likely from too much time indoors. Wearing worn out, faded olive khakis, an ancient, stretched out, threadbare brown turtleneck. More importantly, he carried himself with a natural grace, exuding an earnest and caring attitude. Despite all my desire to find fault, instead I found myself positively impressed. There was no pretension in this fellow, but an open and honest interest in those around him. I breathed a sigh of relief. Jean Claude he was not.

"I should be going," he told me. "I'm sorry to learn that this has been a troubling day for you."

"Yes ..." I turned to Janet. "What have you told him?"

"That one of the administrators was shot and killed on campus."

I turned back to him. "Okay, look, please keep this news to yourself for now. The less said the better. This event's likely to take on a speculative life of its own and we need to get the word out to the board and other key constituents before the press starts messing with it."

"Yes sir."

He and Sarah looked at one another uncertainly.

Jacque nodded at her, walked toward our front door and in a moment was gone.

"You could have been a little more welcoming," Janet told me the moment the door closed.

"Yeah, Dad." Sarah added.

I looked at them with consternation. "Pardon me, I've just come from a crime scene. Do you have any idea what it's like staring at police tape and a chalk outline in the image of a body around a pool of blood where your colleague who you were meeting with an hour before was murdered?"

Sarah, looking chagrined, came up to me and gave me a hug, a peck on the cheek. "Okay, Dad, I'm really sorry." She nodded at both of us. "I'm going up to my room," and left.

I looked at Janet. "I'm completely at sea here. How am I supposed to react to this, this probable boyfriend?"

"She's growing up, Thomas. Just like we did. Let it go. Be supportive. It's her life now. Trust her to make her own decisions."

"Awww, shit ... I know you're right, but there's a part of me that just doesn't want to catch up with this new reality."

"Understandable. I'm having trouble with it myself. But look, I think he's okay. She's made a good choice. We have to let things play out."

"Yeah, I just don't want to lose her."

"Look at it this way, maybe we gain someone worthy of her."

I sighed, "Yeah, I guess. I don't have answers for anything anymore. I'm helpless. This murder has completely knocked me off my feet. At least in the past we had an idea about the who, where, what and why when there were problems. But this? Totally amorphous, seemingly random but then more like it was planned out, intentional but no clue as to why. Out of the blue."

We looked at one another for a long moment.

"I'll bet you could use some dinner."

"Yeah, I could."

It occurred to me in flash of realization that Janet was playing the comfortable role of being my psychologist, that for her my helplessness was actually constructive. Gave her a role to play. The irony and contradiction struck me hard. I would have to think about this. My role in this drama was both one I was not at all comfortable with nor would it last. I heard Zoltan's voice in the background noise of my mind, saying, *Buckle up Buckaroo,* and felt myself smile a rueful smile. *Okay,* I said to myself.

After dinner I went upstairs to check in on Tommie. Getting late but he was still at his computer.

"What are you up to?"

"Ahh, Dad, you wouldn't understand."

"Thanks, son."

"Well, you wouldn't. I'm writing code for the programing of a future row-bot."

"Wow."

"Yeah ... maybe. I want to see what Mr. Diamond thinks."

Diamond was his technology teacher at Schlossler Academy, a good guy who had first identified Tommie's savant capabilities.

"So, how things going at school?"

Squinched up face, eyes ticking, "Dad, I don't. Like I don't fit in with my classmates. Not at all. They're idiots."

"Your sister felt the same way when she was in high school, but, Tommie, you got to come to terms with your surroundings. Everyone has redeeming qualities."

A morose expression. "I don't know, Dad. I really don't know."

"So, tell me about ransomware."

An enthused expression, night and day change. Interesting, no curiosity about why I was asking. "Oh, cool. Whoever wants to do it finds a way to inject malware into a computer system, usually through an attachment or thumb drive. Really clever ones have embedded it in an automatic update for instance. So, once it's in there, it encrypts all the files and then the person or people who did it demands money, usually bitcoin, to unlock the encryption."

"I'm impressed you know all this ... You wouldn't do anything like that, right?"

"Dad, what do think I am, stupid? I'd get caught, although I'm underage so I might get off but it would be nothing but trouble. My tutors at the Center have been all through that with us. It's cri-min-al. You get your ass fried one way or the other and then nobody ever trusts you. You gotta be a ripe asshole to do that kinda stuff."

"Good. Glad to hear you say that. You're okay, Tommie. I'm proud of you."

He smiled but then his face squinched up and went into a spasm of ticks. "Yeah, yeah, yeah. Thanks, Dad."

I went downstairs, passing Janet on the stairs undoubtedly headed to bed. From the living room bar I poured myself a large, neat scotch, went to my den, closed the door and sat in my leather lounge chair in the dark.

Sipping my scotch I thought about Powers, a man I never liked but for whom now I felt a guilty sorrow. I thought about Frank Lusby, the tragedy of his life, and mourned his loss. And I thought about Samuel Kravitz, the jealous, self-righteous, angry scholar, the former provost who held me in contempt and was killed mercilessly when he did not need to die. My eyes grew wet. I took a final slug and headed upstairs.

When I got into bed and began to settle in, Janet turned to me and we embraced and, after a bit of fumbling with bed clothes, made love, deeply and with touches of desperation.

VIII

Back in the Saddle Again

A T 5 A.M. the next morning, I woke, already adrenalized. As quietly as possible so not to wake Janet, I turned off the alarm clock set for 5:30, rose in the dark, grabbed my cell phone from the bedside table and made my way to the bathroom where I saw the text from Alicia, *Are you okay?*

Obviously, she had received a call from Jo Ann as well as my text.

Marginally, I responded, *Expecting a tough day. Will call later.*

By the time I reached Sessions, having retrieved my laptop from the foundation's offices, and parked as usual in the lower parking lot the day was beginning to dawn, dew on the campus lawns and the heavy smell of grass and the nearby woods in the air. I walked hurriedly up the winding, asphalt path to the campus, furtively looking up and around at the sky. At the building's entrance, I took a deep inhalation and entered its burnt dust and urethane-smelling atmosphere.

Berger was already there in the president's office, door open, Jo Ann having yet to arrive.

He was dressed in a light grey suit, white dress shirt, mauve tie, suit coat on the back of his chair. I assumed he had retrieved his clothes from the foundation's suite the prior evening, then spent the night on *Calypso Too* in the company of Jean Claude and in total privacy.

He looked up at me from the president's desk where he was working intently on his laptop, his eyes over large behind his black, center hinged glasses, his mustache twitching a bit.

"Howareya?"

"Not bad. How did things go last night?"

He grimaced. "Awful. Claire was a complete, devastated basket case, their little dog in a panic, running around and yapping at everything. I gave her my best condolences. Neighbors there to comfort her and take care of her. The police, of course, showed up with meaningless questions. They're as clueless as we are, maybe more so. Did Powers have any enemies, any recent disagreements with folks, that sorta thing. Got outta there as best I could. Talked to Jo Ann last night to get some orientation about what's going on here. So, guess what?"

"What?"

"As far as your havin' a place to hang out. These bozos have let all these months go by and haven't hiyard your replacement. Powers didn't want to make the hiryah; wanted to leave it to the incoming president. Jus' what we need, a fucking vacuum in our branding, PR, communications and marketing efforts at a time of total crisis. So, you get to have your old office back in the Communications Department."

"Aw, fuck, you're kidding me. I hate that place."

"Yeah. You think I'm havin' fun here in this mahogany dumpstah?"

"Hah! Right."

"So, I'm on a roll. Jus' talked to Fitz-Hugh. That's the nice thing about Europe bein' six hours ahead. I also was able to reach Blaylock. Whether the board likes it or not, I'm hiring Blaylock to help protect the campus and in doing that perhaps he can help us and the cops, FBI etc. come up with who the hell did this. They'll be in place on the rooftops tomorrow. Other folks will be working on an assessment of and plan for our technology and cybersecurity."

Now I gotta set about canceling everything today on campus,

admissions visits, athletic events, social events everything until tomorrow when we can be assured it's at least somewhat safe around here. Just ruinous.

"You and I and Zoltan will meet for lunch here at noon. First item of business will be a Zoom call with Gregory Blaylock."

"Okay. Good. I'll coordinate with the police on a press conference for tomorrow afternoon. The Powers murder will be all over the papers and the media. I want the cops front and center to take the burden off us. It's their investigation. You'll need to make a statement. I'll write it and send up to you. In the meantime, maybe we can do some independent analysis about what the hell happened."

"Good thinkin', my friend."

"See you later."

"Hey, look, you might as well clean up any mess you find down there too."

"Awww, hell." Meaning that I would now have to deal my old job and with the director of public relations, John "Fine Fine" Stein, as hopeless, clueless and inept a twit as had ever crossed the paths of promotion.

Why had I never fired him when I could have? Too busy, too distracted. Now I would be the one paying the price, not my successor. Can't focus on that now.

No one had yet arrived in the Communications, so I went to my old office, opened the door and stood for a moment, looking around at its bare emptiness and then out the window to my favorite viewing spot of the woods beyond the drive and the parking lot, a beautiful medley of colors.

I found myself letting out a deep, heartfelt sigh, thinking as I did that this was only temporary, but God it was haunting. I felt like running out of the building into those dappled woods.

The lyrics of Gene Autry's *Back In The Saddle Again* began playing in my head, bringing back a memory of a Sunday morning scene from when Sarah and Tommie were kids. They in their PJs sitting in front of the TV with Zoltan, who had been their babysitter the night before. The kids were munching Froot Loops from the box, watching an antique Gene Autry western on a streaming channel. I sat with them for a while with my second cup of coffee and enjoyed the old-fashioned, almost comical simplicity of the dialogue and action while we talked occasionally about whatever crossed our minds.

I felt myself smile derisively at my current scene.

Yeah, God damn it. I began to sing along under my breath in my best west Texas accent, *Back in The Saddle Again, Out Where A Friend Is A Friend, Whoopi-ty-aye-yay.* Somehow, I felt just slightly better as the song kept playing in my head and I kept singing as I went about straightening things up in the office.

My old office chair compared to my new chair in the foundation's office was uncomfortable and awkward. I plugged in my laptop and wrote an email to the department heads informing them of my being back in our offices at the request of the board chair to deal directly with the Powers murder. I was sure this news would bring a sigh of relief to everyone concerned as well as a worry that I might be with them for longer than any of us anticipated. I would disabuse them of that notion when I met with them.

Pushing the Send tab on my email, I picked up my cell phone and pivoted to gaze out into the woods before I called Alicia. A half hour of tranquility remained before staff arrived and I had to deal with the rap music of my former existence and current affairs. The overhead fluorescent lights buzzed in the silence.

It was now just after 7:00 a.m. Chicago time but Alicia answered first ring and acted as if she had been up and working for hours, which she probably had.

"Thomas, I had a call from Jo Ann. Very upset. What the hell happened? Are you okay?"

"Could be better. This is a complete mystery. Our provost, Don Powers, who was serving as acting president, was assassinated by a drone which then dropped a ghost gun after it shot him. No clues as to why this happened."

"That's so terrible."

"Yeah. But I don't have anything more to tell you. Berger's jumped into the breach, now acting as interim president. He's assigned me to temporarily take over my former responsibilities in communications. You can imagine how fucking thrilled I am. He, Zoltan and I meet for lunch in his office at noon ... Trying to get a handle on this mess. So, how are you?"

"Doing well. My father and I made our first site visit to a well-regarded self-help organization on the north side."

"Yeah, how did that go?"

"Dad was fabulous. I was so relieved. He can be so intimidating. His nickname at Piper-Hale, out of earshot of course, is The Bird of Prey. The executive director at this non-profit we called on was a delight, so in command strategically. What they are accomplishing with incentivized training and education programs for disadvantaged individuals and families is fascinating. They are making a significant impact on their clients' lives, transformational.

"But then we met with the chairman of their independent foundation board who's an egomaniacal slum landlord/developer, old guy with corruption written all over him. The more we got into it, the more it seemed like there was some shady self-dealing going on, like maybe laundering money from God knows whom."

"So, what are you guys going to do?"

"Well, we're going to give them $300,000. Our thought is that we don't want to penalize the executive director, their board of directors and the organization for all their good work. In fact, we want to encourage it. And we sure as hell do not want to know any more about their so-called foundation."

"It all makes sense in a perverted kind of way. Welcome to the real world, huh?"

She laughed her beautiful laugh. "Yes. Exactly."

"So you want your old job back?"

"What?"

I filled her in on the ransomware attack and the board's decision to hire Blaylock for a technology audit. Plus, Mark intended to hire them to protect the campus and perhaps help discover what was behind Powers' assassination.

"Oh my God, I'm sure that Gregory Blaylock will at the very least give me a call to update me and sniff around about how happy I am with this new position."

"Makes sense."

"Thomas."

"Yeah?"

"I would still like to see you at some point."

There was an awkward moment of silence while I tried to think of an answer, the conflict of different relationships, guilt and desire welling up in my conscience.

"Hell, I really don't know when the hell that might be."

"You know, I still have my apartment in DC as well our foundation's satellite office there. We'll be doing a fact-finding visit there sometime in January. I'd love to see you and catch up."

"Lord, Alicia, let me see how things shake out here. I'd love to see you but life's complicated, you know?"

"I'm sure it is. Just know you have a standing invitation."

"Okay," I heard myself reply noncommittally. "Let me think about how to work things on this end."

"Okay, Thomas. Take care. I'm worried about you."

"Yeah, thanks. I'll do my best."

I hung up feeling that the day had brightened, until I reflected that my first meeting needed to be with Stein.

He schlepped into my office timorously in his blue blazer missing cuff buttons, butter yellow shirt with its too tight collar amplifying his double chin, bagged out grey slacks, food-stained tie, scuffed up Bass Weejuns.

"How are you, John?"

"Oh, uh, fine, fine!"

I fought with myself not to roll my eyes.

"How's the family?"

Startled look. He wasn't expecting this difficult question, "Oh, um, fine. Um, thanks for asking."

"I guess you know about the Powers murder by now."

Pensive rubbing of hands together. "Yes."

"Mark Berger, as chairman of the board, has stepped into the breach, like he did last summer, and for the next week or two and perhaps longer will serve as interim president. Awkward, but necessary. As you know, I now work for his foundation. He's asked me to assume my old position as director of communications during this crisis."

A desperate half-smile, sweat on his forehead. "Okay."

"Mark's literally is at this moment closing the university for today to avoid any further drone attacks. Could you work with Ms. Bemis on putting out a directive to the university about its being temporarily closed as a matter of caution? Will open again tomorrow when rooftop security is in place. They'll be a press conference tomorrow afternoon in the performing arts center. Think you can do that?"

"Oh sure. Fine." A big desperate smile.

How do you deal with an employee whose upper lip quivers every time you ask him to do something? Obviously, he had been beaten as a child. I often felt that he was so panicked in my presence that what I was telling him or asking him to do was going over his head. So, I always sent him a detailed follow-up email of instructions, so I had a paper trail to fall back on when he screwed up.

After the farce of my meeting with Stein, I decided a better course would be to visit each department head in their own office as a way to get a sense of overall morale and not be as threatening.

It was an okay set of visits. I assured them that this was only temporary, asked their thoughts on how to best deal with the onslaught of press and media inquiries. I told them that I would serve as designated university spokesperson to protect Berger and them, that we needed to set up a dedicated website for daily updates, that we need to set up a prioritized process for handling inquiries, grouping them by priority and wherever possible assembling different groups for tailored updates to help forestall total chaos. To a person, they were quite happy to support me in these efforts.

Then I went back to my office, wrote Berger's remarks and emailed them to him, put in a call to the police's PR rep who I knew fairly well. After orienting one another we brought into the call the Sessions special events department to coordinate all the arrangements for the press conference. Then I reviewed and had our office send out a staff-prepared press release.

By then, it was time to meet with Mark.

IX

A Strange Notion

Jo Ann was in Ms. Bemis mode when I entered the president's office reception area for our lunch, Zoltan already there, having again squeezed himself into one of the university seal chairs.

She was dressed today in mourning clothes, a black jacket and blouse, no earrings, a small gold necklace, black pleated skirt.

She looked past me, as Ms. Bemis usually did, with her patented look of distant dislike and contempt.

I walked up to her desk, leaned over and asked, "How are you?"

Tears formed in her eyes, messing with her mascara, her lips quivered. She blinked several times, looked at me directly, "Not good, Thomas," she told me as Jo Ann. She rose and hurriedly left us.

I looked at Zoltan. He shrugged. "Death never easy."

"Yeah." *You should know*, I thought. Last year in self-defense he had killed the Special Ops agent who had murdered Frank Lusby and then deposited his body in the cadaver laboratory at the medical center, effectively causing him to vanish. My best friend.

The door to the president's office swung open, Berger came halfway out, "Hey, so you guys are here. Come on in. What happened to Ms. Bemis?"

"Indisposed," I told him.

"Oh," he said distractedly as he turned, and we followed him.

At the end of the conference table, IT had set up a monitor and a control unit for our Zoom call.

The food service from the Student Union had set out on the conference table a nice selection of cold cut sandwiches, chips, sodas and water, along with paper plates, plastic utensils and napkins and last but not least, chocolate chip cookies.

"A feast fit for kings," Berger remarked. "Help yourselves."

"More like for administration phonies," Zoltan added, "But we eat it anyway," as he took three sandwiches, bags of chips, three cookies and two diet cokes.

"You should see people at medical center," Zoltan told us as he took a large bite of his first sandwich, talking through the food in his mouth, "Walking between buildings very fast, eyes looking up at sky, panicked like they going to be hit by meteor. Be very funny if it were not possible real worry because no one know what the hell this about. I see same thing on this campus when I get out of cab. Everyone half running around, looking at sky, scared."

"They probably should be," said Mark. "Let me get Mr. Blaylock in here and see what he has to say."

He activated the call. The screen lit up, turned blue and Blaylock appeared. I had always imagined him to be a stealthy secret service kind of spook. Instead, the gentleman who appeared on the screen looked as if he should be teaching a course at Sessions in some arcane Renaissance discipline – a friendly, cultivated, grey-goateed face, a bit flushed from the good life, thinning blond-grey hair combed back, yellow bow tie with a spaniel print, tattersall shirt, midnight blue hopsack blazer.

"Gentlemen," he greeted us, his voice slightly mechanized by the Zoom system, "Can you hear me?"

"Yes," we all replied at once.

"Good, glad we could talk so readily. Thank you, Mark, for your briefing. I'm so sorry you and Sessions are going through such a tragedy, particularly as it comes on top of the Kravitz situation."

"Yeah," Berger remarked, "So, what the hell do you think is going on here?"

Gregory Blaylock paused momentarily, choosing his words carefully before he said, "A vendetta."

"Really?"

"It has all the appearances of that. In our opinion it is most likely that some disturbed person wants to destroy Sessions' administration."

What he was telling us felt exactly right. Still, it was shocking.

"But why?" Mark asked grimly.

"That is the question. Why? We probably won't know until this quite capable, highly motivated, pure evil person is apprehended."

"Yeah. So, what can we do?"

"Mark, we do have immediate remedies. We're guessing that this assassin will continue his focus on the administration building and those leaving and entering it. So, tomorrow I can have team down there with a roof top presence on the several surrounding buildings as well as the administration building. They'll be armed with jamming devices that can be set to jam different frequencies drone operators use. As backup they will be armed in case they need to shoot it down.

"I must tell you that jamming is not ideal, because in jamming an incoming device we risk interference with different communications frequencies being used at the university. Could cause small or even significant disturbances.

"Our folks can meet with your security personnel to discuss this. Once we know the actual frequency or frequencies being used by this person then the university can communicate with staff and faculty about what problems might arise."

"Ok," Berger acknowledged. "But how do we catch this fucker?"

"Good question. There are ways of downing drones using jamming and/or taking over its control. But it would best to have a chase drone follow it."

"Couldn't agree more."

So, we'll do our best regardless to locate the operator and set up an ongoing communication with the local police and most likely the FBI who alerted could try to close in and apprehend this person."

"Excellent."

"Ah, but Mr. Berger, this appears to be a very wily adversary. We will see. And it may be that he changes strategy or that we're not 100% correct in our assumptions, so let me be clear. All of you going to and from the administration building are likely in danger of being killed. But this does not mean that you can yet diminish the rest of the university and medical center being on guard until we are more certain about this assassin's intent."

"Yeah, agreed. Okay. I'll look forward to talking with your folks tomorrow."

"Thank you. I'm hopeful that we can have success here."

Mark grimaced again. "There's no acceptable alternative."

"Yes."

Mark reached over and canceled the call, turned off the screen.

"Isn't it wonderful being back here at Sessions University," I remarked.

"Yeah, fucking lovely," Mark said as he turned to us. "By the way, I'm paying for all our work with Blaylock just so you know in case it comes up as an issue, and it will. Folks everywhere will try to find whatever info they can to criticize us. Human nature, I guess."

His expression narrowed. "Okay, guys. Four agenda items:

1. The ransomware attack,
2. The Powers assassination. Who might have done it?
3. Interim president, Board developments,
4. Dealing with the press, media, alumni and other constituent communications. In essence, damage control."

I thought, *So, this is how he runs things at his companies.*

"Ransomware – we have lucked out. Paid the fucker or fuckers in bitcoin crack of dawn this morning and already have the encryption key and have unlocked the admissions files. Whoever did this at least has some sense of decency. That may indicate a sole actor doing this rather than a group. Dodged a big bullet on this one. Can you imagine what the press and others would be doing with the combo of a ransomware attack and Powers' murder. They'd have a field day questioning whether it was all one big conspiracy. We got enough problems with the Powers situation by itself."

"You got that right. But how do we know it isn't one big conspiracy? The fucker who killed Powers could have just funded his future exploits."

"Oh, Jesus, Thomas," Berger replied, "Don't go there." He paused, considering. "Well ..." he sighed, "I do guess it's something we have to keep in mind. Anyway, Blaylock will also have their new technology division do the audit of our systems and present findings on how to improve them. They'll be working in partnahship with the FBI, other government agencies, other universities combining forces to get some answers about who did this.

"One other thing. Doncha think it's kinda strange that whoever the bastard is who killed Powers hasn't communicated anything about why he's doing this? Nothin'."

"Yes," Zoltan said, "You right. He Sphinx."

"Speaking of that, the police still haven't a clue, calling in the FBI. I talked with Fitz-Hugh. He's as shocked as we are. Says he doubts this was caused by our old Special Ops nemesis, but he'll check.

"I'm getting' calls from all these other university presidents wanting to know what's going on. I can't not talk to these folks, so I'm having Ms. Bemis set phone appointments with them at the end of the day for an hour or so. They have to get in line and may have to wait a day or three. They'll not be happy about that but hell, we gotta few other things going on. Thomas, how do we handle things on your end?"

"The police will be setting up a hotline for calls from anyone who might have any idea about who did this. We'll work with them to plan future press conferences and/or press releases based on any new developments. The press will be hounding the police, us and other agencies. We're already getting overwhelmed by calls in Communications. You had a chance to review the remarks I wrote for you?"

"Yeah, yeah, I express deep remorse for Powers, express our desire to get to the bottom of this working cooperatively with the authorities.

"Ok, so who did this? If it's not Special Ops, who could it be? Someone with pretty big fucking grudge, right?"

Zoltan and I nodded again.

Zoltan added, "And very smart to have figured out how to build a ghost gun and probably the drone too. He probably used his drone to scout the administration building and saw that Powers walk home each night."

"Yeah, that makes sense. So, what's the grudge? Probably not personal, right? Powers from all we know didn't have any enemies."

There was a pause while each of us thought hard about whether there might be some other motivation.

"So," Zoltan said, "Powers killed just because he acting president."

"But like you said to Blaylock, why?" I asked.

"That's the question," Mark answered. "Why? Let's think about what could cause such behayvah. Disgruntled academic? Possible but doesn't seem likely. Generally, academics are thinkers and talkers not doers. Former athlete? Possible. These guys are often hunters, familiar with weapons and even drones used for hunting these days. Employee or former employee? That's a wild card. You just don't know. Have to go through all the HR dismissals, find out who left who had an ax to grind. Zealot? Religious, environmental, cause-oriented? I don't know. Seems hard to make the connection but then again, these folks are sometimes certifiable. Alum? You never know, could be an alum with a combination of the above motivations. Someone from the medical center, say, a crazy scientist, but why would he be after the administration over here? Maybe because of the pharmaceutical companies knocking at our doors? Or our sponsored research programs which for all we know are involved in doing our government's dirty work? So, at least we're identifying areas of inquiry."

During this whole dialog, a notion had begun creeping around in my subconscious, an intuition and feeling that I knew something, that there was a patently obvious answer to our dilemma staring me in face that I did not recognize and strangely enough my jaw began to hurt. Very odd. And then it leapt into my consciousness.

"Holy shit!" I half shouted.

Berger and Zoltan looked at me as if I had lost my mind.

"What?" they asked simultaneously.

"I know who it is."

"What? Who?"

"It's fucking Sammie Kravitz, Kravitz's son, Samuel Kravitz II. Taking vengeance on his father's murder."

Silence. All of us in shock as we considered this possibility.

Finally, Zoltan said, "You could be right."

"I know I'm right. Perfect motive and motivation. Right degree of brilliance. Nasty son of a bitch. Vengeful."

"You sure you aren't sayin' this because the son of a bitch cold-cocked you last year?" Berger asked. "An' how do we know he has the skill set to pull off this murder?"

A long silence while I sat there ruminating about the past.

I thought back to the memorial service for provost Samuel Kravitz, where Sammie had taken his turn at the podium at the university's Patterson Chapel. He had articulated his family's history, his grandparents as Holocaust survivors, his father growing up in a multi-national, multi-cultural environment where respect for human life was a touchstone value. His father's elation only years before when he had had successful prostate cancer surgery.

Sammie had asked the congregation, "Why would he now take his life?"

The silence among us – university administrators, faculty and staff – had been deafening.

"So does someone want to tell me what actually happened?" He had challenged.

No response.

"This does not end here today," he had then told us. "We will keep looking for answers. Trust me."

The family had hired Blaylock to conduct an independent investigation, which is how I had met Alicia, and which had not discovered any certainty about Kravitz's death. Maybe an entity of Berger's purchasing the company had had an influence on their findings, maybe not. I was not going to ask.

Then last Christmas season I had met with Joan and Natalie at the Kravitz mansion at their request. Sammie had barged in on our awkward exchange and, much to Joan and Natalie's embarrassment, had demanded that I come clean about how and why his father had died.

It had all ended in their driveway near their front flagstone vestibule when I turned to tell him something to help defuse his anger and he knocked me senseless onto their cobblestone drive, sending me to the hospital. Thankfully, my jaw had not been broken and my concussion was only mild.

My mind sprang back to the present. "Well, we'll have to find out about his capability but, Christ, he sure as hell has the motivation. That's exactly why I think it's him. He's dangerous. He was sure there was a coverup and that we were all stonewalling, that his father did not commit suicide and he was hell bent on getting to the bottom of his father's murder. Very frustrated and angry that no one would come clean. What's that tell you?"

"What do you know about his present situation, whereabouts?"

"Nothing ... Look, Mark, let's get Blaylock to run a profile on him, get his employment records, any legal documents. Can they hack his email, his texts?"

"I'll talk to Blaylock about sleuthing his background, getting an in-depth profile. But hacking him, that's a different kettle of fish. From what I understand, the police have to have a warrant to do that and that would mean that Sammie would have to be a suspect, so no go at least for the present. But, um, there may be other behind-the-scenes resources for that, if you know what I mean."

Zoltan and I looked at each other. It seemed that Fitz-Hugh and Greta Hauser would be part of our lives forever.

"Maybe you should also pay a social call on his mother," Berger said, "hopefully when the sister ..."

"Natalie."

"Is in town. Never know what they might volunteer out of guilt."

"I don't think Joan Kravitz lives here any longer. She sold their mansion. I believe she's moved in with Natalie, in Chicago. Let me give Natalie a call. Jesus, I gotta think of a pretext. Maybe I go visit them in Chicago to ask whether they'd want to join you with a naming gift in a new administration building honoring our former provost." *Alicia! You could see Alicia!* my subconscious shouted. I felt myself redden.

A brief silence while we shifted gears.

"Okay, so back to my conversation with Fitz-Hugh this morning. Thomas, I know you're having a challenging day and so I gotta apologize for what I'm about to tell you, but, look ..."

I began to get a sinking feeling in my stomach.

"... it was bad enough last spring for me and my various enterprises to have to do this interim bit for two weeks after canning Wentz. Fortunately, nothing much was going on here at the time. Once we figured out the obvious and appointed Powers as interim, all I had to do was clean up Wentz's mess and transfer operations over to Powers once he was fully briefed and up to speed.

"What's going on now is completely different. For one, now I'm board chair, not vice chair, a much bigger conflict of interest. There's supposed to be a Chinese Wall between governance and administration. This ain't egg-zactly it. Second, all hell is breaking loose here and I really can't afford to get caught up in it except acting as a stop-gap to total chaos."

"So, what are you trying to tell me?"

"I cut a deal with Fitz-Hugh that if the national presidential election is not in his favor to come back as interim president. He's already making plans to come back to the States before the election, sees the writing on the wall. He'll leave it to staff to cover the bases between then and when a successor is named. In any case, he can be here as soon as the election is over in November while his family settles into a place they've already bought in Washington's Kalorama neighborhood.

"Aw, God damned," I heard myself say, throwing up my hands in exasperation, "Why would you do something like that? And why the hell would he accept, put himself in mortal danger every time he's on campus?"

"I get a sense that despite his ambition and narcissism he's feeling some guilt about what happened here. Apparently, he had no idea that Secret Ops was going to take out Kravitz, masquerading it as suicide, even though the whole thing was apparently choreographed by Ursula.

"Everyone here thinks he walks on water, board, faculty, parents, students. None of 'em know what happened, the truth behind how and why he left. Plus, he knows the place inside out. Has a natural ability to command and, despite his past conniving, I think he is now desiring to make up for it. And it's not permanent. He wants a big position in one of the think tanks and there are two or three of them who will pay him big bucks to be a fellow."

"That mean Ursula come back with him too, yes?" Zoltan asked with a big shit-eating half grin.

"Yeah, that's part of it."

"You need to keep it zipped, Thomas."

Berger gave us a look, one to the other, knowingly nodding his head. It did not surprise me that he knew of Ursula and my liaison.

"Part of it?" I queried.

"Yeahhhh." Mark looked guilty and bit embarrassed. "As an inducement I also agreed to recommend Greta Hauser, once she's left the State Department, for appointment to our board as well as

Fitz-Hugh once he finishes as interim – two distinguished international power houses."

"Two distinguished, fucking agents of the U.S. government," I countered. "God knows what means they would use to infiltrate this place and our centers abroad."

Berger shrugged, "Sometimes you jus' gotta play the cards you're dealt. You got any other bright ideas? Besides, this plan gets you and me outta this quagmire and front and center back to operating our foundation."

I couldn't disagree with him there, but the thought of Ursula had set off a firestorm of past memories of our lovemaking and then our confrontation at last year's board meeting where she had confessed to her role coordinating Special Ops.

"Back to Ursula for a moment. The last time I met with her was not at all pretty. I basically beat her up about her role at Sessions and with Special Ops. I think it's fair to say, I won't find her a problem should she show up here."

"Good," Berger and Zoltan both said simultaneously.

"Okay, so finally, how're things downstairs in Communications?"

I felt myself let out a long exhalation, running a hand through my hair, a gesture of frustration. "Just fucking dandy," I told them. "Somehow, I mean it defies the imagination, but they forgot about the Speakers Forum. Dates were set last spring, with the first Forum set for the first week of December. No promotions have gone out because no speakers have been lined up."

Berger looked chagrined, then resigned. "Okay," he shrugged, "another thing for me to do. I'll call around the board and see what connections we can line up, write me up a draft email that I can send out to our different division deans asking for recommendations, underlining that we need nationally recognized figures discussing contemporary issues, right?"

"Damn, Mark. You ever thought about a job in communications?"

Berger smirked, "Fuck no. Now get outta here," he said waving at us with the back of his hand.

X

That's the Spirit

THE NEXT AFTERNOON at 3:55 p. m. Nate Tuckett, chief of police, Berger and I sat behind the podium on the stage of the performing arts center on uncomfortable metal folding chairs under hot television lights, half blinded, looking out at the crowd of reporters, journalists, radio and TV media, faculty, staff, students and members of the general public.

I thought about the three of us, *See no evil, hear no evil, speak no evil. Hahahah.* I felt anxiety sweat pouring from my underarms and hoped I was not pitting out my olive-green suit.

The only saving grace from our predicament of this first press conference was that ironically this standing room only crowd had arrived, including most of the administration, without incident. Was this because of our new Blaylock rooftop surveillance teams which had set up this morning to jam and/or chase any suspicious drone that came into our airspace? Who knew? While greatly relieved, I was still worried about whether anything might happen when the press conference was over.

The clock ticked down to 4:00 p. m., time for the shit show. I stood and walked up behind the podium. The crowd quieted. Emily Sayzak sitting in the first row, smiled at me and gave me a small, secret wave of support. I realized that I could smell whiffs of her perfume all the way up on the stage, noticed the bad smell expressions of the two reporters beside her and wondered aimlessly as I grasped the podium and adjusted the microphone whether a random spark might ignite her malodourous presence and cause the whole place to explode.

"I'm Thomas Simpson, director of university communications.

"I'm sure we are all as deeply mystified as we are deeply saddened by the death of our provost and acting president, Don Powers, yesterday. To shed some light on the police investigation of this tragedy, let me introduce our chief of police, Captain Nathaniel Tuckett."

I liked Tuckett, a no-nonsense, forty-something black who had risen through the ranks by sheer determination in the face of below-the-surface and sometimes outright racial resistance. A smart, even-keeled, no bullshit guy, worthy of respect.

Tuckett in full uniform rose and came to the podium, surveyed the crowd for a moment, gathered himself and spoke carefully.

"I'm very sorry to be here today. Over the last few years I've had and our administrative staff and officers have had the pleasure of dealing with Dr. Powers, a thoughtful and fair-minded person, loyal to Sessions University. So, we understand your pain and sense of loss from this horrible crime. We feel it too. I speak for the entire police department in assuring you that our first priority will be solving the mystery of this unprovoked attack.

"That being said, this is obviously a challenging task. To that end, I have spoken with the FBI and they will be giving us assistance as we investigate. At present, to be honest we don't know who or what we are dealing with, individual or group, what their motive might be, why Sessions, why Dr. Powers? Obviously, a technologically clever person or persons or organization has committed this murder. We will do our best to get to the bottom of what's going on here as quickly as possible but will also say it may take some time to break this case. There is so little for us to go on right now.

"To that end we have set up a hotline."

The number and website address for the hotline appeared on the illuminated screen behind us.

"Should any of you think you have any solid information to provide us, please call. Rest assured that your conversations with us will be anonymous. Questions?"

Hands shot up from around the room. Interestingly, he called on Emily first, probably because he knew her, while many of those in the audience were national media whom we did not know.

"Was this a terrorist act?" she asked.

Tuckett responded, having anticipated the question, "At this time, we don't know. We have not ruled anything out. I would also tell you that the facts of the incident do not indicate as yet an act of terrorism. We shall see."

He moved on, calling on different members of the audience.

From my vantage point many of the inquiries were made by people I could only half see.

"What can you tell us about the drone?"

"From all eyewitness accounts, it seems likely that the drone was assembled by its operator, custom tailored for its assault, but again, that's not yet confirmed. It flew in from the northeast and left in the same direction but that does not necessarily mean that it was launched and returned to the same location."

"What can you tell us about the ghost gun that was used?"

"3D-printed and assembled, again in all likelihood by the operator. No prints or DNA evidence were found on it or the shell casing."

"What bullet was used? Was it recovered?"

"The autopsy found what was left of a 9mm hollow point bullet embedded against a back rib. Ballistics could not identify the manufacturer of the round. The same with the shell casing."

"What actions has the university taken to prevent another attack?"

"A private security firm is in place on a number of rooftops around the campus. They have jamming devices and chase drones should the drone appear again. Unfortunately, that doesn't mean that all of you should not continue to take precautionary measures when outside. We realize that this incident is causing the university great difficulties as this is a time of peak admissions visits, athletic events, and social gatherings."

"Why would the drone operator drop the gun after he shot Dr. Powers? Was it intentional?"

"We don't know."

At this point I thought, *Nobody gives a shit about the family, do they?*

The questions continued, many of them repeating what had already been asked from people determined to grab the spotlight for a news clip. I began to daydream as I sat there sweating, trying to look attentive and gravely concerned.

Eventually, Tuckett finished, and it was time for Mark to speak. You could see the crowd's attention shifting to thoughts of their follow-up tasks from the briefing, where they were parked and the best way out of the area.

I made my way to the lectern as Tuckett took his seat.

"Let me introduce our chair of the Session University board of trustees and acting president, Mark Berger."

Mark rose, somber, seeming to carry a heavy load on his shoulders, and went to the podium. A bit of an idiosyncratic figure. No notes.

As I had learned with Fitz-Hugh, those who are brilliant do not need notes because they remember every damn detail of every damn thing. Not only do they remember but they can work with what they remember, shape it, edit it, see it wholly as well as its separate parts. Admirable to those of us living in a world of mediocrity, and at the same time a bit galling.

Mark stood at the podium, looking down at its surface for a moment and then raising his head, his eyes large behind his glasses, blinking. The room grew still. The audience at full attention began imperceptibly to lean forward. He spoke slowly with solemn gravitas. He had them with his first sentence.

"Don Powers was an exemplary individual, a brilliant mathematician who accelerated through MIT and whom Sessions was lucky enough to discover and hire as a faculty member.

"Don was perhaps the most perceptive and even-keeled person I've had the pleasure of meeting in academia, which is why he also became a lynchpin in our administration. He could always be counted upon. Dr. Powers was a saving grace to our university's administration during the challenges of recent years when he willingly stepped into the breach as provost and then as acting president while we continue our presidential search.

"His loss is not redeemable but as an institution of higher learning serving our family of undergraduates, graduates, alumni, parents, friends as well as our community, all of which are counting on us, we must go on."

He paused and let his words sink in.

He isn't remotely using any of my remarks I prepared for him. I thought. I was surprised, but in no way insulted. He had decided to wing it and he was doing well.

"Let me express my condolences to the Powers family. This is an unspeakable tragedy. Our hearts go out to them."

Another pause.

"So, what happens now?"

The silence in the auditorium was deafening, interrupted only by the hum of TV lights.

"We are now talking with several excellent leaders to serve as interim president while we continue our search. We are fortunate to have Thomas Simpson, our former director of Communications return on an interim basis to help lead us through this crisis.

Thank you for being here. It's my fond hope that we will have some resolution to this mystery in the near future and get back to our normal professional and personal lives."

Mark finished by announcing that the family would be holding a private service and that a memorial service for the university would be held at the Patterson chapel this coming Saturday at 10:30 a. m. He then thanked everyone for coming and ended the briefing.

Afterwards we met with Tuckett and one of his lieutenants who took notes while I told them of my thoughts and concerns about Sammie Kravitz. They dutifully took my information, but had no reaction, other than to assure us they would follow up with investigating this possibility. That they did not have an "Ah Ha!" moment was understandable but disappointing. I realized they were being flooded by "tips" from a thousand "sources" and, not having any in-depth idea of the background behind my concerns and any knowledge of the history and culture of the university, not to mention the Special Ops plot we had dealt with, they could place no greater value on my information than any other. To them, on the surface it looked like Sammie was simply a guy angry at his father's death which the police had already found to be a suicide.

Zoltan, I and Berger returned to the president's office and decided after an extended conversation that we needed to act independently to follow-up the Samuel Kravitz II lead, with me being the point person.

All this was great in theory except that I now had the Communications Department to run with a major crisis at hand.

As we ended our conversation, Berger said, "Hey, so I know you'll be thrilled. I did find someone for the Speakers Forum in December.

"You did? Oh, fantastic. Who?"

Berger smirked. "Greta Hauser."

I felt myself close my eyes, put my hand to my lowered forehead and begin to shake my head while I could hear Mark chuckling.

Finally, I raised my head and said, "I'm speechless."

"Desperate times call for desperate measures. But you know, it's a big deal. By that time, she will in all likelihood be the former Secretary of State. Perfect time for her to be speaking at lowly Sessions University. A nice distraction from our assassin and a good time for her to be keeping a high profile. Come on. It'll be standing room only."

"Aw hell, I know you're right. I'll just go with it."

"That's the spirit."

XI

The Return

ONDAY, THE SECOND week of November, autumn beginning to fade from the foundation's view across the city.

The last few weeks had been busy.

For the foundation I had set plans for Jo Ann to join us as my assistant when she was able. We would see what Fitz-Hugh had in mind. Had discussed with Mark his recruitment of Fritz Johnson, the prior chairman of the Sessions board, to become the first member of The Mark Berger Foundation board. Mark was going to follow-up. We had tabled any other board member considerations until we could free ourselves from our continuing obligations to the Sessions administration and to the discovery of Powers' murderer. Blaylock had informed us that as much as they could tell, the ransomware attack had come from within the States. They were working on further follow-up. Not much help.

For Sessions, I had closely supervised John "Fine Fine" Stein regarding the arrangements for Greta Hauser's Speakers Forum presentation the first week of December. Plus, I had helped direct the department to stage a more robust and vigorous public relations presence to counteract the relentless coverage of seemingly fruitless efforts to find the rogue assassin. All the coverage was killing our admissions visits as well as the entire university community's morale.

I was back in our offices for the morning, catching up but all too aware that I had to call Natalie Kravitz and see where our conversation led. A month had passed and no drone sighting or communication, leaving the entire university and medical center in a state of suspended animation, all of us continuing to live in a world of fear and paranoia.

Mark had flown in on two occasions, taken care of mandatory presidential duties and flown back out again. Despite the presidential election outcome being as anticipated, Fitz-Hugh had yet to make an appearance, with no information put forth about when we might expect to see him. *Typical.* I thought.

Natalie flashed through my mind as I made my call to her, tall, elegant, dark-haired, her lovely interaction with Sarah and I when Sarah had been a babysitter for Natalie's children, her eloquence at Provost Samuel Kravitz's memorial service reading a passage from the Book of Wisdom, her deep caring for and attention to Joan, her mother, our totally awkward exchange at their mansion last Christmas before Sammie barged in.

"Natalie, hi, it's Thomas Simpson."

"Thomas? Thomas Simpson? Well ... this is a surprise," she responded.

Yeah, I thought, *I can see why she'd think they'd never hear from me again.*

"How have you been, Thomas? We think of you often. We are still so mortified about Sammie's attack. I hope you've forgiven us."

"I'm fine, Natalie. *Well, not really, but there are more important matters to deal with.* "Now working as the executive director of The Mark Berger Foundation."

"Yes, we saw that news in the Sessions magazine. What a nice opportunity for you."

"Thanks. Unfortunately, given Dr. Powers' death and with Mark serving as chairman of the Sessions board and acting for the moment as interim president, I've been called back into my former responsibilities for the time being."

"Oh ... yes, another tragedy. I'm so glad mother is now with us. We can shelter her a bit."

"How is she doing?"

A sigh, "Not well. I honestly don't think she'll ever recover from my father's death. I'm not sure I will either. She's increasingly frail, more forgetful. Being able to interact daily with her grandchildren is her one salvation."

"I'm so sorry ... Should I ask about Sammie and what he's up to?"

Silence. A long silence. *God,* I thought, *I hope I haven't really put my foot in it.*

Another sigh, "I'll be honest with you, Thomas. We haven't heard from Sammie since he hit you. He's disappeared."

"That's odd, isn't it?"

"Yes, very. We're on the cusp of deciding whether we should hire someone professionally to find him, we're so concerned."

"Perhaps Blaylock could help," I suggested and felt like a total manipulative creep the moment I said it. But Sammie disappearing certainly fit our suspicions.

"I don't know. We'll see ... Thomas, what do you think is happening at Sessions?"

I had hoped our conversation would not go down this path but I was not surprised.

"As best we can figure, someone has it out for the Sessions administration. Motive is unclear, but whoever it is he's quite clever. The authorities are baffled."

"How tragic."

"Natalie, I'm calling at the suggestion of the university's board of directors."

There was a pause while she processed this and chose to make no comment.

"There's some discussion about replacing our current administration building which in many ways has outlived its usefulness. A building committee of the board of trustees is exploring this possibility and, if warranted, will recommend to the board that an architectural firm be hired.

"We've made initial inquiries of other universities who have recently built or are in the process of building new administration buildings and their recommendations are that it be combined with academic classroom and display facilities that would encompass the arts, humanities, architecture, and engineering. In this regard, an idea surfaced about naming part of this space in honor and memory of your father who was highly regarded by the university."

"Oh ..." Clearly this idea caught her completely by surprise.

"Since we know one another, I was asked to call you and see whether the family might be interested in this idea and whether or not you might have any interest in working with us to designate an appropriate part of this new facility to honor Dr. Kravitz and also whether you might want to join in helping fund it."

I soldiered on. "I realize this is a lot to throw at you all at once. I'm actually headed out to Chicago in the next few weeks to meet with a new family foundation recently formed there to compare notes and discuss organization and funding directions. Perhaps I might call on you and your mother while I'm there to discuss these possibilities at least in theory so that we could understand how to advise the building committee and the architects."

Another long silence before she replied, "Let me discuss this with mother and get back to you, Thomas. I'm not at all sure how she will react. It could well be that we'll choose not to be involved. The past is still upsetting to her."

"Sure, I totally understand."

I was not surprised by this reaction. We wished each other well and ended the conversation.

My gut feeling was that, despite her comments about Joan, they would at least agree to my visiting with them. I wouldn't wait for a call, but would force the issue by calling back in a week or so and telling her that I had scheduled a trip to Chicago on certain dates. Only if they agreed would I then book my travel.

I grabbed my portfolio, laptop, and iPad, shoved them in my briefcase, took the elevator to the garage and headed to the university.

I parked in my usual spot in the lower parking lot and hustled up the winding asphalt walkway to the administration building glancing upwards and surveying the sky, as I had done the last two weeks, feeling a bit paranoid at the beginning of my walk because until halfway to the campus the lower parking lot was out of view from the main campus and its rooftop Blaylock agents.

They had informed us that unless they had a clear view of the incoming drone they could not focus their equipment sufficiently to distinguish its signal from all the other signals in the area, so the until the campus building came into view we were effectively SOL.

My plan was to update Mark, see whether he had any new developments to report and then go back to my former office.

Ms. Bemis's eyes widened as I entered the reception area outside the president's office. She was all business today, dressed in a grey pants suit and white ruffled blouse, only a short spangle of grey plastic triangles dangling from her ears.

She held a finger to her lips, motioned me over with a curled finger.

I went to her desk and leaned over so she could whisper in my ear as Jo Ann.

"They are here!" she rasped.

"Who's here?" I asked cluelessly, as softly as I could.

"Them! Fitz-Hugh and Ursula. In the office, meeting with Mark. They been here all weekend. I just found out when I got here!"

"Shit!"

"You got that right, honey."

"Aw, Christ!"

"That too."

I straightened up, caught myself making an involuntary motion to tighten my tie. I found myself wondering why Mark had not let me know about all this. *Well, nothing really to tell me until they finished their conversations,* I thought.

"What should I do?"

Ms. Bemis returned to Jo Ann's face. She picked up the receiver on her phone and punched her direct line to the president.

"Thomas Simpson is here."

She raised her eyebrows and hung up the phone. "You may enter."

I opened the president's office door. Something very odd struck me. Momentarily, I wasn't sure what it was but the room seemed much brighter, suffused with internal light. And then I realized that over the weekend Fitz-Hugh's grip and grin pictures with important dignitaries, politicians, even Hollywood types and his framed proclamations, engraved trophies, artfully rendered clear plastic awards and statuary had been returned to the shelves filling the left side of the room and the backlighting of the shelves had been turned on to highlight them. Plus, there was now a new, last shelf devoted to his service in Brussels, photos of him with international luminaries, royalty and bureaucrats, none of whom I could identify.

As I took in all this with one sidelong glance I thought, *How classic. His ego and narcissism are only exceeded by his magnetism and genius. What remarkable logistics have been applied to transport these gems from Europe to here in a matter of weeks?* I pictured Ursula in her Germanic manner harassing the crap out some diplomatic courier.

Fitz-Hugh rose from behind his desk, Berger and Ursula sitting in front. "Thomas, what a pleasant surprise!" he announced.

His dark blue suitcoat was on the back of his chair, his white shirt with rolled sleeves contrasting with his beautiful tan and his gold Rolex flashing through patches of sunlight as he came around his desk to greet me.

As always, he exuded fitness with only a smidgen of aging around his eyes and a slight softening around the waist, his brown hair with its highlights of blond, his teeth remarkably white, his eyes sparkling.

Mark rose from his chair and turned to watch, as did Ursula, looking far too attractive in a grey shift outlining her attributes, her lips forming a less than earnest smile. She was exactly how I remembered her, perfect complexion, swept back light brown hair, strong jaw line, high cheek bones, cold crystal blue eyes.

What a sucker I was to fall for her.

"Thomas!" Fitz-Hugh exclaimed, "It is so good to see you! Here we are, saving our university again!" As if we had been brothers together in previous times not adversaries.

You slick, double-crossing mother fucker, I thought as I smiled enthusiastically in reply.

We shook hands vigorously, each of us in a contest to crush the other in our attempt to express our bogus sincerity and filial affection. *Yeah, I can think of seven hundred and fifty million reasons for your enthusiasm with my now being Mark's right hand and the steward of his philanthropy.* Strong upwellings of distrust radiated from my abdomen up into my throat.

"Great to see you too," I croaked.

"Pull up a chair," Fitz-Hugh said, motioning to the conference table. I grabbed the faux Chippendale chair at the head of the table and as Mark and Ursula made room for me, put it between them. I could not help looking at Ursula's legs, taut, shapely, fit. I tamped down fleeting images of our former lovemaking, her legs spread wide as I lowered myself onto her.

Fitz-Hugh said for my benefit as he returned to his desk, "I'm here as a stopgap measure to help out our beleaguered chairman during this crisis, while the search for a new president continues. Hopefully for only a matter of a few weeks or months, although I recognize it could be longer."

My heart sank at his mention of months, but it was entirely realistic.

"I trust that Sessions is still moving forward along the same lines put in place during my administration as The Global University. I'm not here to forward that agenda but to simply provide administration, academic as well as operational and board liaison. Celeste and the children are settling in at our new home in Kalorama in Washington, DC and I'll need to be spending time there as well as here.

"Ursula, of course, will capably serve as my right hand in my absence."

Ursula smiled and turned to me, "And we are so glad that Mr. Berger as board chair was able to bring you back to Sessions for this period."

"Yes," Fitz-Hugh readily agreed, "You are an invaluable asset, Thomas."

"Thanks." *Blowing smoke up my ass.*

"To continue, for our safety, Mark is generously providing us with suites at the Intercontinental and a limo to ferry us to campus with a security guard here escorting us to and from the limo, that way hopefully eliminating the possibility of an attack from above.

"Over the weekend Mark has been gracious enough to brief us fully on your foundation's initiatives with Powers as well as all the administrative issues at the university.

"Gregory Blaylock and I had a good exchange this morning. The bad news he had to tell me is that their team here spotted a drone yesterday. At a very high elevation, out of range, it seemed to be scouting us, although there's no way knowing if this was the drone that killed Powers or some warped idiot trying to scare everyone."

Berger turned to me.

"Thomas, give us a brief update on communications. You're handling quite a load with this current crisis."

I brought them up to speed, our progress enhancing our communications, PR and marketing outreach to offset and complement admissions' own efforts, our planning for Greta Hauser's presentation for the Speakers Forum. I then told them about my morning's conversation with Natalie Kravitz, which brought a serious focus from each of them and a nodding of heads, including approval of the purpose excuse for my visit, a relief to me.

"And finally," I told them, "I need to talk to you about Ms. Bemis."

Curious concern from Fitz-Hugh and Ursula, Berger nodding knowingly.

"Strangely enough, Powers terminated Ms. Bemis hours before we met with him. She let me know prior to our meeting and I offered her the opportunity to be our assistant at the Foundation which she readily accepted."

I was watching their expressions and could not get a read.

"But then with Powers' death and Mark's service as interim president, we agreed that it was more important that she continue to serve temporarily the office of the president. This is all a bit awkward, but I want to get closure on whether and when she might sometime in the near future join the foundation. Fact is, with the announcement of The Mark Berger Foundation, even with the information being provided that its philanthropy would be limited and predominantly on behalf of the university we're being flooded with clueless inquiries and proposals that need to be at least acknowledged."

Fitz-Hugh nodded his head, put his fingertips together, "Thank you, Thomas, for bringing this up. Not awkward. Of course, we would be delighted for her to join the foundation, a good move for her, and her familiarity with Sessions, Mark and you brings all sorts of dividends. Give us two weeks. That gives us a chance to get up to speed and get a temp in here and orient her or him. Thanks for your patience."

"Thank you!" *Damn, the Foundation carries some weight, doesn't it?*

"Okay," said Mark. "Good. So look, I gotta get back to Bahston for a time. Got an em-par to run, or so they tell me. As usual, need anything, call, but for now it's Ciao. In the meantime, Thomas will shuttle between here and the foundation. Actually, since you guys are staying at the Intercontinental, check in with Thomas and take a look at our offices. First rate, as is the executive directah. From here on, Bryan, you are officially in charge."

I found myself wondering whether Ursula's proximity might cause a problem. No. Old news.

"My pleasure, Mark," Fitz-Hugh responded. "Ursula and I will do our best."

"I bet you will ... but no spooks!" Berger smirked.

That got a laugh out of me, while Fitz-Hugh and Ursula were momentarily stunned.

Back in my office in Communications, I sat in my chair and rotated it around to contemplate the woods, leaves now well past their prime, falling to ground as I watched, and ruminated about this morning's developments. The HVAC system came on, blowing its usual polluted air which I could hear lightly ruffling the papers on my desk. It occurred to me that I wanted and needed Zoltan's feedback. I rotated back around and picked up my cell phone.

"Yes?" he answered his cell phone.

"Got a lot of new developments going on. Fitz-Hugh and Ursula are here for starters. Just finished meeting with them."

"My God ..."

"Why don't you come out for dinner tonight? We can take a long walk with Sparky afterwards like we used to. It's been a while."

"Yes. That good idea. You tell Janet to cook good meal?"

"Uh, in that regard I won't be telling Janet anything except that you're joining us. She doesn't respond well to orders or requests even, but if you don't say anything, she'll soldier on."

"I should order food. Good Hungarian food."

"You don't have to do that."

"I order food."

"Jesus, okay."

"I come by administration building and meet you at 5.

"Make it 6."

"Yes. And we run together to car. Maybe I bring gun."

"You don't own a gun."

"Yes, but pawn shop nearby."

"You bring a loaded pistol into our house Janet will freak the fuck out."

"Hmmmm ... that true. Maybe I just not tell her."

"Aw, geez. Give me a break."

"Never. Hahaha. See you at 6."

I ended our call and sat for a minute gazing at the open doorway and then at the papers on my desk, a jigsaw puzzle of bureaucratic bullshit.

The was a polite rap on my doorframe. I looked up and was startled to see Fitz-Hugh standing there.

"May I come in for a minute?"

"Of course."

He entered, quietly closing my door as he did so, and sat in the office chair fronting my desk.

He smiled, mused for moment, then looked at me directly, "Perhaps one of F. Scott Fitzgerald's most notably quotations: 'The test of a first-rate intelligence is the ability to hold two opposing ideas in mind at the same time and still retain the ability to function. One should, for example, be able to see that things are hopeless yet be determined to make them otherwise.'

"That quotation popped into my head this morning as I was thinking about you, Thomas, and all that you have had deal with over the last three years, even as you have progressed admirably professionally. It's been quite a tumultuous time, hasn't it?"

"It sure has."

"I wanted to tell you from the heart how much I appreciate your steady and, frankly, proactive and even inventive stewardship during this period. Things would have turned out far worse except for your vigilance.

"It occurred to me that I've been remiss in acknowledging your importance to keeping our mother ship of the university righted and afloat. You are owed a debt of gratitude that will probably never get properly acknowledged given the circumstances, but I, for one, wanted to let you know of my appreciation."

"Thank you, Bryan," Was all I could muster, as I was significantly moved by his remarks. This was the Fitz-Hugh I knew and admired for his multi-faceted brilliance, one of his attributes being able to perceive the right moment and time to express exactly the right sentiment. At the same time, I acknowledged to myself that he was gaming me. Ursula had probably suggested that he visit. Nevertheless, I appreciated the trouble he had taken.

"Glad to have you on our team again, Thomas. Together let's hope we can set things right."

"Yes, sir. Thanks."

He rose and left, my office, a bit dimmer for the lack of his presence.

No matter how much I hated him for his duplicity and what he had done to Sessions University, I found it impossible not to like him.

XII

Chase

A T 6 P.M., as always carrying my damn briefcase with my iPad, portfolio, laptop, and other paraphernalia in it, wishing it contained some kind of weapon, a sawed-off shotgun perhaps or a jamming device, I found Zoltan waiting for me in the indoor protection of the atrium, the security guard eyeing him warily.

We left the administration building, breathing in deeply the fresh fragrant air of a crisp November day while we glanced around nervously at the clear blue sky, noticing students scurrying to their classes, their eyes also to the heavens, the sidewalks devoid of any joggers or folks out for an evening stroll. Our world was being held hostage to the whims of a nut case, probably the vengeful, undone Sammie.

Just before the entrance to the Farr Botanical Garden, we took the walkway that wound down the grass-covered slope toward the lower parking lot, woods off to our right, open lawn to our left.

"This is Emily Sayzak's favorite place to ambush me," I told Zoltan, "And ask questions I have to stonewall while she propositions me."

"Ah, you lucky boy," Zoltan said, a half grin appearing momentarily in place of his usual scowl.

"Hey," he said, turning. "You look." He pulled up the back of his sport coat and then the back of his black mock turtleneck. Nestled neatly against his hairy lower back, tucked inside his black jeans' beltline was a Kevlar holster holding a compact automatic pistol.

"Aw, hell, why did you do that?"

"It nice Glock. It crazy cheap at pawn shop. They throw in holster with it. Extra clip. Ammo too. Why not? We need protection."

All I could manage to do in response was shake my head.

We walked on, the stillness of late afternoon surrounding us, a few traffic noises from nearby roads sounding faintly in the background. Below us the drive that wound through the wooded park bordering the university came into view, my car in the lot further below.

"You call Janet about our dinner and food delivery?"

"Yeah, I let her know about you coming to dinner and to expect the arrival of Hungarian food beforehand.

"Thankfully, she was enthusiastic about our dinner plans. Not only because she did not have to fix dinner, but because the kids would love seeing "uncle" Zoltan and because as it happens, Jacque, Sarah's boyfriend, will also be joining us, an opportunity for him to meet another member of the family even if you are something of an imposter."

"But I real deal. Family where you find them. Not by birth. I look forward to meet boyfriend."

"Yeah."

I had by now on several occasions had the opportunity to interact with Jacque and found him to be a thoughtful and considerate young man, well read and interested in world affairs, reality based, despite his apparent technological brilliance. A good influence on Tommie. Sarah could have done so much worse that I was actually, grudgingly, admitting to myself that Jacque was okay. Maybe even an asset.

"I also called Jo Ann. Fitz-Hugh's okay with her starting at the foundation in two weeks, so she was thrilled."

"Yes. She be big help. Scare off all the sucks."

"Hah. Yeah."

I began to hear a faint buzzing off to our right.

A chill went through my heart.

We turned around, glancing at one another in alarm and then searching the sky.

There it was, a drone, a speck high in the sky, following the lower drive's route through the woods, descending toward us. I could not believe it. This was real, a bad dream forcing itself into reality. Panic.

"Oh, shit!" I heard myself exclaim. "We're out of view of any of the campus buildings!"

The realization came to me that the drone had surveyed the campus that morning and its operator had figured out that our current location was unprotected and then had spotted us this afternoon leaving the administration building.

"You head for woods," Zoltan said, motioning urgently at them, "I head for parking lot. Yes?" He started fumbling behind his back for his Glock as he began to run.

"Yeah, yeah ..." I told him as I dropped my briefcase onto the walk, turned toward the woods and ran, sprinted across the lawn like I had not done since high school, every fiber of my body, knees, feet, hips, hamstrings shouting 'What the hell!' discomfort and pain as I moved into high gear.

By now the drone was only a few hundred feet away. Damn, it was fast. It passed overhead, turned and then began a descent toward me, its buzzing increasing as it dipped and picked up speed, amazingly quick and adroit, grey plastic body with four engines whirring on extended arms, a camera below and below that a ghost gun, but I noticed immediately, an automatic.

Christ, I thought as I now pounded toward the trees that were jiggling in my eyesight more than fifty feet away, *I'm a dead man!*

From my side vision on my right I saw the drone swerve and dip and come for me from behind. On my left I saw Zoltan who was surprisingly quick on his feet make a U-turn back toward us and sprint toward the drone. He had the Glock out now, carrying it in his right hand.

No more looking as the drone chased me as I put my full attention toward making it to the tree line in hopes that the drone could not follow me through the underbrush.

The buzzing was loud now, a death knell, slowing as it lined up its shot and just as I was thinking that I was having my last flashing memories on earth of Janet and the kids, tinged with the deepest regret, the buzzing changed and grew up and down erratic. A shot rang out, I jumped at the crack of its sound, but I was okay. Within a heartbeat a car window shattered far in the parking lot below us.

Now completely out of breath I halted, almost lost my balance and turned. The drone was about ten feet behind me, about five feet off the ground weaving spasmodically in mid-air under the weight and suffocation of Zoltan's herringbone sport coat, a hole blown out of its left armpit, a whisk of smoke rising from the hole.

Zoltan, his Glock back in its holster, smashed at it with both fists and knocked it and his coat to the ground. The drone's automatic fired again, three rapid shots from under the sport coat, blowing large holes in it as we both cowered. But these shots were sent harmlessly along the ground into the woods. Zoltan leapt on top of his sport coat and the drone with both feet and stomped on it, Godzilla trampling a city, plastic splintering and crunching noises, until its buzzing went silent.

He turned to me and said between breaths, "Fucker ... ruin ... my nice coat! I realize ... as I make turn and come up ... behind you that Glock useless. I shoot at drone I hit you."

"Good thinking!" I responded, equally out of breath, "But you ... sure ... stomped the shit out of it! Nice job!"

"You run fast for pansy ass white boy."

"You didn't do too bad yourself."

"Yes. It is my walking. It pay off. But now I need new coat."

"Ah. My treat."

"I visit Goodwill tomorrow."

"That coat was getting pretty old and worn out anyway. Probably your body odor is what was starting to kill the drone. You just finished it off."

"Oh, look at you now. Big 'I Am' wise ass when moments ago you scared little pussy running into the woods."

"Hey, we were both scared shitless."

"Yes, that true. I have to get wallet and spare hard drive, keys, extra clip, other things from my coat. You put them in your briefcase, yes?"

"Sure."

He bent over and gingerly lifted a lapel, removed the miraculously undamaged items, glanced back up at me. "What we do now?"

Within a moment I called Nate Tucker's cell and told him what happened. Then I called Gregory Blaylock and let him know, mentally patting myself on the back that my communications officer's obsession with keeping a wide array of contact information had paid off.

A police cruiser arrived below us on the drive at just about the same time as two Blaylock agents pounded down the walk. The cops, hustling up the walk, waved them off but allowed them to gather around as they pulled on evidence gloves and gingerly removed Zoltan's coat from the drone, a now-mangled animal-like contraption looking like it had been hit by a car. The smell of gunpowder lingered in the air.

They drove their squad car up from the drive over the lawn and carefully deposited the coat and the wreckage in its trunk, and then drove down to the lower parking lot to examine the car whose window had been blown out and to locate its owner.

While they were doing that, I called Janet.

"Uh, we're gonna be a little late, like maybe real late."

"Why? What happened?"

"You're not going to believe this. Zoltan and I just got chased by the same drone that murdered Powers."

"Thomas! No!"

"Yeah. Luckily Zoltan caught it from behind while it was chasing me. Tossed his sport coat on it and brought it down. Smashed the hell out of it."

"Oh, Thomas, thank God you're safe."

"Yeah. We're going to be here for a while. They need to interview us. Blaylock agents are here too."

No sooner had I finished talking with Janet, my phone rang, startling me. Berger.

"Hey, I just heard from Gregory Blaylock. Are you guys okay?"

"We are. Close call though. It's just beginning to hit me how close it was. Anyway, we're still here. Where the hell are you?"

"Stuck in the God damn airport. Our chartah's grounded. Fog in Bahston. Probably can't get outta here until tomorrow."

"What'er doing for dinner?"

"Don' know. Haven't gotten that far yet."

"Well, come on over to our place. Zoltan's ordered what I'm sure is an oversupply of Hungarian food. You're more than welcome, plus we can strategize."

"Hungarian? Never had it in all this time. Is it edible?"

"Hah. Yeah, very."

"Sure. Okay, good idea. This drone fucker is a little too smart for his own good. Blaylock said that he'd added an automatic ghost gun to his drone and that in all likelihood he's already built a replacement or three for the one you guys busted up. He reiterated that they can't figure out anything from the generic electronics he's using and the unit you just trashed is likely clean, clueless. Anyway, I'll call my limo and get the fuck outta here. Be on the lookout for a delivery of wine. I got an idea to share with you guys and our good friend, Fitz-Hugh, is the one to make it happen."

"Oh shit, I can see where this might be going."

"Yeah. Not that I'm happy about it."

"Greta Hauser to the rescue."

"Yeah, somethin' like that."

"Guess it's going to be one of those evenings, huh? Lord, I could use a drink."

"You got that right ... Hey, so the word from Blaylock is that we need to keep this latest attack totally secret if possible. No need to set off a shit storm of more publicity and fear. The thinking is that this attack with its limited focus proves that all our preventive measures are actually working, so we'll innovate on how to protect that lower parking lot area.

"Okay, makes sense, if you can pull it off."

"We'll figure out something."

"Sure."

XIII

A New Uncle

FROM THE MAIN road we drove up a steep, curving hill, turned left and entered our neighborhood, a neighborhood of large, pretentious C+ construction houses on smallish lots for second-rung wannabes, a mistake in our lives made on behalf of nearby public schools, a community swimming pool, a clubhouse, and cut-throughs on each street that avoided children having to walk on roads.

I smiled a cynical half smile as I thought about Tommie now in private school and he and Sarah enrolled in the Sessions program for gifted and talented students, at how the clubhouse was rarely used and how the emphasis by our helicopter parents on straight A's and our neighborhood swimming team's competitions burnt out kids so that many, when they entered college, with the absence of their parents to cajole them, did poorly.

We drove down streets cluttered with the last piles of leaves awaiting county pick-up.

"What we tell family and Sarah's boyfriend about drone?" Zoltan asked.

I shrugged. I was too stressed to think about it. "We'll just wing it I guess. Let's just not go into any depth. Okay?"

"Yes. We be normal secret-keeping butt holes."

"Hah. Yeah. It's fucking stressful, you know?"

"More for you than me. No family involved. I not tell Kristina anything."

"Smart man."

"Yes."

We parked in the garage and as usual entered the house through the side door to the laundry room which led into the family room and growing scents of Hungarian food.

As she did every evening, Sparky came running to us, barking her pleasure at my return, jumping and running in circles.

Janet came out of the kitchen and ran to me, embracing me in a strong hug, gave me a passionate kiss. I was shocked. Demonstrative displays of affection did not happen in our household, ever.

Holding me tight, she said, "Oh, honey, I'm so glad you're okay. Your call really scared me."

Zoltan looked at us curiously, raised his eyebrows. I could read his mind.

Over Janet's shoulder, I mouthed, *Shut UP!*

His expression changed immediately to one of faux innocence, as if to say, "*Me?*"

Sarah and Tommie emerged from the kitchen with Jacque following them. They also rushed to me and Janet and hugged us, while Jacque stood back awkwardly.

"Wow," I said, my voice muffled by all the closeness, "All I have to do is have a near death experience for you guys to show a little affection?"

They laughed as Tommie said, "Dad, don't be a dufus."

My wonderful teenage son.

Sarah took a step back. "What was it like Dad?"

Zoltan said, "He run like grizzly bear about to bite him in ass."

We laughed.

"Actually, that's true," I told them, "God, I'm sore as hell. I was trying to get to the woods, but I wouldn't have made it. Zoltan saved me."

"Yes. I throw sports coat on top of drone. Thomas say my B.O. kill it."

More laughter.

"Actually, he clubbed it with his fists and stomped it to death while it fired off a couple random shots into the woods."

My family went silent, looking at us anxiously.

"Maybe I shouldn't have said that last part. Anyway, as you can see, we're okay. Look guys, you can't breathe a word about this to anyone. That's from the police, okay? They want to avoid another panic, like last time, when everyone went nuts and they had to deal with all the publicity, conspiracy theories etc. Got it?"

They nodded affirmatively. No wise remarks or uncooperative looks.

In my heart-of-hearts I was startled to see the family so caring. It made me realize that I was loved, not just taken for granted, a strange, unaccustomed feeling that penetrated my soul.

While Janet and the kids went back into the kitchen and dining room to finish preparations for dinner, Zoltan and I walked over to our bar in corner of the family room. I pulled out two of our best, heavy crystal glasses, poured myself a liberal neat scotch and him a similar neat vodka. We looked at one another meaningfully, silently clicked our glasses, toasting our continuing lives, and downed our drinks.

We stood looking at one another as the raw liquor blasted at our taste buds, burnt its way to our bellies and then built a warm fire. Moments later we felt a very helpful, stress-reducing rush.

"Whew, baby," I heard myself remark.

"It a good baby. Yes."

The doorbell rang.

I opened it to find Mark in his *Calypso* outfit with a heavy foul weather jacket over it, a driver behind him carrying a case of wine.

"Hey, is this the Simpson residence?" he smirked.

"Maybe."

"Chateauneuf Du Pape at your service."

"Well, well, come right on in, my friend."

"Mr. Berger's here," I heard Tommie say from the kitchen, "They're all gonna get smashed."

Berger's driver placed the case of wine on our kitchen counter. I pulled out a bottle and uncorked it, retrieved a decanter from the bar and poured it in, a luscious vinous scent penetrating the air. I went into the dining room to the scents of wonderful food, placed the decanter on the table, added another open bottle for good measure and checked out the spread before me.

They had set the table with our best silverware, wine glasses and China, linen napkins and placemats, everything we used for only the rarest of special occasions. There were plates of stuffed cabbage, chicken paprika, cheese biscuits and bowls of goulash and beef stew and egg noodles. Again, I felt an unfamiliar emotion of intimacy, touched by their display of affection.

We took our seats around the table, with me sitting at the head with Mark at the other end, Sarah and Tommie sitting on the kitchen side and Janet and Zoltan the windowed side.

Tommie stood suddenly, his eyes blinking rapidly in a spasm, his face twitching, holding up his glass of water. He said haltingly, "I would like to pro-pose a toast."

We all stared at him, shocked at his departure from self-obsessed Asperger's, so unlike the Tommie we knew, a wonder to behold. My kid was growing up.

"To my Dad being here. 'Cause if he weren't, Sarah and I would have to find shitty jobs bagging groceries, working at Mickey D's or something."

We howled.

"Oh, and Uncle Zoltan too. We wouldn't be able to do crazy opera and crazy science experiments that stink up the house."

Zoltan stood and held up his glass of Chateauneuf Du Pape, only half full because of a large slurp he had taken a moment before.

"And I would also like to propose toast, 'To my adopted family, the Simpsons. I love you guys. And to Mr. Berger, who's okay for Jewish midget.'" He grinned his awful grin and sat down.

Mark stood, raised his glass, "Thank you, Zoltan, and you're okay too for a giant scientific, cancer-killing, genius turd. Anyway, glad to be here with youse alls and Jacque. Sometimes bad weather in Bahston pays great dividends."

To our bemusement, Zoltan stood again. "I have what my father used to call 'brain wave.' I think it be wonderful idea if we now adopt Mark Berger as uncle too."

We looked at one another, smiles all around.

I stood, "I second that notion. What do you say, Mark?"

Berger paused for a moment. It was interesting to see. He was touched, just a bit emotional.

He raised his glass to us. "I would be honahed. You know, uncles can sometimes be useful folks. I had an Uncle Herman, who in addition to driving a Mercedes 230SL Pagoda, was an attorney. He became very handy many years ago when I got divorced from my wife, a dental hygienist who was attempting to floss me good. So, I stand ready to help the family in times of need or distress. Jus' call."

I held up my glass, "To Uncle Mark," I toasted.

We all stood and toasted him. "To Uncle Mark!"

Berger actually blushed.

We sat down with large smiles and began to pass plates and bowls around and refill already empty glasses.

As we began our meal in earnest, Jacque said, "If you would not mind, may I make a comment about Tommie's thought about so called 'shitty' jobs?"

"Sure," I told him, always impressed by his innate politeness.

"In actuality, were such an unthinkable and unfortunate event were to occur as your *disparition*, Sarah and Tommie would not be subjugated to such so-called jobs. Tommie is already proficient enough in his technology skills that he could be hired as a programmer, but of course, with the consent of a parent or guardian, and with limited hours, close supervision and no compromising his education and Sarah could easily be hired as a translator part time during the academic year and full time in the summer."

"Which gives me an idea," Mark said, "At the right moment as you guys get ready for employment, I hope you'll talk to Uncle Mark first. We got lots of needs for good folks in our various companies. Jacque, for instance, you and I should talk about our need for integrating AI into our enterprises, particularly our hedge fund but also about how to best manage inventory, purchasing, that kinda thing. I'd be interested in your thoughts."

"Oh, certainly." Jacque looked pleased. The rest of us were momentarily silent, shocked at a glimpse of a possible future.

"Jacque," Berger asked, "Tell me a little bit about yourself. Where you grew up. Where you went to university. That kind of thing."

I found myself feeling guilty that I'd never made this kind of inquiry myself. It felt so obvious now that Mark had brought it up. Jacque was just so polite and a bit shy and self-effacing that I had not wanted to pry.

"Ah," Jacque began, bringing his hands together, "My parents own a property, you would call it a farm, in the Loire Valley. It is over a thousand acres and for our livelihood we do a little bit of everything. Our grapes produce a nice Sauvignon Blanc, so we bottle just over 1,300 bottles a year, and sell them locally and regionally. We also have forests that we manage and livestock and crops to manage. We keep very busy. We hunt and fish, which helps keep food prices down. Nothing is better than a dinner at sunset and under the stars on our back terrace overlooking our fields and forests, dining on our own roast, cooked with our own firewood, drinking our own wine and eating potatoes and vegetables from our own gardens. Perhaps one day you could all visit our farm. I spend most summers there."

My thoughts about the sudden appeal of spending time in the Loire Valley was interrupted by Janet.

"You mean you actually shoot animals?" she asked.

Uh Oh, I thought and wondered what her reaction would be if she knew Zoltan was packing a Glock automatic. The horror.

"Yes, of course. I had my own rifle at nine years old. We live off the land."

"Oh."

I could see all the preconceived notions in Janet's mind clashing with this new disclosure, her fondness and respect for Jacque versus OMG firearms, animals being murdered and eaten even as we helped ourselves to seconds of beef stew.

Jacque continued, unaware or choosing to ignore Janet's discomfort, "As for my education, I graduated from the Sorbonne with a master's in Information and Knowledge Systems. I have always been interested in children, so I applied to Sessions for a teaching fellowship in the Center for Gifted and Talented Youth and I had the good fortune of being accepted. And now I get to help students like Tommie realize the merit of their special talents."

"Like building a Row-Bot," Tommie said.

"Most impressive," Mark commented. "Thank you."

From that point our dinner evolved into a more and more exuberant affair. Wine flowed freely.

After dinner, as the kids and Janet took our dishes into the kitchen and straightened up the table, Zoltan went into the family room and emerged with the bottle of vodka.

"No, no, no," I told him.

I took the bottle from him, went behind the bar, found my flask, filled it, went to the hall closet and pulled on my winter coat, placed the flask in its jacket pocket.

"Time to walk Sparky," I told him and Berger, who nodded their heads knowingly.

With Sparky on her leash, we headed to the cut-through near the house. I took out the flask, took a slug and passed it to Berger. All was still, except for the occasion barking of a dog piercing the cold air. Thankfully Sparky ignored the barking in her quest to sniff every pile of leaves, every bush, fire hydrant, mailbox post. The moon was up. Our breaths streamed out before us. There was a faint, dank smell of burnt leaves in the air.

Berger took a hit and passed the flask to Zoltan.

"After Blaylock," Mark told us, "I also got a call from Nate Tucker. He's obviously on the defensive and wanted to update me. They're checking in the different neighborhoods surrounding the university to see whether anyone has seen any drones being launched. No such luck. I mean, not that there aren't a bunch of hobbyists in the parks around here flyin' em, but nothing suspicious. They've even talked to a bunch of building supervisors about checking their rooftops to see whether there might be evidence of activity. No luck there either."

"So, Mark, you mentioned Fitz-Hugh?"

"Yeah, well, I'm thinking we now also ask Fitz-Hugh to talk with Greta Hauser about whether she can procure satellite downloads of the drone flying on the day of Powers' assassination and of earlier today when one tried to off you two. Find out where they're being launched."

"You think she can get those downloads?"

"Piece of bureaucratic cake. Sure she can. Will she? I don't know. A good test of Bryan's influence with her. But he sure as shit has done her bidding in the past. Let's see whether she returns the favor. By the way, I ought to have Sammie's research results from Blaylock in the next two weeks or so."

"What about hacking Sammie's email, texts etc.?"

"I'm leaving that to Bryan via Hauser. That Sammie is Kravitz's son and that Bryan remembered his testy eulogy at his father's memorial service carried some weight."

"So, what we do now?" Zoltan asked, passing the flask back to me.

Berger shrugged. "Wait. I'm headed back to Bahston tomorrow. I gotta charter on hold if I need to jet down here ASAP."

"Good."

XIV

Chicago

MONDAY THE FIRST week of December. On my flight to O'Hare I had spent most of the time beating myself up for bad planning. Unwitting bad planning but bad planning, nonetheless. Too many priorities from two job responsibilities plus being point person on our quest to figure out whether Samuel Kravitz II was Powers' assassin.

The result was I had scheduled this trip to Chicago, squeezing it in before Greta Hauser's Speakers Forum presentation on Wednesday, to call on Natalie and Joan Kravitz and to see Alicia. As it turned out, the Speakers Forum, given the attraction of the recent Secretary of State, had then taken on a life of its own, eliciting far more interest from the general public, not to mention the media, than we had ever experienced before.

I should have had the foresight that the media would immediately create a national stir with speculation about whether the Drone Assassin, as he was now being called, would choose this event for a slaughter fest. It was not that they did not know by this time that in all likelihood the assassin was primarily interested in offing our administration. They just chose to ignore that in favor of creating a tasty morsel false narrative.

About a week into these developments John "Fine Fine" Stein had collapsed under the pressure, had begun talking gibberish and arriving to work even more slovenly dressed than usual and sitting paralyzed in his office. I had sent him home for the duration, had talked to HR about the need for him to seek psychological counseling and how we could part with him in the future. I had then taken over his coordinating responsibilities, working hand in glove with our Special Events department which thankfully was solid and cooperative.

Early on we made the Speakers Forum a ticketed event where the purchaser had to provide ID. This would allow us to control the crowd as well as provide the names of all the purchasers to the police. We had arranged for campus security to cordon off the campus, admitting only ticket holders and those with university IDs, and hiring shuttle buses to also transport ticket holders from the lower parking lot and other remote locations. Our local cable station and national news organizations had lined up to broadcast the event, which created another whole logistical challenge. Given all this and the quickly sold out event, all audiences were encouraged to view Madam Secretary's presentation elsewhere, while we secretly hoped for bad weather.

Police presence and campus security presence were increased substantially with Berger behind the scenes paying anonymously for whatever was needed. We understood from the police that the FBI would be present but had no information about what that entailed. Classic.

Our auditorium, we understood, had been thoroughly reviewed by a team of campus security, the police and the Secret Service to be sure it would be secure before, during and after the event. Blaylock beefed up their rooftop presence. I felt bad for their agents freezing up there, although they had by now set up tents with heaters and other amenities.

Needless to say, I was very much on edge, feeling guilty that my trip to Chicago could be a badly timed, stupid and unnecessary boondoggle. Then again ...

My plane had touched down at O'Hare three hours before, snow pelting against the window two seats away. My phone's weather app told me that it was 5 degrees outside.

In anticipation, I had dressed in my heaviest three-piece suit, a full-length winter coat, a wool pullover hat, scarf, fur-lined gloves, hiking boots, my dress shoes in my suitcase, and yet walking outside to get a cab when the piercing wind gusted, I felt naked.

My itinerary: dinner with Alicia, then an 8 a.m. meeting the next morning with Natalie and Joan in Highland Park. Natalie had assured me that this would be the best time to talk with her mother. Then an Uber to the airport for a mid-afternoon flight back home and back to my home office to continue to prepare for the Greta Hauser presentation the following afternoon.

I was staying at Berger's The Hotel Britt in Chicago's Near North neighborhood, a contemporary building with a black facade, each floor sectioned by brushed aluminum balconies, its interior high end, modern glass and steel with dark terrazzo floors.

The hotel also housed a well-known jazz themed restaurant, Connie's, which is where I now sat, waiting for Alicia.

A jazz trio of electric piano, bass and snare drum were playing a soft and mellow tune. Given the ambiance of the place and having looked through the menu and seen two-inch steaks pass by, I had uncharacteristically ordered a Stolichnaya martini because it seemed appropriate for this more sophisticated occasion. Alicia had texted me that, given the weather and rush hour, she might be late. Hell, in this environment I was happy to wait.

The band's tune ended. They announced a brief break and, as I sat rehearsing my conversation with the Kravitz's, my phone buzzed in my pocket. I pulled it out, glanced at the screen. Berger.

"Howaryah?"

"Hey, I'm at your Hotel Britt. What a terrific place!"

"Yeah, that's what they tell me. I've never actually been there."

"Well, stop in the next time you're in Chicago. First rate."

"Yeah, so do me a favor. Step out into the lobby. They'll be a clerk there to direct you to a secure phone."

In the lobby an obsequious tall and thin fellow in a hotel uniform, asked, "Dr. Simpson?"

"Yes."

"Follow me, please."

We walked down a hallway off the lobby where he punched in a door code on a non-descript door, which opened revealing a small, bare-walled office with a small, cheap desk, rolling executive chair behind it, two cheap, leatherette chairs in front.

I sat behind the desk and picked up the phone while the hotel clerk made his exit. The desktop had a layer of dust on it. The air in the room was stale.

"So," Mark told me, "When we realized the Special Ops folks were tracking us last year, I had secure phones set up in all the places I might visit. Never got around to The Britt, but now that forethought has come in handy 'cause some of what I got to tell you is totally secret shit and, hell, I don't trust any hackable communication these days. In fact, Fitz-Hugh has again indicated that we'd be best off from now on to again go back to encrypted burner phones, so I've just sent off six of those suckers to the foundation."

"Geez, okay."

"First, an update: As it turns out, no matter how hard they've tried, Blaylock still hasn't found a way to electronically cover that little dell where the walkway goes to the lower parking lot. They stationed a guy there in a car in the parking lot and now a communication's going out to those in the administration to not park there — I think everyone in the administration's been avoiding it anyway — but to park in lot by the administration building which will now be patrolled. Students and others will be directed to the lower parking lot, thereby making everyone unhappy but such is life. This oughta pretty well prevent the assassin from having any administration targets, which in theory at least should prevent any further attacks.

"Second, some bad, complicating news. Fitz-Hugh was actually able to get information on the flight path of the two drone attacks. A miracle. But ... The first flight took off and landed at different locations and the second flight took off from another different location. The mother fucker assassin is mobile. Can't track him down. More than that, they're being launched outside the city limits, which increases the search area dramatically."

"Damn it."

"Yeah. I'm beginning to really hate this guy."

"I already did."

"Yeah, so I also got downloads on Sammie from Blaylock and from Fitz-Hugh. Very interesting."

"I'll bet."

"Here's what I've put together from both conversations: Being Kravitz's son and growing up in that household, it won't surprise you that he's a brilliant and extremely well-read son of bitch.

"Not surprising too that he graduated two years early from high school and, interestingly, like your kids was enrolled in the Sessions gifted and talented program. He then went to Sessions on a reduced-tuition, child-of-a-faculty-member ride.

"Unlike his dad, Sammie's not just a renaissance guy in the humanities, languages etc., but he's gifted in other areas. Built his own race car while double majoring in the humanities and, get this, engineering. First person to graduate Sessions with that double major and did it in two friggin' years what with all the credits from the gifted and talented program. Dad must have been very proud.

"From there he went on to Yale where he got a PhD in modern languages. Dad musta been over the moon on that one. Then things get really interesting. What kinda job you think he got with that background?

"No clue."

"He parlayed his engineering degree and his multi-lingual talents into securing a job at RDP Technologies, Inc. in their international marketing division, writing copy for the research and production of their drone products and my guess would be learning the ins and outs of building the suckers."

"Holy shit."

"Then whadhedo?"

"Tell me."

"Shortly after he planted his fist in your face, he went the fuck off the grid. Just disappeared. No trace. RDP, the family etc. were mystified. Thought maybe he'd been kidnapped or joined a cult or something. But then he texted Natalie anonymously from a burner phone that he was okay, on a personal quest and would be in touch occasionally."

"So, Natalie fudged a bit when talking to me."

"Yeah."

There was a momentary pause while I thought about what Mark had just told me, "You mean to tell me that the fucking Special Ops folks have been listening in on Natalie and her husband, her mother and Sammie ever since Samuel Kravitz was murdered?"

"That would be the implication. They sure as shit did it to us."

"But with us they stopped, right? Why are they continuing to monitor Natalie and her mother?"

"Good question. I think they did stop with us, but who the hell knows for sure. My guess is that they see Sammie as a loose cannon. They've tied up all the other ends of this mess, but if Sammie ever does figure out what's going on, all hell could break loose."

"And so they don't know anything more than we do about where he is, which is why they continue to monitor the Kravitz's."

"Yep. Probably."

"So they think too that he's our guy?"

"Yep."

"Hell, yes. I knew it! So, what are you going to do with all this information?"

"Nuthin'."

"You're kidding me."

"Thomas, I tell anybody but you and Zoltan and my ass is in big trouble with people it doesn't pay to be in big trouble with, as we well know through Kravitz's and Lusby's demise."

I felt myself gulp. "Uh yeah. So, what the hell can we do?"

"Oh, I'll let Blaylock give hints to the cops and the FBI. You know, they're just methodically checking all these bogus leads. While we know that in all probability it's Sammie, they aren't giving that possibility any emphasis at all. Frustrating. So, I think it's up to us with the help of Blaylock and Fitz-Hugh to figure out how to apprehend Sammie, and put it in the cops and FBI's lap, I guess. That is if they actually believe us. I mean the burden of proof on this is colossally difficult. Essentially, we gotta catch him in the act, or the cops or FBI do. Tough assignment, especially since he's not helping us out by not doing stupid mistake communications or manifestos or even launching new attacks.

"As for you, you'll have your conversation with Natalie which is entirely appropriate. Ask her about Sammie. See whether she has anything further to say."

"You know, Mark, here's what I'm worried about, since Sammie seems to hate me."

"He doesn't hate you as much as he hates what you stand for."

"Okay, but what do you think the chances are of his launching a personal attack on our family? Something like that?"

"If he wanted to do that, he would have already. Naw, his vendetta is against Sessions and its administration and board. He wants to make a big showing about eradicating the bastards that covered up his father's killing. That's why he's focusing on the administration building. Easier than trying to get us where we live, like me bein' in Bahston."

"Yeah. Okay. So, no emails or texts to go on?"

"Fitz-Hugh reported that nothing prior to the murder was worth anything. I mean, yeah, Sammie apparently was upset about his father's death and who did it, all of which we know, but no smoking gun of any plans or intent to do anything about it. I mean, he coulda been using a non-traceable computer like at a library or other venue to plan his going off the grid. I don't think we'll ever know."

"Damn."

"Yeah, we got a very smart adversary."

"No shit. Right."

"Okay, my friend, I gotta go. Hope you have good luck tomorrow. I'll see you on Wednesday morning at the foundation in advance of Greta Hauser's presentation that afternoon. Be a good time to brief everyone and figure out next steps."

"Yeah. Thanks. Look forward to it."

"Ciao."

XV

Alicia

I WENT BACK to Connie's and my warm, unfinished martini. The band was back from their break and had begun a more upbeat tune. As I was ruminating about my conversation with Berger and trying to decide whether to order another drink, I also contemplated my well-rehearsed talk with Alicia, where I told her about the drone attack and how in the aftermath my family's reaction made me realize how much we cared for one another, that I had lost sight of that, how much it meant, how important it was. It had made me realize that my relationship with Alicia was headed in a direction that could cause problems, problems at home. So, we probably should step back ...

There was a sudden awkward hitch in the band's playing, then a quick recovery.

I looked up. Alicia had entered the room and was walking toward our table. I watched as all eyes followed her, a striking beauty with a confident walk. As she took off her tan wool hat, her blond hair cascaded onto the shoulders of her dark blue, pinstriped, wool pantsuit jacket and her indigo blue, cloisonne-patterned scarf. I was taken in by her bright blue eyes and her radiance.

Her entry, I realized, had caused the trio to hiccup mid-tune and had caused every patron and wait staff member there to stop and stare. And, of course, she was oblivious, waving to me, a big smile flashing onto her face. I felt my heart sinking and my knees going a bit soft. Memories of her paled at her actual presence.

Christ, I thought, *You're in big trouble.*

I stood and we bussed cheeks. The fresh hay scent of her hair exploded in my memory. I felt myself grow embarrassingly erect and sat down quickly.

"I'm so sorry I'm late," she told me, "Traffic only gets worse."

She looked at me, looked at my drink. "You look harassed. Is that why you're nursing your drink?"

"A bit more complicated than that, but no matter," I waved a hand. "How are you?"

She reached out and put her hand on top of mine. "Better now."

I found myself speechless. Thankfully our waiter came.

"I'll have the same," she told him, "and he'll have a refill," she smiled.

"How was your day?" I asked.

"Busy. The world seems to have discovered our foundation and that's resulted in a tidal wave of proposals. Of course, most of the submissions immediately indicate that the sender never read our guidelines or did and is tortuously trying to bend their inappropriate request to them."

"We're going through exactly the same thing. These folks submitting think they're playing the lottery or something. I'm blessed now that Jo Ann has arrived as our foundation's executive assistant. I've drafted polite turn-down letters to fit the different categories of submission and as fast as these suckers come in, she's sending out rejections. I'm thinking we should put out a directive that we're closed to submissions at this time."

"Good idea! Brilliant in fact, especially given Mark's focus on Sessions. Unfortunately, our guidelines are much broader, encompassing all of Chicago. It will be an immense challenge just trying to make a difference.

"By the way, Jo Ann is so happy to be working for you.

Apparently, Fitz-Hugh ran everything through Ursula, so it was like Ursula was her superior in every Teutonic sense of the word. Wentz, however brilliant he was, was a total lout, as you know. And Powers was simply contemptuous. But, yes, I also have to hire help ASAP. We have piles of unopened proposals."

"Not cool."

There was a pause while our drinks came and we ordered dinner – two medium rare steaks with all the trimmings and then she looked at me earnestly, her hand on mine again.

"So, how have you been, Thomas? I've been reading about the murder of your provost and the terrorizing of the campus. It must be wreaking hell on everything."

"It is. A stressful time for me and our family. I haven't told you the latest. Totally confidential."

I watched her eyes widen and felt her hand tighten on mine as I told her about Zoltan and my close call. I left out, of course, anything about our working together with Berger to get to the bottom of who was the murderer and our follow-up dinner after the drone attack. I also found myself unable to bring up my prepared remarks about our relationship. The words stuck in my throat and were washed away with several sips of my new martini.

I told her briefly about my meeting the next morning with Natalie and Joan Kravitz and my discussion with them about their considering a gift in honor of the former provost.

Dinner came, steaks that sliced like butter and that erupted wonderfully against our taste buds, and our conversation lapsed into reminiscences. Our initial Blaylock interview and what each of us was thinking. Our lunch for her to thank me for warning her to leave Blaylock, the incredible food at a local Italian restaurant and our conversation, then her seeing me late at night in the hospital after Sammie had given me a concussion, our lunch in Washington, DC and discovering our mutual appointments to serve as executive director of our foundations.

Our conversation flowed even as we finished dinner and

continued as naturally as we took an elevator to my room. A part of me was shocked by the easy manner of our ascent but it was quickly overridden and dissolved by my excitement in Alicia's presence. Any negative thoughts, any resistance evaporated. I was all in.

We embraced and kissed the moment the door clicked shut, tender, loving, unhurried, exploring one another. Caught up in our growing passion, it seemed as if our clothes found a way to leave us. Her lips were soft, pliable, her tongue playing against mine. Her skin was impossibly warm and soft. I could feel her heart beating fast against my chest. Her body was lean, athletic, supple, yielding, her breasts with hard nipples were pillowed against me, my member up against her hip. And then we were in bed and I felt her grasp me, soft, slick and rasping all at once. Heard myself let out an exclamation and her a simultaneous moan and we were off to the races. God, we were nailing it. A rhythmic teamwork evolved from our initial thrashing. Suddenly all was right, coordinated and we descended into a subconscious world, reaching levels of impossible ecstasy and reaching for the next levels, continuing on into the depths where the entire universe consisted only of our mutuality, and then a hint, growing into a reality of release and finally our explosion together, multiple shouting out of our pleasure, extending it, unwilling to let it go. Until gradually it did, even as a paralyzing afterglow possessed us.

Eventually, I slid off her and we both lay in bliss, breathing heavily. Unable to speak. The smell of sex surrounding us.

After a time of almost dozing off, I heard myself say, "Christ, I hope we didn't wake anyone."

"Possibly the entire floor. Maybe even the entire hotel."

"The band and entire dining room came to a halt."

We began to laugh helplessly.

"Lord."

"I need a shower. Care to join me?"

"Ohhhh, mayyybe."

No two people had ever been as clean as we were after that

shower. I think we would have been happy to spend the rest of our lives happily soaping one another's bodies.

Alicia began to dress. "I still have work to do, I'm afraid."

I was disappointed. "Okay ..."

Finally, as I sat on the bed with a sheet over my legs, I shrugged and asked the question I had been torturing myself with for over a year.

"Let me ask you something. What the hell do you see in me? I mean, face it, I'm just a mediocre guy, plus I'm married with children. I mean, you're obviously gorgeous, could have your pick of anyone. Why me?"

She looked askance at me. "This from a guy who three years ago was an associate professor, then became head of marketing and communications at his university and now is executive director of a significant new enterprise?"

"Ah, I feel like it's all a lucky and happy circumstantial accident."

"It's not. And don't kid yourself, Thomas. For starters, I'm not very appealing to members of the opposite sex. First, most guys after an initial attraction, discover I have a law degree, am a former private investigator, have an Aikido black belt and sorry to say, am something of a workaholic. Just a bit daunting. Second, most guys are boring, self-absorbed narcissists with a completely undeveloped appreciation for the opposite sex. However sophisticated they might be, underneath it all they just want big-boobed fuck bunnies who tell them how wonderful they are."

"Good way of putting it."

"You on the other hand first, aren't bad to look at, but more than that you have an open, appreciative vibe, you listen, seem to understand and resonate with whomever you're with, which goes along with your being perceptive and politic. And perhaps most important, people naturally trust you. Don't ever underestimate that. Being agreeable doesn't hurt either."

"So, I'm a yes man."

"Way more than that, my friend, you're a great ally and as I suspected, not at all bad in the sack."

"Jesus."

"As for your being married with kids ..."

My God, I thought, *She's actually bringing it up!* I felt a great sense of relief.

She paused, thinking, obviously wanting to choose the right words, "I'm happy for you and your family. I don't want us to be an issue. I value you as a friend and as a colleague and more deeply as someone for whom I have deep affection. Let's just let time play things out and see where it leads us, somewhere or nowhere. Let's maximize what we have while we have it."

"My God ... okay."

XVI

Discoveries

ANOTHER COLD CHICAGO morning, light snow, overcast, the temperature hovering around ten degrees. I put on my full and insufficient winter regalia and, after a power bar and cup of coffee breakfast in my room, took an Uber from the hotel out to the Kravitz's house, an attractive, two-story millstone, slate-roofed mansion on a private, dead-end lane.

The Uber dropped me off at their front yard gate. The house was set back about fifty feet, the yard elevated, contained by a stone wall topped by a bare hedge fronting their snow-covered lawn, a big, bare oak back to the right. There were several steps up to a white gate.

The steps and walkway were covered by salt and sand over snow. The air was so cold and dry that my boots made crunching noises in the packed snow as I made my way to their mahogany front door. The door opened before I reached it. A fellow stepped out, black wool hat and long, black cashmere winter coat, black scarf, his breath steaming out before him.

I jumped, thinking for a moment it might be Sammie, but then saw a very different person. Pleasant, freshly shaved, open face which started at seeing me. He was carrying some mail and obviously headed to put it in their mailbox.

"Hey," he said, puzzled, and then remembered, "Ah, you're here to see Natalie and Joan. Good."

He walked up to me. We shook gloved hands, our breaths billowing out.

"I'm Walter Berenson, Natalie's husband. You're ..."

"Thomas Simpson."

"Ah, yeah, that's right. You're the guy Sammie hit."

"Yeah, that's me."

"Sammie's such a shit. Never should have done something like that. Natalie was mortified. Joan was crushed. Sammie's a thoughtless, God-damned bastard at times."

Probably always, I thought. "Yeah, where is he these days?" *Might as well go for broke.*

Walter shrugged, "Who the hell knows. He bought some damn big RV apparently, with all the comforts of home, even a workshop in it, and vanished. We think he's still back on the east coast somewhere. But he's pretty much gone silent. Could be anywhere. Anyway, it's good to meet you. I'll let you in the house."

"Thanks."

As we crunched our way to the front door, I tried to tamp down any show of excitement about Walter's information. Now we would have a better idea of the kinds of places Sammie might be hanging out. This was followed by a quick realization that it also meant, as we had recently discovered, that he was mobile, could be anywhere at any time, which explained his drones' multiple take-off and landing locations. So much for tracking drone flights. *Damn it.*

At the front door Walter punched a code into a small security panel. There was a click, and he opened the door. We walked into a comfortable, warm vestibule with a wide wood plank floor, a large, all-weather rug at the door, the living room and dining room off to opposite sides, stairway at the end.

"Hey, Dad, we gotta go!" Natalie's son, Ben, croaked as he walked in from the family room. He was now a sturdy, athletic beginning teenager, his voice changing.

My old friend, Marcel, Joan's standard poodle named after Proust, trotted in and to my surprise obviously recognized me, came to me, rose and placing his paws on my thighs told me how glad he was to see me again as I petted him and rubbed his ears. I noticed that he was now a bit grey around the muzzle. Time was passing, the kids were, what? Probably 15 and 14. What would I expect given our experience with Sarah and Tommie?

Molly, Ben's sister, came in. Totally transformed from her childhood three years before, now in slacks and a cardigan sweater, stylish boots, her brown hair now long and over her shoulders. I could see in them different genetic resemblances to both Walter and Natalie. *Thankfully,* I thought, *No resemblance to Samuel or Sammie Kravitz.*

"Hi," she greeted me with a small wave. "How's Sarah?"

"She's doing really well. Skipped her last two years of high school and is in Sessions' gifted and talented program."

"Wow, that's great! Give her our best."

"Sure will."

And then there was Natalie, tall, brown-haired, elegant, in jeans and a blue turtleneck.

"Thomas, so good to see you. You've met Walter, I see."

"Yeah."

"Sorry for this daily cacophony. It'll be quiet momentarily."

Walter said, "Gotta get to the mailbox and take the kids to school. Kids go to the car. Open the garage door. Good to meet you, Thomas."

"Mother's in the living room."

I took off my hat, overcoat, gloves and scarf, placed them on a nearby chair and glanced around as we walked in

It was a large, high-ceiled room with overhead lights. The back wall had French doors leading to a snow-covered patio, latticed windows on each side. The décor was modern, designed to amplify light. Lustrous oak floors were covered in places by handcrafted rugs. The walls were pale yellow with white trim, white bookshelves held neatly arranged items from children's artwork to family pictures to knickknacks and cocktail table books, spots focusing on oil paintings of Lake Michigan scenes, water vistas and dunes, sailboats. Off to the side in its own protected alcove was a black ebony Bosendorfer grand piano, a glass-paneled cabinet full of music scores, a metronome, and other odds and ends, a wireless, foot-activated iPad page turner on the floor. All testimony to Natalie's being a professional pianist.

Joan and Natalie sat on a tan leather sofa while I took my place on a facing blue print upholstered chair. Between us was a gabled table set with a silver tray, pots of tea and coffee, a bone China plate with small muffins and sugar cookies, bowls of marmalade and strawberry jam, silver butter knives, small, crested napkins. This, I reflected, was a house with staff.

I had expected Joan to have declined since I last saw her but was not fully prepared for how much of a decline, even in the comfortable, secure home of her daughter with her grandchildren present.

When I had first met her three years ago, she was a vibrant, active woman prior to Samuel's passing, a bit PhD disorganized but obviously cultured and brilliant. Active around Sessions in attending performing arts and a volunteer with numerous organizations from animal welfare to civil rights.

Now I saw a shell of a woman, arthritically bent over and frail, in part I was sure from the burden of our former provost's death.

Inwardly I felt so bad for her and for my task at hand. Felt like I was a fraud and a cheat in this assignment. Given all I knew about her husband's death and now having to see whether I might extract money from the family for a memorial, perhaps I was. But duty called and their participation in honoring our former provost could be a good thing for the family, help bring peace and finality to their mourning. *Yeah,* I thought, *you fucker. You can rationalize anything.*

"Thomas," Joan asked as I sat down, her voice now with a quavering to it, "How is your family?"

I brought them up to speed on Sarah and Tommie.

She was particularly pleased by Tommie's progress.

There was a momentary pause while they looked at me expectantly.

"So," I began, "I wanted to make sure we could meet personally. Mr. Berger asked that, given Provost Kravitz's longstanding role at Sessions, that I update you with our plans for our administration building."

Natalie and Joan looked a bit puzzled, but I continued.

"As you know and undoubtedly remember, the current building is something of 70's dinosaur. God knows what notions and decision-making led to its design and construction, but it has now outlived its purpose in any number of ways and is becoming a maintenance nightmare.

"Actually, I'm sure Samuel commented about it because like me he had to work there."

"Oh yes," Joan said, brightening for a moment, "Often. He hated that building and what he said about it was far less polite and good bit more profane than your commentary."

I laughed. "Oh, I'm sure!" *Just like Kravitz,* I thought, *the priggish bitch. Oh, but we must be respectful of the deceased.*

Natalie laughed along with us.

"As you know, I'm now the executive director of The Mark Berger Foundation and you may also know, Mark is the incoming chairman of the board at Sessions. You won't be surprised when I tell you that he is as unhappy or perhaps even more unhappy with our antiquated administration building as everyone else.

"Mark wants a new administration building for Sessions and he's willing to put his money where his mouth is. Now what I'm telling you from this point forward is confidential. The current administration and the board building committee have done research and have also contacted other universities who have recently completed or are in the process of completing new administration buildings. In this new world of ours where a university's administration is often not looked upon fondly, it turns out that such new buildings are better received and also better utilized when they also help further the university's educational goals.

"For instance, Sessions has significant needs for visual arts, design arts and other display space from many departments in the humanities as well as engineering, architecture, and technical disciplines. This space as part of a new administration building would not only be of educational benefit to the undergraduate and graduate students but at limited times, like the weekends, could also serve the general public. The thought is that the first and perhaps even a lower level the new building could be used for these purposes while the upper levels could house the administration."

I paused to gauge their reaction. They had been nodding along amiably but still a bit puzzled at my intent in sharing all this information.

"What's happening," Natalie asked, "with the presidency? Would a new president be on board with this development for instance?"

Mentally I breathed a sigh of relief. Thank God she did not get into Powers' murder, which would have only brought up memories of Kravitz's so-called suicide and unleashed a Pandora's Box of uncertainty. I could tell that she did not want to go there any more than I did.

"Good question, Natalie. Let's put it this way, I very much doubt the board would hire any candidate that was not fully on board with this plan."

"That makes sense."

"We're fortunate now as luck would have it to have Bryan Fitz-Hugh, who's more or less between assignments, back to serve as interim president. It's anticipated that once his job is done at Sessions, he'll become a fellow at one of the more prominent think tanks in Washington. In any case, he's doing a fabulous job, like he did before, of running a tight ship." *A lie? Hard to know.*

"Mark has in mind that if the board's building committee decides to go forward and hire an architecture firm to create a conceptual design for the new building, he will, probably anonymously, personally or through our foundation, fund that work. Also, he will likely make a significant naming contribution toward the building's completion.

"The reason I'm here today is bring you up to speed on these developments and as well seek your advice."

They were listening carefully now.

"Several of the building committee members *A lie* have told us that they still feel somewhat bereft about Samuel's death and have asked, should this new plan go forward, whether a fitting memorial might be considered for the new administration building to honor his tenure and his dedication to the humanities."

I watched as Natalie immediately understood where I was headed with my conversation whereas Joan seemed both pleased and uncertain. She had not fully processed what I was about to say.

"Mark sent me here to brief you on these developments and to keep you informed as they progress with the thought that at a later date perhaps you might consider joining him and others in naming an appropriate part of the new building in honor and memory of our former provost. No need to make any decisions at this time," I added hastily, "This is just something for you to consider over the next year or so. In fact, as all the planning is finalized, I'll be in touch about visiting again, if that's okay with you."

Tears formed in Joan Kravitz's eyes and she reached for one on the small napkins to stanch them.

Natalie looked at her mother with concern, then turned to me. "Well, Thomas, thanks for this briefing. We'll look forward to receiving more information as time goes on. Of course, as you note, we cannot make any consideration at this time."

"Oh, of course." *I'm just glad you're not just throwing me out on my ear. At least Sammie's not here.* Thanks so much for your time."

I thought momentarily about bringing up Sammie and his whereabouts, but I already had the information I needed from Walter. Best not to press my luck and upset Joan even more.

She and Joan ushered me to the door while we exchanged the

usual pleasantries. I ordered an Uber from my phone. We stood there awkwardly for a few minutes and then I left them, crunched down the walk, through their gate and to the road where the Uber was pulling up. Breathed a huge sigh of relief tinged with sadness and guilt as I got in the car.

At O'Hare I was early for my flight, which was fine by me. Once I was at the gate, I gave Berger a call.

"Howarya?"

"Okay I guess."

"I was jus' getting ready to give you a call. As discussed, I'm flyin' in late tonight to meet with you, Fitz-Hugh, Ursula and Zoltan at the foundation tomorrow morning, 8 a.m. Hotel will be in there early to take care of the prep, coffee, croissants etc. Let's get some movement on Sammie. Plus, I gotta meet with Fitz-Hugh separately on all the other university bullshit, including the program for Greta Hauser's presentation in the afternoon.

"So, how'd it go in Chicago?"

"Natalie and Joan are pleased that we've thought of them and wish to keep them informed. I lightly put forward that once the new building has been approved, I would come out and review the plans with them and see whether they might wish to join you in naming and dedicating a specific memorial in the new building in honor of Provost Kravitz. They'll at least hear me out."

"Any news about Sammie?"

"Yep. I ran into Natalie's husband, Walter, on my way into the house and he let it be known that Sammie before he disappeared had bought a large RV with its own workshop and that he suspected that he was still on the east coast."

"Wow. Well, that's explains why he's so mobile. All he has to do is drive around and figure out randomly where he wants to launch and pick-up."

"Yeah, changes our thinking quite a bit. For starters, unless we can track his drones in real time, we're SOL."

"Yeah."

"Plus, the police are at a useless pursuit trying to find him at local apartment buildings etc. You think they might get a hint from us that they might consider looking at RV camps and such, places where Sammie might be overnighting. That kind of thing."

"To be honest, I dunno. I'll give it a shot. As far as figuring out the make and model, getting the license plate number for his RV, I'll bet he bought it under a different name, like shell LLC or something. He's that smart. I'll get Blaylock to figure all that out. God knows we can't count on the cops or the FBI to give our interest in Sammie any credence. I'm getting the feeling they think we're nut jobs wasting their time."

"You're probably right … So, something else occurred to me. I'm surprised we did not think of this already."

"Yeah?"

"If Sammie is at the center of this, and he's caught, he's going to be the focus of a very public trial and go to prison for a very long time. Another huge tragedy for the Kravitz's. I can't see them ever wanting to make any future contributions to the university in that case."

"Yeah, good point … Tell you what. That happens, I'll make the entire God damned contribution in the provost's honor and memory, with their permission of course. The fucker at least deserves that. He served Sessions well for decades before Fitz-Hugh and all this shit started flying."

"That would be exceptional, Mark."

"Well, let's hope it doesn't come to that, but it damned well might."

"Yeah."

"How'd your other meeting go with the ED from the McDonald Foundation?"

"Very well. You know, despite our different objectives, I think we should stay in touch with them. We're facing a lot of the same issues administratively and who knows what the future holds with our joint missions over time."

"Makes sense. I'd be damned interested in meeting Gaylord McDonald at some point. He's a friggin' legend."

"So are you, my friend."

"Ah, bullshit."

On the seemingly endless, gaining an hour flight back home, I contemplated the new reality of Alicia and me.

I had anticipated that at some point I would be hit with a wave of guilt, pangs of anxiety about the danger of hurting my family. I kept searching my subconscious for their arrival and ... well, all I felt was my normal anxiety about the universe I inhabited.

With Ursula, it had been a much more intense and a much riskier situation, a liaison with a co-worker which, if discovered, threatened an explosion – the loss of my job, public humiliation, devastation to our family, certain divorce.

What was most confounding about my relationship with Alicia was that it seemed to exist in complete independence from Janet and our family. Two separate worlds.

I pictured Alicia and I arriving independently at various foundation educational conferences in the U.S. and abroad. Three to five days of romance and then back to our regular lives.

I kept wondering whether I was fooling myself with this perception, but no matter how I approached the situation, while I did not want to admit it, I actually felt rather superb, buoyed by this new love and its unencumbered happiness, joy even.

I wondered what Zoltan would say about the situation. I had an immediate strong feeling that I would tell him.

I felt myself grimace.

XVII

Welcome Home

MY PLANE ARRIVED back at our airport just before 4 p.m. and who would you guess was there to meet me? My loving and supportive wife? No, she was still at work.

Sarah and Tommie, my dear kids? Well, no, they, and perhaps Jacque, were probably hanging out at home snacking on whatever they could find in the fridge.

Zoltan? Hell, he was undoubtedly in his lab, lost in space, probably having forgotten about my trip, perhaps thinking about texting me to see whether we should meet at the university club.

So, who was there to meet me?

Oh, of course, Emily Sayzak, standing back on the concourse when I exited the jetway with my roll-aboard, other passengers before me looking askance at her as they passed and met with a waft of her perfume.

I must admit that, as usual, she looked good, in a red cloth overcoat, bright red scarf, too tight black slacks, her stiff blond curls sticking out from of all things, a red plastic beret. Until one came close it was difficult to notice her excessive makeup.

But there she was, waving at me like I was a soldier returning home from war.

Christ, I thought, *Fucking welcome home.*

"Emily, what the hell are you doing here?"

"I don't even get a hug? You have no idea how much I've missed you, Thomas."

"God damn." I gave her a perfunctory hug. At least that was the way it started until she held me tight and planted her right breast against my chest and her pubis against my thigh. I had to get away from this woman.

"Emily, what do you want?" I asked her as I pulled away and began hustling to my car, trying to remember where I had parked it and where I had securely stored my parking ticket.

"How did you know to meet me here?"

"That cold bitch at the foundation told me you were in Chicago on business and that you'd be back today. The rest I just figured out. Only two direct flights arriving here daily; only one in the afternoon. Met some nice folks in the bar before your flight came in."

She was walking beside me, her chicken legs in a rapid cadence, keeping up. Her perfume, of course, accompanied us.

"No one seems to have a clue about this drone guy. I thought maybe you'd know something. You always know way more than you let on. Oh, and thanks a lot for lying to me about that little Jewish guy in the expensive three-piece suit, Mark Berger. He's your new chairman of the board and rich as hell, like one of the richest people in the world."

"Yeah, true. Sorry." I said insincerely.

"He's single, isn't he?"

"Very." *Aw, shit.* I could see where this was going.

"Could you introduce us? I'd love to do a profile interview with him for the paper. Give him and Sessions a lot of good play. Not focus on all the other crap that's been going on."

And jump on his bones. Thank God, honey, you don't know all the crap that's gone on.

"I don't know that his publicists would want that. He's pretty private. Plus, he's crazy busy."

"But you work for him, right?"

Reluctantly, I nodded, "Yeah." *I can't get to my car fast enough.* I picked up my pace, the roll-aboard clanking along over the flooring. Emily was almost running now.

"But, Thomas, don't they have leads on this drone guy?" Her voice quavered with her efforts to keep up.

"I have no idea. I'm not involved in the investigation of course. And how do you know it's a guy?"

"Just stands to reason."

"Okay, if you say so."

"You have to admit, I have good intuition, which I why I'm here now. How about you buy me a drink? Could we have dinner? I could fix you a nice dinner at my place."

Oh, I bet. Emily a la mode.

"Emily, I have to go home to the family. I'm sorry to disappoint you. I appreciate all the trouble you've gone to meet me here."

"How disappointing," she told me, sticking out her lower lip in a childlike pout.

Sensing the end of our conversation, I slowed to a stop. In her favorite move, her hand snaked out and through the opening of my overcoat and suit coat and grabbed my left love handle. "Well, Thomas, keep in touch will you?" she said, drawing closer.

"Sure thing," I said, as I turned away and thought, *Never!*

Times like this, Emily Sayzak scared the crap out of me.

I walked out to a cold, wet overcast afternoon and heard myself chuckle. It was such nice weather compared to Chicago. All a matter of perspective. Remembered where I had parked the Bimmer and finally located the lot ticket in the back of my wallet.

As I drove home, I felt a profound exhaustion creep over me. Once there I went into my office, closed the door and played catch-up with the day, making phone calls, answering emails and breathing a sigh of relief that all the logistics, security, streaming and media services were lined up and ready to go. Even better, tomorrow promised miserable weather, overcast, foggy, drizzling, temperatures in the low 40s. Someone up there in the heavens liked us perhaps, or it was just good luck? I breathed a long sigh of relief.

I mumbled my way through dinner and the evening, Janet look-ing askance at me several times. I apologized. Gave her a brief, tip of the iceberg summary of my meeting with Alicia and with the Kravitz's, enough that she understood that I had not only been hew-ing to a tight travel schedule but that while my meeting with Alicia was collegial on behalf of our mutual new foundations, my meeting with the Kravitz's had been a stress-inducing tightrope walk and that I was on pins and needles about the Speakers Forum. The kids were, as usual, self-absorbed and oblivious, Sarah on her cell phone with Jacque and Tommie only taking time away from his computer to stuff his face with our pre-prepared, grocery store chicken burritos.

By 9:30 I was in bed, asleep.

XVIII

Madam Secretary

THE NEXT MORNING, I arrived at the foundation early to the welcome smell of fresh brewed coffee, croissants, and pastries in the conference room. The hotel kitchen crew was finishing setting up a serving table.

The door to Mark's suite was closed. He had obviously arrived late and spent the night there as a matter of practicality. As I transferred my portfolio and iPad to the conference room table, he emerged in dress slacks and a white dress shirt, still looking a bit groggy.

"Mornin'. Need coffee. You get some rest?"

"Yeah. More or less."

"Madam Secretary arrived last evening late with a Secret Service detail. Even though she's officially out of office, I guess the detail sticks around for a while. Another great use of our tax dollars. Interesting, she insisted that we accommodated them on a different floor, which we had to clear. Anyway, perhaps it's my deviant mind but I imagine she and Bryan maybe stayed together last evening. I'm sure Ursula was thrilled by that." He smiled. "Yeah, just another daunting Sessions University day."

I shook my head.

Bryan was next to arrive, brimming with confidence but with a hint of nervousness, a smidgen of self-consciousness under it all. He poured himself a cup of coffee and sat at the end of the table.

Zoltan came in scowling as usual, greeted none of us but went to the coffee urn, poured a cup of coffee, drank it down, refilled, grabbed three muffins on one of the small plates and paying us no attention, sat down at Bryan's end of the table and began devouring the muffins.

"Sociable, aren't we?" Berger told him as he took his chair at the other end.

"Mmmmfff ..."

"Such a sweetheart."

"Mmff ..."

Ursula walked in, sleek and cold, dressed in a mauve shift, as always momentarily making me wish she were not such a knockout until I was hit by the recollection of her coordinating the operations that led to Kravitz's and Lusby's deaths. She took a seat in the middle, giving us a perfunctory nod as she booted up her iPad.

I sat across from her, opened my portfolio.

Mark cleared his throat, "So, I have bad news," he told us. "Thomas here discovered that our possible assassin initially bought an RV, which helps explain why we couldn't locate him anywhere. Moving target.

"Blaylock with some research was able to identify Sammie's LLC, which had bought the RV, and with that info and the general timeframe of his purchase, discovered that in Delaware he had bought a 35-foot Superstar RV with a workshop. These suckers cost well over $250 grand. We got the registration and plate number, etc. With this new information we convinced Captain Tuckett that it might be worth his while to have the police check out all the RV sites and other places frequented to see whether they could find him. Two problems."

We were all staring intently at Berger. He had our full attention.

"One, police, double checking with DMV, discovered that he's fucking sold the RV. Two, Tuckett's now pissed off that he sent his folks out looking for an RV, wasting their time."

"Ah shit," I heard myself say. I glanced at Bryan and Ursula.

Stunned silence as they absorbed what Mark was telling us. Zoltan's normal ax murderer expression was unchanged.

"Well, there's one interesting thing about all this. He sold it in a nearby state, another indication that he's our guy. But at the same time, I don't think we're going to be able to count on Tuckett being cooperative from this point forward."

"What we do now?" Zoltan asked.

"Turns out Sammie sold the RV for cash. A falsified seller and address bill of sale turned up with the VIN number of the RV, so the police are going after the RV dealer that bought it. But there's no way to trace Sammie.

"So, I talked all this over with Blaylock. They think he's probably found a way to finagle the use of some other vehicle, paid cash, say, and just driving it with the former owner's plates and registration and they think he probably also found some place to rent so he can hide out where no questions are being asked of a cash customer. All this make sense?"

"God damn it," I heard myself say.

"Yeah. We're back at a dead end. Plus, it's a long ass dead end. The police have been checking out the drone Zoltan trashed and they reckon that it has a range of over twenty miles. That's a hell of a big search area, goes out into the surrounding counties. Fortunately, thank God, no one's leaked any info about the attack on Thomas and Zoltan, so at least we've avoided another conflagration of publicity."

"Which brings us back to Zoltan's question," Fitz-Hugh said, as much to hear himself speak than anything else.

"Blaylock suggests we set up a trap," Mark told us, "Where the so-called Drone Assassin thinks he can off another victim, then scare him off before he can attack and surreptitiously follow the drone to its pick-up point, close in on him there or follow him to his hiding place."

"That would require real time surveillance," Fitz-Hugh observed. I realized Mark had been setting up Fitz-Hugh for him to make this observation.

"So yeah, you're right, Bryan," Berger said, looking directly at him, "To pull off a trap apprehension would require real-time surveillance. Nice trick if you can do it. Maybe you could help with that, Bryan?" he asked.

Fitz-Hugh raised his hands, a signal of helplessness. "At this juncture, that's very unlikely. All of us former officials are now in a kind of powerless limbo. We retain some of our reputed importance but that's it. Maybe the FBI could pull it off."

Zoltan's balled fist hit the table. Coffee cups jumped and rattled on their saucers, spilling coffee over its surface.

Zoltan's normal savage expression had gone livid.

"You, Mr. Acting President," he said loudly, snidely, "Are worst kind of leader, greedy ambitious fool!"

I looked over at him, shocked and astounded, *What the hell are you doing?* I thought, *Are you crazy?*

I looked at Ursula. She was as shocked as I. Mark was looking at him, his head back, eyes wide with surprise.

Zoltan was unfazed. "Yes, you do great things here. Moved university in right direction with global thinking, green campus and lot of other shit. Create enthusiasm. But then you corrupt us with Special Ops. People get murdered, Kravitz, Lusby, Powers, their families and we here at university devastated. And now whole university and med center be held hostages to crazy drone person who may be fucking Sammie Kravitz out for revenge. This all because of you!"

From all appearances Fitz-Hugh was not fazed. I could not believe it.

He looked at Zoltan evenly and said flatly, "Zoltan, I can understand why you feel this way. While you're certainly right about the facts, please understand, these situations developed in ways no one could anticipate with tragic and unfortunate consequences."

Zoltan threw up his hands, "Ah, you simply same slippery bullshit artist you always been. You fake leader. Lead us and university to destruction. You failure!"

And Fitz-Hugh just took it. Said nothing, his jaw set, head held high, his expression hardened.

I looked at Ursula, same expression.

After a long silence, Mark said, "Can we get things back on track? Internal bickering is not gonna help save this place."

"I agree," I said much more loudly than I had intended.

"So," Mark continued, "The only way anyone can see that we can flush this sucker out is for someone to play decoy. The assassin, given Thomas and Zoltan's attack, has obviously figured out that Blaylock can't monitor the path to the lower parking lot. Now we've prevented any further attacks by switching the administration parking to the lot next to the administration building and having students and others park below, thereby preventing anyone from the administration from walking down that path.

"Now we could have somebody routinely traveling from the administration to the lower parking lot each day to entice our assassin to make another attack, try to scare him off and track the drone to its landing place. Make sense?"

We all looked around the room and I found their gazes all settled on me. I felt my insides well up into a total panic.

"I've got a family!" I blurted out.

There was an awkward pause.

And then Zoltan said, "I do it."

He looked directly at Fitz-Hugh and then to Berger. "Someone got to be man around here. I do it if you give me bulletproof vest and weapons to carry. At end of each day I walk down to lower parking lot like we did before. I act like I have car parked there. I have shoulder holster with laser sight handgun, big bore with shells filled with heavy kind of shot. Make so I cannot miss taking out drone if plan fuck up and I must kill it."

"I don't think that's gonna work," Mark said immediately, firmly. "First, he'll recognize you from before, where you killed his other drone. Second, no one is stupid enough to risk their life twice on that path. Naw, the decoy would have to be one of Blaylock's guys or a cop or FBI. We'll have to consult them. Maybe they, particularly the FBI, can help with real time observation. I'll talk with the authorities about that possibility. We're kinda SOL unless we can figure that out."

There was noise from the elevator door. I jumped. Too early for Jo Ann. Who the hell was this?

I stood and went out to the reception area to find Madam Secretary, Greta Hauser, stepping off the elevator accompanied by a burly Secret Service agent. She was dressed in a very expensive, beautifully tailored, medium grey Harris Tweed power suit, cream-colored silk blouse, pearl necklace, pearl earrings.

I found myself speechless, stunned. She was exactly as I had remembered her from our shaking hands at last year's board of trustees meeting in Washington, DC – short gray hair, Germanic, piercing blue eyes that immediately reminded me of Ursula's. Her presence seemed to fill the space of the reception area despite her open and even friendly expression.

She smiled at me. "Good day, Thomas."

My God, I thought, *She remembers me.* Then instantly, *No, you dummy, Ursula briefed her.*

"I've heard so many good things about you from Bryan ... and Ursula."

"Thank you."

"I thought that as an incoming member of the board of trustees that it might profit me by knowing a bit more about this terrible tragedy of some obviously deranged person holding the university hostage and your efforts to rectify this travesty."

"Oh. Um, well, you're welcome to join our meeting." *What else could I do?*

The whole room stood to attention when she entered. Even Zoltan seemed shocked.

"Let me get you some coffee, dear." Bryan said solicitously.

"Why thank you, Bryan."

The agent pulled a chair from the table and sat in the near corner where he could see the door. I pulled out a chair for her. She nodded thank you and sat down.

"You've previously met Mr. Berger, I believe?" Bryan asked as he poured her coffee.

She smiled, "Oh yes, I feel like we are old friends. We sat together on the dais two years ago at your board meeting, plus some years ago we also sat together at a state department dinner on behalf of the OAS where I learned that he is not only a financial wizard but also has a PhD in political science from Boston University. I observed that his success in many ways may very well be attributed as much to his PhD as to his business acumen."

"Hey, say what you want, Greta. It's all okay by me."

That Berger and Hauser knew one another made us all slightly more comfortable.

"So, here's the deal, Greta," Mark said to her directly, "We're working with the Blaylock Agency who I'm sure Bryan has told you about, and also the local police and the FBI in trying to track this assassin down. Thanks to Thomas we early on figured out who it might be and everything we keep finding out seems to point to same guy. But he's elusive as hell, just changed his way of operating so we're again at a dead end of figuring out where he is. He can launch his damn drones from almost anywhere and have them return almost anywhere, so unless we have the capacity for real-time surveillance, we're kinda screwed."

Greta Hauser looked at Mark meaningfully. "I see."

In a heartbeat I knew she not only perceived what Mark was asking but also understood in all the dimensions past, present and future what their implications might be. Fascinating.

She smiled at Mark. "I'm sure you understand that I can offer no comment. But I thank you for sharing with me this information. A very troubling situation. I very much appreciate the update."

With that she stood, turned and left the room, the agent hustling to be close behind. Her cup of coffee now fronting her empty chair, a few sips taken from it, a pale gloss lipstick mark on its rim.

Once we heard the elevator doors close, Berger turned to Bryan. "Hey, so Bryan, how would you interpret that last remark?"

Fitz-Hugh smiled knowingly, shrugged. "She'll do whatever she can to help us."

"That's kinda what I was thinkin'. Good. Maybe you are some fuckin' help after all."

Zoltan snorted and crossed his arms.

Bryan watched him for a moment impassively, stood and walked to the elevator, Ursula following him.

When the doors had shut, "Zoltan," Mark said, "With your skill set you should probably run for political office somewhere."

Zoltan unfolded his arms, smiled his everyday rictus grin, "Yes, Berger, I am blessed with gift. It not easy always saying wrong thing at wrong time."

"That's for sure. Luckily, it just all rolls off Bryan."

"Yes, he very slippery."

"Hmmm ... Yeah."

We stood to leave, but Mark said to me, "Hey, stick around for a minute."

He turned to Zoltan. "Hope you enjoy the show later today."

"Yes. She very interesting lady. Smart, careful. She a killer. Would not want to be her enemy."

We both nodded as he turned and left us.

"So, have a seat," Mark told me.

"Sure."

We sat down and he looked at me in a puzzled way, his hands together in front of him, fingertips touching. "So, I noticed something today. Kinda blew me away."

Uh, Oh, I thought.

"Ursula and Madam Secretary."

"Yeah?"

"It's uncanny. There's a family resemblance."

"Oh."

I thought, *Shit, I know this secret and I'm the only one because of*

Ursula and my liaison and I promised to never reveal it. But I'm not going to lie to Mark. No way.

"Whatyaknow about that?"

I leaned my head back and closed my eyes, then brought my head forward and looked at Berger dead on. "Ursula Mueller is Greta Hauser's biological daughter."

Berger's eyes opened wide. "My God."

"Yep."

"Who's the father?"

"Guess. He just left here. Dr. Slippery."

"Goddddd Damn!"

"Yeah. Bryan and Madam Secretary had Ursula in their final year at the Kennedy School. They were both headed to other parts of the world, Bryan as a dean of students for a west coast school for international studies and she as an assistant to our U.S. ambassador in Germany. So, Ursula was put up for adoption. A Washington, DC family adopted and raised her. Lovely folks from what I understand. When she was at MIT, she researched her birth parents and sought them out. Bryan hired her as his assistant when she graduated. Now you know why she's so remarkably loyal to both."

Mark thought for a moment. "Okay, so this secret stays with me. I appreciate this confidence and will respect it."

"I'm not going to lie to you, Mark."

"Yeah, I know. Appreciated that more than I can tell you."

"Thanks."

XVIX

The Speakers Forum

W E STOOD OFF stage on the right, Berger, Nate Tuckett, the head of campus security and me, comingling with stagehands and technicians. Across from us on stage left was a pensive Ursula and Special Events staff.

The auditorium was packed, house lights up, waves of conversations flowing through the air, last-minute arrivals hastening to their seats.

On the stage Bryan Fitz-Hugh and Greta Hauser sat in comfortable red leather armchairs on a bright Persian rug behind a lectern with a prominent Sessions University seal on its front, on top a microphone stalk. A reading light illuminated a single sheet of State Department stationery with some headings on it, Greta Hauser's reminders.

I was accustomed to Bryan speaking at length extemporaneously, so it did not totally surprise me that Madam Secretary would have simple reminder headings for her remarks.

The four of us on stage right were breathing a collective sigh of relief. Despite Tuckett being pissed at us, we nevertheless had bumped fists and offered raised eyebrows and back slap congratulations to one another. No incidents or disruptions in crowd management, parking, shuttle buses or even Will Call. Rooftop surveillance reported no sightings, the temperature hovering in the low 40s, the sky overcast, with patchy fog and drizzling. Nasty, impossible day for flying. Good day for us.

At 4 p.m., the house lights dimmed, and Berger walked out to the lectern and into the spotlight. I was stuck by his self-effacing, dutiful manner, especially as compared to the relaxed superstar confidence radiating from Fitz-Hugh and Hauser. The crowd quieted. The mike made noises as Berger adjusted it.

"I'm Mark Berger, the board chair here at the university." He paused momentarily to allow everyone to quiet, settle in and focus.

"We are deeply honored today to welcome our most recent Secretary of State, Greta Hauser, to this year's first Speakers Forum. Our interim president, Bryan Fitz-Hugh, will introduce Dr. Hauser. Interestingly, Dr. Fitz-Hugh and Dr. Hauser first met as students at the Harvard Kennedy School many years ago and have remained friends and colleagues since.

"Many of you are familiar with Bryan, our former president, who has recently returned to the U.S. from his service as assistant undersecretary of the European Union. We feel so fortunate to have Bryan back with us while our current presidential search is underway. His work with us, as before, has been exemplary.

"Bryan ..."

Fitz-Hugh rose and, exuding a pleasant confidence, came to the lectern. He made a respectful and filial nod to Berger as they passed one another. All eyes were on him, none disapproved. I was always fascinated by how in a heartbeat he took command of a room, in this case a 950-seat auditorium and, I was sure, a large television audience. He was made for this.

At the lectern he looked out approvingly to the audience and into the TV cameras, drawing everyone in.

"You have no idea," he began, "What Mark Berger means to this university. An alumnus with a PhD and a law degree his first loyalty has always been to Sessions through thick and thin. We would be a much lesser institution without his leadership. Mark, I applaud you." He turned toward Mark off stage and began to clap and the audience, and Greta Hauser, who stood and faced him, applauded.

Mark took a step forward onto the stage momentarily and gave Fitz-Hugh, Hauser and then the audience a small wave of appreciation and then stepped back out of the limelight. His eyes were moist, and he was struggling to contain his emotions.

As the applause faded, Fitz-Hugh turned back to the audience, then began again.

"As Mark has mentioned, I had the very good fortune many years ago now to have a certain Greta Hauser as a classmate at the Kennedy School at a small backwater place called Harvard."

A small wave of indulgent laughter from the crowd.

"It may be difficult for you to believe, perhaps, given our present careers, but we were once starving graduate students going through many of the same struggles as today's students.

"All the while, we were being enlightened by the faculty and through our own late-night discussions and thought sessions.

"We began to see and develop a rudimentary understanding of the world – countries, history of their development, ethnicities, languages, traditions, politics, economies, challenges, conflicts within and from outside, a dizzying array of complexity.

"Today, having just returned from my duties at the European Union, and having the good fortune to return to Sessions temporarily, I can tell you that I look back on those times with fond affection and nostalgia for their simplicity and for world's simplicity then.

"Today's world is a far more complex and fraught place, as we all know well.

"I will also tell you that all the complexity and challenges of the European Union, which I have been dealing with over the last three years, twenty-seven countries and twenty-four languages, and a maze of bureaucracies, pale in comparison to the complexity and challenges faced today by our Department of State.

"So, it is with great admiration as well as being honored by the time she has taken to be with us today that I introduce my close friend, our most recent Secretary of State, Madam Secretary, Greta Hauser."

It's unusual that a speaker receives a standing ovation upon introduction, but that is what happened, the crowd as one unit stood and applauded, a long and sustained and enthusiastic appreciation for Madam Secretary.

She rose and came to the lectern, a serious, stylish, and commanding figure.

She began, nodding toward Fitz-Hugh and then facing the crowd. "Thank you, Bryan. Bryan has always been a great friend, ally, and resource. In those days of which he was just speaking I could always count on him for important and critical information ... especially regarding free food and/or beer."

Surprised, strong laughter swelled upwards from the crowd.

She paused for effect, letting the audience shift its perspective. This was, after all, the Secretary of State just weeks ago.

"I did not come here to recount to you all the many attainments of the Department of State during my tenure or to provide you with an assessment of the world's challenges during these troublesome times, which might take days. I will leave the first assessment to posterity and the second to my successor whom I have the pleasure of continuing to brief as he engages.

"What I do want to accomplish today, hopefully, is to provide you with some perspective about our Department of State and its rather extensive and remarkable role in world affairs.

"Why?

"Because in our headline-centric, media-driven, nanosecond-attention span society, we are not provided with the slightest knowledge of what our institutions do or accomplish.

"Instead, what the public sees is me or a counterpart dashing around the world to trouble spots, meeting with key leaders, assessing situations, articulating hopeful solutions.

"But what about the rest of the State Department during these times? What does it do? How does it function?

"I'm sorry to say but the general notion is that we help out with passport difficulties and host or attend a series of very pleasant world, local, regional, national and international meetings and dinner parties which accomplish little.

"While these functions do represent a smidgen of our overall work, let me use this occasion, in this academic environment, to provide what I hope is a teachable moment.

"Today's State Department has more than 270 diplomatic missions worldwide.

"Since 9/11, our mission, role and responsibilities have grown dramatically in response to our world's developing complexity and conflicts.

"Key areas of responsibility are:

Anti-Corruption and Transparency - We prioritize anti-corruption and seek to make it even harder for criminality and terrorism to take root and spread, to promote governments that are more stable and accountable, and to level the playing field for U.S. businesses to compete in every region.

Arms Control and Nonproliferation - We work to counter threats to the United States and the international order caused by the proliferation of weapons of mass destruction and their delivery systems, advanced conventional weapons, and related materials, technologies, and expertise.

Climate and Environment - U.S. climate and environment diplomacy aspires to realize economic growth, energy security, and a healthy planet. The well-being of the natural world affects millions of U.S. jobs and the health of our people, and so we work with partners to advance U.S. interests on issues such as addressing the climate crisis, combating wildlife trafficking, fostering resilience, conserving nature, water security, and reducing harmful pollutants.

Climate Crisis - Bold action to tackle the climate crisis is more urgent than ever. The record-breaking heat, floods, storms, drought, and wildfires devastating communities around the world underscore the grave risks we already face. Through our actions at home and our leadership abroad, the United States is doing its part to build a zero-carbon future that creates good jobs and ensures a healthy, livable planet for generations to come.

Combatting Drugs and Crime - Effectively combatting transnational criminal organizations requires a comprehensive, committed, and well-coordinated approach between us, other federal agencies, and our partners around the world.

Countering Terrorism - As the threats posed by terrorist organizations continue to evolve, we work to build global consensus to degrade and defeat these adversaries. We also work closely with the Departments of Defense, Homeland Security, Justice, Treasury, and the Intelligence Community to lead an integrated whole-of-government approach to international counterterrorism.

Cyber Issues - In partnership with other countries, we lead the U.S. government's efforts to promote an open, interoperable, secure, and reliable information and communications infrastructure that supports international trade and commerce, strengthens international security, and fosters free expression and innovation.

Economic Prosperity and Trade Policy - Our economic officers focus on building a strong U.S. economy that creates jobs and underpins national security, highlights economic considerations in policy formulation, and builds the relationships needed to expand commercial ties that drive American prosperity.

Energy - We promote U.S. interests globally on critical issues such as ensuring economic and energy security for the United States and its allies and partners, removing barriers to energy development and trade, and promoting U.S. best practices regarding transparency and good governance. We also work to deny terrorists and rogue nations access to funds derived from energy production.

Global Health - Outbreaks of infectious disease do not respect national boundaries. Halting and treating diseases at their points of origin is one of the best and most economical ways of saving lives and protecting Americans. We actively work to prevent, detect, and respond to infectious disease threats.

Global Women's Issues - The United States is committed to advancing gender equality and the empowerment of women and girls through U.S. foreign policy. We have identified four key priorities to advance gender equality and the status of women and girls around the world: women, peace, and security; women's economic empowerment; gender-based violence; and adolescent girls.

Human Rights and Democracy - The United States uses a wide range of tools to advance a freedom agenda, including bilateral diplomacy, multilateral engagement, foreign assistance, reporting and public outreach, and economic sanctions. We work with democratic partners, international and regional organizations, nongovernmental organizations, and engaged citizens to support those seeking freedom.

Human Trafficking - We lead U.S. global engagement to combat human trafficking and support the coordination of anti-trafficking efforts across the U.S. government. The United States follows the widely used "3P" paradigm — prosecution, protection, and prevention — to combat human trafficking worldwide. We also employ a "4th P" — for partnership — as a complementary means to achieve progress across the 3Ps and enlist all segments of society in the fight against modern slavery.

The Ocean and Polar Affairs - The United States works to efficiently and effectively develop and manage ocean resources with neighboring countries and the international community to preserve their health and wealth for many generations to come. The changes today in the Arctic — economic, social, and environmental — transcend national borders, opening new opportunities and making international cooperation critical for the Arctic's continued sustainable development.

Refugee and Humanitarian Assistance - The primary goal of U.S. humanitarian assistance is to save lives and alleviate suffering by ensuring that vulnerable and crisis-affected individuals receive assistance and protection. U.S. funding provides life-saving assistance to tens of millions of displaced and crisis-affected people, including refugees, worldwide.

Science, Technology and Innovation - We execute public diplomacy programs that promote the value of science to the general public. We also implement capacity-building programs in emerging markets that train young people to become science and technology entrepreneurs. Our efforts contribute to scientific enterprises that hasten economic growth and advance U.S. foreign policy priorities.

Treaties and International Agreements - Treaties and other international agreements are written agreements between sovereign states (or between states and international organizations) governed by international law. The United States enters into more than 200 treaties and other international agreements each year.

To carry out this wide diversity of mission programs the Department of State employs a workforce which includes some 13,000 members of the Foreign Service, 11,000 Civil Service employees, and 45,000 locally employed staff.

Greta Hauser paused. The audience by this point was a bit stunned. They had not known what to expect from her address but this much information, however surprising and informative, was not it.

She continued with a rueful smile, "Now, I am sure you are asking yourself, 'Why is she telling me all this?'

"Boastful, self-promotion?"

There was a stir and some mild laughter from the audience.

"No. My intent is simply that this is the one opportunity I will have to educate the public about a government agency that is not well known, despite its importance to our everyday lives and, most important, to our freedom as Americans."

"Anddddd, I do also have an ulterior motive. What else would you expect?"

Laughter.

"Seriously, when you look at our many programs all over the world, what do you see? On your behalf, I'll tell you what I see in two words: Career Opportunities! For those of you who have interest in world affairs, particularly if you are multilingual, and many of you are these days, where else can you find employment where you can travel the world and influence the course of history, help provide for our security and our continuing freedom by serving your country?"

"So, just when you think our country is in decline and that patriotism is fading, you or those in your family may actually be able to make a real difference, an historical difference in our future. I ask you today to consider that. I can tell you from my life experience and I can attest to Dr. Fitz-Hugh's experience that we have never regretted our choice of careers, as challenging as they have been. I encourage your involvement. Thank you!"

The audience began their applause. It was a bit tepid at the beginning but as Greata Hauser continued to stand at the lectern, looking at them beneficently, and as the audience began to reflect even momentarily on what they had just heard, the applause deepened and then people began to stand.

I thought, *How in the hell did she just do that with some simple notes.* I was in awe, and then a host of ambivalent feelings crept into my admiration.

How was it that people like her and Bryan, brilliant as they were, could operate with no conscience about their being directly responsible for murders and their cover-up. Even while they hid behind various bureaucracies and undoubtedly justified such acts as occurring in the line of patriotic duty, there was the blood of innocent people, good people on their hands. How did they justify their liaison? Bryan being married with children and regularly sleeping with an assortment of women, even a board member's wife? Did greatness entitle one to simply disregard all the rules and expect no penalty? That's the way it seemed. The only thing I knew for certain is how bad all this made me feel. Yet, ruefully, I reflected on my own behavior over the last three years with Ursula and now Alicia. Was I any better? I hoped so, but in truth, I was not sure.

Madam Secretary turned, gave Bryan a smile as she went back to her seat.

Bryan rose, still applauding, and came to the lectern.

The audience quieted and took their seats.

"Thank you, Greta," he said turning to her. "I'm sure we are all better off for your remarks, deeply appreciative of your being here today and we thank you from our hearts for your service to our country."

He turned back to the audience, "Have a safe trip home or to your next destination. Thank you for coming."

XX

Black Eyes

MONDAY, THE SECOND week in December, I sat in the foundation's offices on another overcast winter day, gazing out at the city's bare brick and wood frame buildings, concrete sidewalks and leafless trees as they sloped to the distant faint silver sliver of the harbor. Crusts of snow were everywhere on roof tops, walks and culverts, wind buffeting against my window sending off small waves of chill.

It was a morning to catch up on the deluge of proposals. I now had Jo Ann screening them for my final review. Then declination letters would go out. There were actually a few proposals from local organizations that held some potential for a partnership with the university. I was holding them to discuss with Mark who was flying in this morning for a 2 p.m. meeting at Sessions with Fitz-Hugh, Ursula, Zoltan and me to review the latest developments concerning the Drone Assassin.

I was thinking about how the threat of the assassin actually seemed to be fading, despite the ever-present danger of another attack.

Zoltan and my adventure with the drone, thankfully, against all odds, was still a secret. So, all the public knew was Powers' murder, which was beginning to seem long ago.

Greta Hauser's presentation at Sessions had also helped draw attention away from the murder. Standing room only, with national news coverage and with no drone or other incidents. Its success had led to a dramatic pickup in admissions visits and the university and medical communities feeling that they could now move about in a more normal manner even if cautiously.

More cause for concern, as everyone, it seemed, was letting their guard down.

Plus, we had heard not a word about the possibility of real-time surveillance for the next drone attack, presuming there was one. Maybe Fitz-Hugh would have something to tell us, but the absence of another attack had created all sorts of questions about whether the assassin had vanished or was just biding his time in the face of a stout defense. Were we winning the war with our adversary or just fooling ourselves?

Of course, the press continued to have a field day with all sorts of reasonable to wild conspiracy theories about the assassin and the murder.

The use of the drone had captured the imagination of the country. Journalists, media types and reporters had stalked the university and medical center, interviewing anyone who would talk to them, while the real players, Berger, the board, Fitz-Hugh and the authorities made themselves less and less available.

On our part and that of the authorities there was an increasingly distant hope that the assassin would reveal himself through communicating some kind of message or manifesto. But he was too smart for that.

My cell phone buzzed on my desk. I lowered the footrest on my chair and, rotating, picked up the phone and glanced at the screen.

Emily Sayzak. *Aw, shit.* I let it go to voicemail, then listened.

"Thomas, Emily. I'm downstairs in the restaurant. You need to buy me breakfast." She released a small laugh. "I met this strange guy. He kinda worries me. I need to tell you about it. I know you're here because your car is in your parking space, so don't stall me."

She had me at 'strange guy'. While Emily kept showing up at

totally inconvenient moments, the one other time she had made a similar call to me she had provided me with the black and white pictures of Wentz and Lusby in a bathhouse with underage boys. Berger had used these to secure Wentz's resignation. Wentz, who on viewing them, being overweight and in shock, had collapsed in an asthmatic heap, whereupon Mark had arranged for him his admittance to a health spa out west along with his wife, Florence, a lovely alcoholic.

I pressed Return.

"Hi, Thomas!"

"I'll be right down."

I walked out to the reception area.

Jo Ann had a pile of proposals on her left and a smaller pile on her right, sitting back in her chair, feet on her desk, reading one, with a bemused, slightly disgusted expression. Unlike at the university, where she dressed to be on display, at the foundation on days when we had no appointments, she went casual, today jeans, a red turtleneck, a big, shapeless lamb's wool sweater and Uggs lined boots.

"You goin' somewhere?"

"Yeah, Emily Sayzak, just turned up in the restaurant downstairs. Wants me to buy her breakfast."

Eyebrows up, a clear nail polish stiletto fingernail to her cheek. I had briefed her on Emily's predatory nature. "So long as that bitch don' come up here."

"Not a chance," I smiled.

"Good." Eyes back down to the proposal.

The Intercontinental restaurant had survived the hotel's extensive renovation after Berger had bought it and had become more upscale. I found Emily in a booth at the back. By now, past 9:30 a.m. the place was mostly empty. Good choice of seating. No one around to overhear us.

She smiled and waved.

"Sorry to barge in like this," she told me as I sat down, "but I figured I'd better let you know what happened, a bit more that I wanted to cover in a phone call, plus you never know who's listening in these days."

I thought. *If you only knew.*

She looked reasonably civilized today, tan winter wool pants suit and white turtleneck, tan wool overcoat lying beside her. And, of course, her perfume filled the air.

The waitress came for our order, wiggled her nose and gave me a puzzled sidelong glance while Emily ordered the full breakfast special, scrambled eggs, waffles, hash browns, sausage, a biscuit and coffee. Why was I not surprised by her appetite? I order coffee, black.

As the waitress left, Emily began her story, "So, Thomas, I know you probably think I sleep around."

I felt my eyebrows rise. *Probably?*

"But contrary to popular opinion I actually have some scruples. They may be my scruples, but I have 'em, and one of 'em is I don't sleep with co-workers, particularly my bosses, like my editor who is always trying to get into my pants."

Somehow this last analogy left me with a rather queasy image which I managed to suppress.

"But so my editor is always asking me out and on a rare occasion, just to keep him on my side, I'll accept an invitation if it assures no chance of compromise."

Where the hell is this story going? I wondered. *And what's all this urgency about?*

Her breakfast and my coffee arrived. I loved quick service. Very impressive. All the wonderful scents of her breakfast mixed in with the smell of her perfume. Nauseating.

Emily covered the scrambled eggs and hashbrowns with enough ketchup to resemble a crime scene and dug in with gusto and between mouthfuls began her story again.

"Anyway, last Friday, he shows up around my desk and says he has Saturday tickets to an afternoon concert out at the Shorrock

Playhouse, you know in the dell beyond the reservoir, for Jesus Bonachea, one of my favorite jazz guitarists. His date has come down with the flu. Could I go? Sure, I say, and we went. Terrific performance and on the way back he sez, let's stop at Gertie's for a beer. You know, Gertie's, right?" She said as she stuck a large piece of buttered waffle, dripping with syrup into her rather small, canted mouth and chewed.

I did know Gertie's, a local institution. In the early years it had been a Rock 'n Roll hangout. Then it had become a bikers' bar. A place you wanted to stay away from. But then as the suburbs grew it had over the last decade gentrified and become in and trendy. Any motorcycles you might see in the parking lot now were BMW's driven by business owners, brokers and bankers from around city. So now it was the weekend hangout for families and friends, housing a very popular bar, and had expanded with indoor and outdoor dining areas and live music.

She swallowed and reached for her coffee. "Anyway, Gertie's was fine by me and so we go and sit at the bar. The place is hopping. We have a beer or two, order some burgers and he has to use the men's room. Then as soon as he leaves this guy comes up, hitting on me. A spooky guy, black curly hair, big black beard, dressed like a redneck, but he isn't, just faking it. I'll chat with anybody, so we start talking. You know, and the conversation is about who we are and what's up with our lives. He says he's between jobs and on a kind of sabbatical, like he really doesn't have to work. He's an engineer working in aviation," she said, as she lifted a forkful of scrambled eggs.

Holy shit. My attention zoomed from half-listening to fully focused alert.

"His name wouldn't be Sammie, would it?"

She swallowed and reached for her glass of water. "He said his name was Tom, which I didn't really believe. As usual in a bar, no last name provided."

"Okay."

"So, he asks what I do and when I tell him I'm a reporter, he gets very interested, I mean scary interested. I mean, he has these intense black eyes that make me feel real insecure, like he's fucking dane-ger-rous.

That's Sammie all right, I thought.

"He immediately wants to know what I think of what's been happening at Sessions University, what with a provost and acting president dying in the last three years.

"And I kinda put him off, telling him my beat was more City Hall and that kinda thing, only got over to the university once in a while when university stuff intersected with the city."

"So, then, really weird, he asks if I know you."

"Whoa!"

"Yeah. So, I say, 'Oh you mean that PR guy over there?' like I could barely recall who you are. Yeah, I know who he is but that's it."

"About then my editor shows up and gives this guy a pissed off look, and he makes a polite exit. But something about this whole exchange didn't seem right, felt weird, made me suspicious.

"So, I ask the bartender if she knows this dude. Turns out for the last couple months he's been a regular there, but real standoffish, loner type. Will occasionally try to chat up chicks but no success. Apparently lives further out in the country in some little former tenant farm he's recently renting. For some reason, my instincts told me I oughta tell you about this. Ring any bells?" she said as she moved on to smearing butter on her biscuit.

"Wow," was all I could muster as a response, my mind racing with the potential of her discovery and what to tell her.

"So, Thomas, what could be the deal with this guy?"

Instinctively, I tiptoed around the truth, "I'm not sure." *I'm damn sure!* "But this could be the guy everyone's looking for."

"You mean the Drone Assassin? Holy Cow!"

"Maybe. I have to share this with some folks to see whether what happened to you fits this guy," I said, stalling.

"Someday you ever going to tell me what the hell's been going on at Sessions the last three years?"

"No. I can't tell you and you don't want to know. BUT let me tell you how much this information could mean to me. If it pans out, I'll find a way to secure that interview you want with Mr. Berger." *Anything to keep you away from investigating this current lead.*

"Oh, Thomas," she reached across the table and put her hand on mine, "That would be so cool. Thanks! But I still want to know what's going on with this guy."

Aw, Christ. "Okay, so let me go. I've got some work to do."

"Sure you couldn't hang around a bit?"

"Aw, Emily. Look I really may owe you on this one. Thank you."

I rose to leave and then turned back.

"Emily, do me a favor."

"Sure," she said, pausing as she was preparing to decapitate a sausage.

"If and when you interview Mark, ditch your perfume, okay?"

She looked a little bit shocked and a bit offended.

"He's deathly allergic. You wear perfume, it'll ruin the whole interview."

"Ohhhh," a relieved expression, "Okay."

"Thanks."

XXI

The Feds

ACK IN THE office I noticed that the door to Mark's suite was closed.

"Is he here?" I asked Jo Ann who was now sitting upright while continuing her proposal review.

"Oh, yeah, marched right through here, gave me a wave and went into the suite to change."

"Okay."

"Hey, Thomas, does he always dress like that?"

"Hah. No one's gonna tell him otherwise would be my guess. Was he in his sailing garb?"

"Oh yeah, *Calypso Too*."

"Okay. Get used to it."

"Sure," she shrugged.

About twenty minutes later Mark appeared at my office door clean shaven, dressed in slacks, V-neck sweater, button down shirt and sport coat.

"Howarya?"

"Have a seat. You're not going to believe what happened to me about an hour ago."

"Yeah?"

I told him in detail about my breakfast conversation with Emily.

"Yeah, I remember her from the Powers murder scene. She has hots for you, right?"

"Maybe more for what she thinks I might know."

He put his hand to his chin, musing, "You don't think she's just makin' all this up just to get your attention?"

"Not a chance. This is real. She's the one who gave me the pictures of Wentz and Lusby. Despite being a pain in the ass reporter, she's also a trusted source."

"I never knew she was your source for those pictures."

"Yeah, same deal. She hangs out places and people approach her, especially guys. That's what happened here. Uncanny."

Berger thought for a time. The wind buffeted against my window. Out in the reception area Jo Ann coughed.

"You know what's gonna happen at our meeting with Fitz-Hugh in couple hours?"

"Of course not." *I'm always the last to know.*

"The FBI has a guy who can act as a decoy. They've kinda appeared out of nowhere and asked Blaylock and the cops to stand down. The big boys are taking over kinda vibe. I mean, they might as well be saying, "Greta sent us" or something like that. Anyhow, seems like she's worked her behind-the-scenes magic. At least that's what Fitz-Hugh would like us to believe.

"Apparently, they now have the capacity of real-time tracking of the drone. Whether they always had that and didn't want us to know or whether Madam Secretary somehow caused things to happen, I don't know, but they got it. Anyway, it looks like they're now going to set up rooftop operations and have an agent decoy trying to entice a drone attack.

"I don't know how effective them taking over will be but it'll save me a ton of money," he smiled.

"Great. But what does that mean? Some dude trying to look like a university type marches up and down the walkway to the lower parking lot daily and we all wait and see whether Sammie is stupid enough to swallow the bait?"

"Yeah, that's pretty much it. Plus, should the drone appear, they'll fake chasing it, but instead follow it in real time to where it lands and be directing a team on the ground to apprehend whoever picks it up."

"And how long will this last?"

"The fucker could wait us out."

"Yeah."

"I know what you're thinking, Thomas. Now that we know where Sammie hangs out, we could just track him back to his place, right?"

"Yeah!"

"So, who's gonna do that?"

"Um, you trust the cops and FBI to ID him at Gertie's and follow him?"

"I don't know. Just seems like rich potential for screwing things up. He gets one whiff of the cops or the Feds, he'll vanish. Plus, I get the distinct feeling that the cops now think we're a bunch of conspiracy theory idiots who've led them on a wild goose chase. Plus, the FBI is not gonna go for our Sammie focus either, any more than the cops did. To them, he's just a guy mourning his dad's suicide. And Blaylock, if we put them on this, they have no authority to do anything. Plus, the cops and FBI, because Blaylock is owned by one of my entities, are likely not to believe them any more than they believe us."

"Yep."

Another long silence.

"Well, Thomas, let's meet with Fitz-Hugh and these guys and see what they're thinking. Let's not say anything about what we now know."

"Yeah."

Mark rose to leave and at my doorway, he stopped, thought for a minute and turned back to me.

"So, if we wanted to take this on, sleuthing out where Sammie is. How would we do it? I mean, the guy is a murderer. Do we really want to get in this deep?"

"We'd have to have Emily positively ID Sammie for starters.

He's changed his look, now has a beard. I gotta see him in the flesh before I'm 1000% sure it's him. Very distinctive walk and mannerisms. Exudes hostility. The fact that he asked her if she knew me, that makes me certain it's him, but it would help if she would ID him first."

"A reporter? Are you crazy?"

"Suppose she has the wrong guy?"

"Yeah. But I don't like her bein' involved."

"I've been thinking about this. If Emily and I go out to Gertie's and hang out in the parking lot some late Saturday afternoon about the time Sammie usually shows up, and Emily confirms it's him, then I just fake it and say, damn, that's not the right guy, and take her home. Zoltan can be in Gertie's, where Sammy won't recognize him, toward the back door. I text him and he comes out, while I'm taking Emily back to her place, puts the tracking device on Sammie's vehicle, gets an Uber back to our house. We can then track the device on our cell phones, iPad etc. Then at some point we just follow his trail to his hideout."

"Yeah, that could work. Need to be sure about how well the tracking device works. Can we trust Emily not to pester us about what's going on?"

"No. But I've been stonewalling her for three years now on Kravitz and she's tolerated that. Maybe she's an idiot or maybe she's just playing the long game. In any case, to toss her a bone, I told her that in appreciation for her help I'd arrange for her to do a puff piece with you as the incoming chairman of the board at Sessions."

"You asshole." Mark was definitely annoyed. "So, we find him. Then what the fuck do we do?"

"That's the part I haven't figured out yet. Maybe get pictures of him coming and going. It would be great to wait 'til he leaves and go take pictures from inside his hideout, his drones set up, then the FBI would have to believe us, right? But you'd think, given his technology prowess, that he'd have motion detector cameras set up, maybe even a booby trap."

Berger stared at me for a time. Then said evenly, "Let's just bide our time, see what's going on at Sessions. We can make decisions about the best strategy later. If at all possible, I'd much rather have The Feds just do their job and give them all the credit."

"Sure."

*

IN THE WAITING area outside the president's office, as Mark and I entered, an interesting dynamic was taking place.

I had heard from Jo Ann, who kept in touch with her friends at Sessions, that the timorous temp agency secretary who had replaced her, named Donna, had already been nicknamed Donna Doormat because of everyone walking all over her.

Now she had been confronted by the presence of giant, menacing Zoltan and looked ready to dive under her desk.

She looked utterly relieved at Mark and my arrival, picked up her phone and announced us.

Fitz-High greeted us at the door and was in his top drawer, resplendent form, exquisite wool suit, white on white shirt, university tie, tan, fit, white toothed and brown with blond highlights hair perfectly coiffed, greeting us with enthusiasm just short of unctuous as we entered.

Ursula, in a dark grey, well-tailored pants suit, red blouse, as always seriously tempting, was sitting to the right of Fitz-Hugh's seat at the head of the conference table, looking baleful.

"Let me introduce you to our guests," Fitz-Hugh said as we took our seats. "Agents Pfaff and Gomez."

Pfaff, on Fitz-Hugh's left nodded hello, as agent Gomez, sitting next to Pfaff, imitated him.

I took a good, hard look at Agent Pfaff. Mid-forties, paunchy, bland, thinning black hair, five o'clock shadow, uniform dark suit and tie. His beleaguered expression revealed an individual struck unexpectedly by the hypersonic velvet missile of bureaucratic command which had thrust him into a situation upon which his future in the Bureau would be decided, a situation where he would be treading in the dark on different jurisdictional islands of eggshells surrounded by quicksand.

His cohort, Gomez was short and slight, brown-haired buzz cut beginning to grow out, beginnings of a goatee, wearing an acetate turtleneck and new chinos and, incongruously, black wingtips and black socks. The human decoy, I took it. *Well,* I thought charitably, *He could be an imitation techie.*

"Glad everyone could be here today," Fitz-Hugh told us. "Agent Pfaff, perhaps you could enlighten us about your plans for helping to find and subdue our assassin."

Pfaff nodded, "Thank you, Mr. President." His voice was as neutral as a manual transmission between gears.

"We've asked the local police to let us handle this case. They were more than happy to do so I must tell you. Say you've been leading them astray. Won't let them do their job. Fairly pissed off.

"The Blaylock folks were happy to be relieved of this assignment. Freezing their asses off. Very cordially transferring some of their equipment and shelter to us, have briefed us in detail on the drone frequencies employed, that kind of thing. We'll have communications in place and visual equipment to monitor the drone's flight, so even if we lose its signal, we can follow it in real time to its landing place. There's an on the ground team that can be dispatched to follow its flight path and be onsite once it lands.

"Agent Gomez here will be our decoy. He'll arrive each morning at the unprotected lower parking lot at 9:30 a.m. and make his way to the administration building and then return at 6:30 p.m. These arrival times coincide with the times that students, employees, faculty and others use that walkway the least, so he'll be an inviting target. We may also have him leave and come back for lunch here and there."

I found myself nodding along with the rest of the table.

Zoltan turned to Agent Gomez, "Where you live?"

"I can't disclose that," Gomez replied in a quiet voice.

"You have lawn where you live, trees and such?"

"Yes."

"You rake leaves?"

"Yes."

Everyone was looking at Zoltan quizzically.

"Then you change clothes you have on to leaf-raking clothes. Clothes you have on too fresh. Look bogus. Particularly you get rid of damn clodhopper shoes and stupid socks. Wear dirty sneakers or whatever you use to rake leaves. Then you look like someone here at university."

Gomez turned to Pfaff, who gave him an affirmative nod.

"What car you drive? Need to be shit car. FBI car not work. Also, got to have university parking sticker. Assassin smart, not above tracing your license plate."

Again Pfaff nodded to Gomez.

I felt myself smile, visualizing a fleet car without a parking sticker covered with campus cop parking tickets.

"So, how long do you think it'll take before this decoy plan plays out?" Berger asked.

An unhappy expression flashed momentarily on Pfaff's bland features. "In all honesty, we don't know."

"Great," Berger remarked evenly.

A concerned look crossed Fitz-Hugh's and Ursula's faces simultaneously.

We all rose to leave and following my PR/communications instincts and training, I approached Pfaff.

"Agent Pfaff?"

He turned and faced me. "Yes?"

"Despite our so-called useless wasting of everyone's time, would you mind giving me your contact information just in case we actually by accident come across something that might be of interest to you?"

He hesitated, glanced around and found Fitz-Hugh and Berger staring at us. Reluctantly, he reached into his suit coat pocket and produced a single white business card with nothing but a number on it and handed it to me.

"Thank you."

*

WITHOUT A WORD being spoken, Zoltan, Berger and I exited the president's office and walked to the university club, glancing at the sky as we walked along. No drone. Just a chilly clear blue sky and the rustle of the wind gusts playing randomly with the remaining dead leaves piled up in the botanical garden and up against the bushes lining the empty president's mansion.

The club was welcoming with its warmth, a small, artificial Christmas tree in the hallway alcove, decorated with lights and colored glass bulbs and tinsel, the angel from on high at the top bent to the left. 3:15 in the afternoon and the bar area was empty. We were able to get the attention of one of the staff who quite considerately fixed our drinks and served them and bar snacks on the small table we had chosen in the corner that looked out into the bare trees in the woods.

"So," Berger said once we had settled in and had a first welcome sip our usual drinks, "Whatdidya think of that charade?"

Zoltan did not hesitate, "Cluster fuck."

"Yeah," Mark agreed, turned to me.

I shrugged in agreement, although I wasn't really sure.

"Look, if Sammie has got half a brain, he'd have his drone scout the whole scene from the administration building to the lower parking lot. My guess is that he'd figure a way to do that without being detected – very high elevation and probably switching frequencies so his signals get lost in all the others around the university. Okay, so a guess, but this guy's no fool.

"Fact is, they stationed a guy there in a car in the parking lot but a lotta good that has done. Fact is, since your ambush no one in the administration has been parking there. Hence, no attacks.

"Great, except now out of the blue, Sammie can suddenly now spot one guy who he doesn't recognize going to and from the administration building to the lower parking lot. So, if you were Sammie, what would you do?"

"Try to figure out who the hell this guy is."

"Right. So, how would you do that?"

I shrugged.

"What I'd do is take my damn car registered to someone else and drive by and check out his car. Maybe photo this guy. You think Sammie's smart enough to hack into DMV records and also gain access to facial recognition databases?"

"Wouldn't surprise me," I said.

"You be good crook," Zoltan added.

"Very funny. Hate to tell you but there are a number of folks of that opinion already. Anyway, if I'm Sammie, something doesn't smell right about this whole scene. Either the car or Gomez or somethin' doesn't add up. He doesn't know this dude for starters. He knew who you guys were. I don't know. I see this whole thing where the FBI has Gomez walking up and down that path on a day-to-day basis from now until eternity."

"Yeah," I sighed, "I agree with you."

"So, Plan B."

"I'll call Emily."

We explained to Zoltan my conversation with Emily and Berger and my discussion earlier that morning.

"Okay. Thomas, can you get in touch with Jacque? Would he be around campus now? We need his technical advice."

"Uhhh, I guess so."

Within fifteen minutes, while Berger and Zoltan sipped their drinks and chatted about our plan, I managed to get Jacque's phone number from Sarah and called him. Yes, he was in fact not only on campus in the Center for Gifted and Talented Youth offices, but he was actually at the moment tutoring Tommie. I asked him to join us at the club and to bring Tommie along, which he did, both of them arriving looking a bit awkward and slightly intimidated by the club atmosphere and the three of us serious-faced adults.

We made room for them and they pulled up chairs from other tables. Tommie very politely moved the snack bowls over to his side of the table and began helping himself. I looked around and saw that we were all smiling at him.

My peripheral vision suddenly picked up motion to my left. I turned toward the doorway.

Ursula had just walked in. She had spotted us, was walking our way. Collectively, all of us at the table froze.

She reached us, smiled and kidded us, "Gentlemen, isn't it a bit early to have the enjoyment of a drink?"

I was the first to recover, "Serious university business," I told her with mock seriousness.

"I can certainly see that."

"Let me introduce you to my son, Tommie."

"Tommie, this is Ms. Mueller, our university president's assistant."

"Oh, so pleased to meet you, Tommie. I have heard so many amazing things about you." she said, as she walked around the table and proffered her hand, "Your Dad is very proud of you."

Tommie stared openly at her, paralyzed, his face ticking, his eyes blinking. It was a very awkward moment until he finally stuck out his frozen hand.

Ursula wrapped her hand gently about his and made an almost phantom shake. Very loving. I had never seen this side of her before.

"And this is Tommie's tutor, Jacque." With Jacque and everyone else looking at me, as I hesitated, my brain searching for the right word. *Boyfriend?* Finally, I said, "Who is also Sarah's friend."

"Ahh," Ursula commented to Jacque, "I commend your good choice. So pleased to meet you, Jacque."

"Why thank you," Jacque responded in his usual calm and pleasant manner.

"Well, you gentleman enjoy your meeting."

She turned and walked off toward the back of the wing, all the right things working in her physique, leaving me to wonder what the hell *she* was doing in the club.

"Who was *that*?" Jacque half-stammered.

I looked at him, bemused by his uncharacteristic reaction, "Bryan Fitz-Hugh's assistant," I told him, and before I could help myself, I added, "She's a killer."

Zoltan and Berger gave me eye-pop looks.

Quickly I changed the topic, "You guys want something to drink?" I asked Tommie and Jacque.

Perrier for Jacque. I ordered water for Tommie who frowned at me. No way I was going to let him have sugar or even worse, caffeine and preservatives.

"So, Jacque," Berger said," We were having a discussion about the recent increase in car thefts around here. My various enterprises are having the same problem. We need your best technical advice. Can you identify a good car tracking device where we can easily install it on our cars, like in the wheel well or bumper and follow the car on our iPhone, computer, iPad, etc.?"

"Ah," Jacque remarked, "Not a difficult task. Thank you."

He pulled out his cell phone and worked the screen for a short time, came upon what he was searching for and shared the screen with Mark.

Mark looked at it, raised his eyebrows, turned to Jacque. "Egg-zactly what we're lookin' for. Thanks."

He handed the phone to me and I shared it with Zoltan. Perfect. A small, waterproof, wireless, GPS tracking device with a magnetic base, iPhone-linked, low-cost, delivery tomorrow.

Zoltan handed Jacque's cell phone back to him.

"Send me the link," I told Jacque.

"Of course."

He texted it to me and I placed the order.

"You guys are excused." Mark told Jacque and Tommie. "Thanks so much for your help."

We watched as they walked out into the hallway.

"So, what are doing for Christmas?" I asked Mark.

"Well, so not much. I just take myself to my favorite Dim Sum restaurant and join about three hundred Chinese for brunch, which is okay. You ever notice they have all the really good-looking daughters bringing the trays around? Not bad."

I couldn't remember the last time I had Dim Sum. Mark's observance seemed a bit lonely. Somehow inviting him and Zoltan to join us this year did not seem right. The Powers murder and the mystery of it in many respects had killed off some of the joy and spontaneity of our friendship.

"Whataryouguys doin'?"

"Beats me. Believe it or not, Janet and I haven't even discussed it. Hanging around the house. Seeing what the kids are up to."

"Sounds pretty idyllic to me."

"Yeah, I won't mind. That's for sure."

Zoltan told us, "I going down to Washington and visit with Kristina. We cook meal together. Quiet time. See *Nutcracker* for thousandth time. Never get tired of it. Walk along canal if weather good."

"So, I'll be in touch with you guys once I talk with Emily."

We all nodded at one another and rose to leave.

XXII

ITBOT One

CHRISTMAS DAY. I had hoped against hope that I would be able to sleep in, but no, I woke in the dark before 5 a.m., lay there for a time hoping I might doze off. Not a chance, my mind working through various scenarios over the next week involving Emily, Sammie, Zoltan, Mark and me, wondering whether I would ever be free of this mess.

I rose in the dark and pulled on a pair of old corduroys, a turtleneck, wool socks, and heavy sweater, grabbed my cell phone, glanced at Janet who was in deep sleep, wrapped in sheets, blankets and our bedspread, resembled a mummy, and snuck downstairs.

Let Sparky out of her cage, grabbed a banana, fixed a cup of coffee while she pranced around me. Fixed her breakfast. Downed the banana while she woofed her food. Poured my coffee into a small thermal cup, pulled on my winter jacket and wool pullover hat from the hall closet, stuck my feet into my winter boots, leashed Sparky and headed out into the cold gloom of the neighborhood.

The day lightened as we walked, Sparky sniffing at every wet leaf, fencepost, and hydrant. I breathed in the cold, dry air, reflecting on the year that had passed and all our blessings. Despite the tragedy of Powers' death and the lingering threat of Sammie Kravitz, we were healthy. Janet seemed less at sea now that she had anointed me as a quasi-client. Sarah prospered at Sessions and had a decent boyfriend. Tommie was showing signs of maturity and awareness of others.

I was very much looking forward to spending Christmas with our family. It always seemed to me that the hassle of daily living and the demands on each of us prevented meaningful interaction.

The sky at sunrise was incarnadine and orange with slate-colored clouds rumpling the heavens as we made our way back home, passing brown bare lawns, leafless trees and lifeless houses, the scent of wood and fake wood smoke from last evenings' flaming hearths still in the air.

Our house stood out as brightly lit and welcoming by the time we returned. I opened the front door to scents of waffles, butter, coffee, bacon. Mood enhancers for sure.

Janet was in the kitchen and as I entered, she handed me a plate with a stack of waffles, bacon and buttered toast. I grabbed another cup of coffee, sat at the kitchen table where she joined me with a bowl of fruit and yogurt.

"How was your walk?"

I shrugged. "Pretty normal, which is just a fine way to start the day."

"Yeah," she smiled. "Nice to have couple days off."

"You bet. Just to have some clear space. Welcome relief. Just wish I could sleep longer."

"Yeah. Work never leaves you, does it, Thomas?"

"No, unfortunately."

We ruminated for a time, the house quiet, the heat coming on.

"You know," Janet said, "I've been thinking, do you think Jacque was sincere with his invitation to visit his family's farm in the Loire Valley?"

"Jacque is a very sincere guy. Sure."

"Wouldn't that be wonderful?"

I was taken by her idea. Obviously, I had been too damn preoccupied to think of it myself. "Absolutely, the kids are at the right age where they might appreciate and get a lot out of such a visit, Sarah particularly given her proficiency in French, and it would get us out of the damn rut we live in, do something new and adventuresome. Could you and Sarah start looking into it?"

"Sure. We'll start by talking with Jacque."

"Of course, I see an itinerary where we spend a few days in Paris first before our visit."

"Makes sense. Could be a really exciting adventure."

We sat there for a time thinking about our future trip.

Then Janet said, "Sarah tells me you called her asking for Jacque's phone number."

I had known this inquiry was coming the moment I had called Sarah. I was sure Jacque would not share his conversation with us with Sarah, which would result in this inquiry from Janet, so I was prepared.

"Yeah, I wanted to suggest to Jacque that if he and Sarah ever got married that they should just elope, save us a ton of money."

Much to my amusement, she bit.

"Thomas! What in the hell would cause you to say something like that? That's an awful thing to say!"

"No one gets married these days anyway, so not to worry."

"Thomas, really! But why did you call him?"

"It was at Mark's request. Do you know how many vehicles his various enterprises own or lease?"

"Of course not."

"Well, turns out its thousands. Can you imagine? Anyway, he and I and Zoltan were at the university club, and Mark was saying he was concerned about the increasing auto theft that's occurring and that he's considering installing tracking devices on these vehicles. It occurred to him that Jacque, being a tech guy, might have some useful ideas and knowledge about that, so he asked me to call him, so I called Sarah to get his number. Turns out he was tutoring Tommie at the Center, which is practically next door. So, he and Tommie came over to the club. Jacque immediately IDed a company that made such a device. Okay?"

"Oh, sure. Sarah and I were just curious."

"Understandable. So, something else. Mark has asked that Zoltan and I check out a place out in the sticks for him next Saturday. Zoltan will be meeting me there and then Ubering back here just to hang out a bit. I've got to pick up and drop off one of Mark's hotel staff who'll check out this place with us. I think maybe Mark wants to have an event or meeting there. Didn't say why, just wanted our impressions. Wants to keep it confidential. So, next Saturday afternoon, Zoltan and I will be doing that. Just wanted you to know."

Geez, what a crock of shit. I thought. *The lies I have to tell. They wear me out.*

"Okay. For as open and trusting a guy as Mark is, there's another side of him, isn't there?"

"Yep."

"Well, he is your boss even though he's a family friend."

"Exactly."

I could see something else was on her mind. "So we're not finished here, are we?"

"Um, no. I've been thinking about how to tell you this but Sarah is quietly making some hints that she intends to sleep over at Jacque's on occasion."

"Aw shit." I heard myself say, even as I realized that for some time this possibility had been occurring to me.

"How do we react to this?" I asked Janet.

"It's her life."

"Yeah, but ... but ... hell, it's not like I didn't know this would happen and I haven't been sure how I'd react, but, ohhh ... shit, I'm kind of decimated." I laughed a rueful laugh. "Well, it's a little late to tell her no, to 'forbid' her, to 'demand' that she break off things with Jacque. If only he wasn't such a good guy."

"My thoughts exactly."

"Hell, she's just 17, not even legal."

"That's true, but she's a very grown up 17."

"Yeah."

I realized as our conversation was going forward that of course as usual I was the last to know and that Sarah and Janet had been discussing how to break this news to me for some time whereas I had just wanted to turn a blind eye to the obvious situation. Well, I probably got what I deserved.

Now I understood that the whole morning's conversations about going to France and this new revelation about Jacque and Sarah had been choreographed between Sarah and her mother.

Christ.

Noises from upstairs, steps on the carpeted stairs, as if on cue, Sarah walked in.

"Bonjour! Maman et papa." She looked at us thoughtfully. "Am I interrupting something?"

"No," I said a bit churlishly.

I put my dishes in the sink and went to my office.

I was feeling a rising anger because I felt powerless. Powerless to change my daughter's developing relationship. Powerless to prevent she and Janet from scheming. Powerless to affect Sammie Kravitz from terrorizing our world.

What in the God damned hell was I supposed to be celebrating for? The birth of Jesus? The onslaught of the commercialization of the holiday? Okay. Okay. I knew I needed a better attitude and thought back to my reflections with Sparky just a short time ago. This too shall pass. But I needed some time in the den with the door shut to gain a better attitude.

I shut the door behind me and called Alicia.

She picked up on the first ring as usual. "Thomas! Merry Christmas!"

It felt so good to hear her voice and feel my soul and body react to it.

"Thanks. Big plans for the day?"

She laughed her beautiful, melodious laugh. Of course not! Well, there's a neighborhood party, if you can call it that in the parents' mansion-filled enclave. We're going to that and then back home to a nice dinner prepared by their staff. Then open presents. It'll be okay. How 'bout you?"

"Happily stuck with the family. You recall me talking about Sarah's boyfriend, Jacque. Seems his family owns a large farm in the Loire Valley, and they might welcome us this coming summer. Janet and Sarah are looking into it."

"That would be fabulous. Say, there's a three-day Foundation Association meeting in Washington in the last week of January for new foundation founders, officers and staff. I'd love it if you could join me there. Dad and I will fly in one or two days early and call on different national organizations we're interested in for our work in Chicago."

"That would be great." *Uh-Oh*, I thought and then immediately swept aside any concerns.

"Where are you going to stay?"

"My apartment is only a one bedroom, so I need to put Dad up somewhere."

"I'd stay at the Tribone Hotel. Mark owns it. You know, he expressed some interest in meeting your Dad. I wonder whether he'd be available?"

"What a good idea."

"I'll check."

"Well, Thomas, you can be assured that I will be spending this Christmas wishing you were here."

"Hmmm ... Good."

"Gotta go. Enjoy!"

"You too."

I ended the call ready to now face the family and the day in a much better frame of mind. I worried momentarily about the psychology of what had just transpired, but then dismissed it.

Tommie had now joined the breakfast table and was hammering away at a stack of four waffles slathered in apple sauce to avoid syrup.

"Merry Christmas everyone!" I greeted them as I fixed a glass of ice water from the fridge.

A sidelong, mildly cynical look from Janet. Sarah pecking away at her iPhone gave me a distracted nod, Tommie kept eating. My joyous, wonderful family.

I could tell by his squinching and ticking and his eyes fluttering that Tommie was even more wound up than usual.

I had no sooner sat down with my ice water than he suddenly pronounced, as he looked across the room and not at me, "Dad, we gotta get rid of Tommie Town and all my old kids' toys."

I was taken aback but also realized that Tommie Town and the old toys had been sitting in the basement unused for almost two years.

"Really?" I told him. "But you and I built that together." Actually, I had done 90% of the work while Tommie pantomimed his share of the project.

"Yeah, Dad I need that space for my lab-bor-ra-tory," he said, pronouncing 'laboratory' like he was in a Boris Karloff movie, his face ticking and his eyes fluttering again as he pronounced it.

Lord, I thought, *what a colossal bitch of a job dismantling the whole set of towns and the plaster and chicken wire mountain, all the train tracks, the landscaping, the model villages. Oh, damn.*

"Dad, pull-lease!"

"Well, okay, each weekend we can work on it."

"What will you do with it?" Sarah asked.

"I have no idea."

Janet chimed in. "Perhaps some non-profit would want it, the Boy Scouts perhaps or another hobbyist.

"I don't know."

"You could put an ad on Facebook or other online apps, Craigslist too," Tommie enthused.

"I'll let you figure that out, okay?" I shrugged. A hope dawned. "Maybe someone would come and remove everything. That would be fabulous."

The doorbell rang.

"That's Jacque!" Sarah exulted and was gone like a shot.

He walked into the kitchen carrying a heavy, serious-looking case and a canvas bag. The case was black fiberboard with gray, pop-riveted steel reinforcements lining each joint, hinged on one side with a center clasp lock on the other, about five feet long, two feet in depth and width.

"What the hell is that?" I asked.

"A surprise," Jacque smiled.

Tommie shouted triumphantly, "I know what it is!" launching a piece of waffle he was putting in his mouth back onto his plate.

Jacque set the case on the floor, opened its clasp. "Come look."

We gathered around the case as he removed a top layer of protective foam.

"Oh, my God," Janet remarked in wonder.

In the case was a four-foot-tall robot with a rudimentary, eyeless, composite head, its torso and limbs formed of different pulleys, springs, carbon fiber rods, and pneumatic actuators, steel cables, colored electric wires, and battery pack in its chest.

Jacque pulled the robot out of its surrounding foam casing and with Tommie's help steadied it upright on our kitchen tile floor.

He then retrieved a controller from the canvas bag and handed it to Tommie.

"What's its name?" Sarah asked.

"ITBOT One, 'cause it's an IT, the first IT."

"Okay."

"Tommie, tell them about ITBOT One?" Jacque asked.

We could see Tommie reaching into his memory, face ticking, eyes fluttering, but his expression turned to normal as he said, "ITBOT One is an untethered, autonomous, full-sized, walking, humanoid robot with four moving limbs and a head."

"Tommie did much of the programming for ITBOT One. In fact, ITBOT One is essentially his guy."

Tommie grinned giddily.

"Tommie, why don't you show the family how ITBOT One works," Jacque suggested.

Tommie grew very concentrated and serious as he flicked what was obviously the ON button on the controller.

ITBOT One straightened up with small whines and some clicking from its parts.

Tommie worked the controller, and ITBOT One began taking very short, uncertain steps in a shuffling walk across the floor its mechanisms whining and clicking. I thought for sure ITBOT One was going to fall but some gyroscopic feature seemed to right it when it was on the brink of toppling.

"Damn, Tommie," I heard myself exclaim. "You ARE a damn genius."

Tommie was grinning ear to ear as Janet cooed at him, "So, wonderful!"

Sarah asked, "Is that all ITBOT One does?"

A maniacal, devilish expression came to Tommie's face as he pushed a button on the controller.

ITBOT One said in a synthetic voice, "Shut up, you worthless human scum."

"Ohhhh, how cute," Sarah said defensively.

ITBOT One's arm came up with a middle finger salute.

Tommie was beside himself laughing, his body twisting as he almost lost his balance.

"Hmmm," Jacque commented with a contrite smile. "I honestly did not know about this last innovation. Enough, Tommie. I think I can speak for everyone. We're amazed by ITBOT One."

A disappointed, "Ohhh, okay."

Suddenly, ITBOT One went dead.

XXIII

ID

AT THE FOUNDATION'S office the Monday following Christmas, after I had brewed myself a cup of coffee, settled into my office and gazed for a time at the winter cityscape, thinking regretfully about the week ahead, I placed a call to Emily Sayzak, picturing her small coquettish face as I did.

She answered immediately.

"Thomas?"

"Hey, Emily. How was your holiday?"

"Oh, you wouldn't be interested. I had some friends over for a potluck dinner, fixed a big turkey, drank too much Chablis. How about you?"

"Oh, quiet. Time with the family and Sarah's boyfriend. All good. Relaxing. Look, remember that guy you told me about?"

"Sure."

"This Saturday could we go out to Gertie's around, say six, and sit out in the parking lot until this guy arrives?"

"You mean like on a date?"

"No. I just need you to point him out. I need to be sure we have the right guy."

"You mean like we're parking like in high school?"

"No. I just need your help to be a thousand percent sure he's who we think he is."

"You mean the Drone Assassin?" she asked, excitement resonating in her voice. "Oh, I'd love to!"

"Well, let's not jump to any conclusions." I felt like I was walking on very thin ice. Felt myself shaking my head. *Christ, I hoped this would work. Otherwise, we could be so screwed in so many ways. A front-page headline on the daily paper shrieking Drone Assassin Identified ran through my head. Jesus, the police and FBI would be furious. So would everybody at Sessions. Mark would probably have to fire me to cover things up. Why the hell was I doing this? And it was my own stupid idea!*

"This could all be wrong," I told Emily. "We're just playing a hunch."

"Who's we?"

"Just Zoltan and I."

"Oh," a note of disappointment in her voice. "The cops think you've been leading them on a wild goose chase."

"Yeah, I know. That's why we're being so careful. They could be right." *If I heard the 'wild goose chase' phrase one more time I might burst into flames and explode.*

"Well, okay, I'll play along, it's always nice to see you, Thomas."

Oh shit. "Yeah. Thanks. How about I pick you up around 5:30?"

"Sure."

She gave me her address. By the street name I knew the neighborhood, brick and slate roof row houses just outside the city line built in the early fifties and populated by retirees and young families. Not where I would have expected her to live. I started making up excuses for when I dropped her off on why I could not come in.

We hung up. "Christ, what have I done?" I heard myself say out loud.

About a half-hour later I placed a three-way call to Berger and Zoltan. I filled them in on my conversation with Emily. Using standard phrasing like 'the place' for Gertie's and 'him' for Sammie we planned for 'Z' Zoltan to take an Uber to Gertie's and hang out of sight at the back of the place to be sure the 'maybe' Sammie was not there before 'my passenger' Emily and I arrived.

I told them that if he did show up and Emily IDed him, I'd tell her that he was not the right guy and that I needed to let Zoltan know, then text the make and model of his vehicle and his license number to Zoltan and leave. Zoltan would take the back exit out of Gertie's, plant the tracking device and take an Uber back to our house, where I would meet him after dropping off Emily.

"Well, okay, we got a plan," Berger told us. "Let's hope the fuck it works."

"Yeah."

"It work," Zoltan declared. "Then what we do?"

"See where he's hanging out," I told him.

"We want to go there?"

"I don't know, man. Not real safe. I don't feel like getting killed this or next weekend, do you?"

"No, maybe following weekend. But die from too much sex not Sammie automatic."

"God damn you're brilliant. Thanks for sharing."

"Yes."

"One thing for sure. I'm not calling the cops or FBI. They'd just laugh at us."

"You right."

"Okay, guys," Mark said, "Be in touch on when he goes and where he goes."

"Sure."

*

SATURDAY AT 5:30, driving the family beater to be as inconspic-uous as possible, after cleaning out Sarah and Tommie's fast-food trash, I picked up Emily at her rowhouse. Her place was fronted by a few concrete stairs, a short concrete walk and then a second set of stairs to a roofed porch and her front door. She was wearing a pleated grey wool skirt, an unbuttoned red winter coat, a red turtleneck that showed off her nipples, half-boots, her red beret. She gave me the usual frontal Emily hug before we walked to the car, her blond permed hair bouncing and her breath visible from the cold air outside, blinking at me with her heavily mascaraed eyes. As usual she also wore too much makeup and bright red lipstick.

"Wow, Thomas, you really went all out on the car." She told me as she got in. "I'm very impressed."

"Our family beater. Don't want to look obvious."

"Yeah. Makes sense."

She sidled over, her skirt riding up on her legs, and gave me a nice wet peck on the cheek.

I noticed immediately a change.

"Um, Emily, you aren't wearing your perfume?" I commented, trying to suppress my enthusiasm as she slid back to her side of the car.

"Yeah. I can tell you don't like it."

"Oh."

"Every time you get near me you try not to but you end up making a face like you just stepped in dog shit."

I felt myself smile an embarrassed grin, "Geez, I'm sorry."

"It's okay," she said, shrugging lightly. "Anything to please you, Thomas."

"Okay. Thanks."

On our way out to Gertie's we made meaningless conversation to fill dead air. Traffic congestion from too many workaholic people now in a panic to get all their errands done over the weekend. How she would like to vacation in the Virgin Islands. Had I ever been there? I told her about visiting when I was still single, chartered a sailboat with friends, the highlights of the BVI, Tortola, St. John's, Foxy's, Virgin Gorda, all of great interest to Emily.

At Gertie's I found a good parking spot with a view of the lot but toward the rear where we would not be noticed and backed in. Pulled out my phone and texted Zoltan, "You here?"

"Yes."

I pictured him hunched over a table in the back sipping a straight vodka, empty seats on either side, patrons staring at him with "Who the fuck is this guy?" expressions.

The moment I put my phone back in my overcoat pocket Emily was on me, her lips on mine, her tongue working hard. Worse, I liked it.

I pulled away, "Hey, hey, hey. Come on, come on. We need to pay attention."

I went to push her away and my hand brushed across the warm ingot of her left nipple.

She drew in a breath. "Oh!"

"No, no, no. I'm sorry."

"Don't be. I liked that."

"Aw, come on Emily. Please. We'll miss this guy."

She moved toward me. "Ok. More time for us."

"Come on. This is really very serious."

Our activity had caused the car's windows to steam up. I began to wipe the windshield frantically with my bare hand, opened the door window a crack for fresh air to clear the steamed-up glass.

Emily drew back, pouted. I gave her a quick once over. Jesus, she was hot, everything about her.

I looked out at the parking lot. A few cars had come in and parked but the folks getting out of them were couples. Well, maybe our 'maybe' Sammie would show up with a date, although I doubted it.

"Thomas ..." Emily said affectionately as she moved toward me again.

"Yeah," I heard myself say guardedly.

"I've always really liked you."

"Aw Christ, Emily ... Could you please ..."

A door slammed nearby, a creaking bang. Emily and I turned to look out at the parking lot.

Emily jumped and yanked at my arm. "There he is!"

He had parked in the row facing us, a few spaces beyond us. It was Sammie all right. He'd gained some weight and now had a full beard. Dressed in overalls, plaid shirt and hunting jacket. Amazing what you can find at the Salvation Army. I actually might not have recognized him. Suddenly, I was very glad Emily was along.

He had just left a derelict Ford F-150 pickup with a camper top. I looked away while he passed close by just in case he glanced toward us. He made his way into Gertie's with the same forceful stride I remembered from Christmas season a year ago.

"Aw, shit," I said to Emily, as convincingly as I could, "That's not him."

"Ohhhh ..." from Emily.

"Let me text Zoltan."

I pulled out my cell phone, texted Zoltan, "It's him."

I entered the make, model and license number and "It's a derelict old truck. He just walked in there."

'Yes," came the reply.

I texted, "I'm leaving with Emily. Put the tracking device on the inside of his rear bumper, then take an Uber to our place. I'll see you there."

On the way back to Emily's, not unexpected but to my total regret, as if she had suffered a personality change, she turned into a reporter.

"So if that guy isn't the Drone Assassin, then who is he?"

"I have no idea."

"But he knew you."

"He knew of me maybe, knew who I am, but I've never seen that guy before. I'm very confused about this whole situation, his whole line of questioning. Maybe he's one of the undercover guys for the FBI, the cops, or even Blaylock. I just don't know, but I'm going to try to find out."

Emily became very serious, upset, "Thomas, there are some things you're not telling me, like everything else. I've always trusted you and what do you do? You just keep lying to me."

"No shit. Look Emily, I really care about you. Yes, there are things I cannot talk to you about. And as I've told you, despite your profession, it's better that you don't know. Things that scare me. You can take it as a crock of shit, but I don't want you to get embroiled in all the crap that's gone on and is going on. It's dangerous."

"But Thomas," and as she spoke, her face reddened and she began to cry, real tears streaming down her face, her mascara bleeding into it, "But that's what I DO! I take risks for stories if I need to. And you're just treating me like a child."

This could easily be manipulation. I thought.

"I'm so sorry, Emily. I shouldn't have asked this favor of you."

"Yes, you SHOULD have," she said, her voice cracking as she pulled a tissue from her coat pocket and began to compose herself. "That and a lot more."

"Yeah, sorry, I can't do that."

"GOD DAMNED YOU!"

Oh, Jesus, a woman's fury.

"Thomas, I can take care of MYSELF!"

That's what we all think, until ... The Mike Tyson quote flashed through my mind, 'Everyone has a plan until they get punched in the mouth.'

We pulled up to Emily's place and it did not surprise me that she did not invite me in. She was thoroughly pissed-off at me and who could blame her. Hell, I was pissed-off at me. She did reach over and give me a light buss on the cheek, then exited the car, frosty as a windshield on a cold winter morning. On the way up the concrete stairs a gust of wind blew hard enough to lift her coat and skirt, revealing her buttocks. No underwear.

I shook my head, saying to myself, *Maybe I'm a lucky man, after all. Maybe her being pissed at me is just as well.* I shrugged and laughed a small, bitter laugh. Hell, I could rationalize anything.

As I inspected myself in the mirror on the back of my sun visor, whipping off lipstick smears from my mouth and cheeks, checking to make sure there were none on my clothes, I found myself very anxious to get back to the sanctity of our home, even with Zoltan there waiting for me.

XXIV

The Hideout

8:30 P.M. AT our house.

Zoltan and I sat in my office with the doors closed, Zoltan nursing his after-dinner vodka and me my scotch. Zoltan was in my leather lounge chair, the only chair he could fit in, barely. I was pulled up next to him in my desk chair, both of us looking intently at the screen of my iPad.

"He on the move," Zoltan said as we watched the tracking device icon travel roads from Gertie's out into the country.

Janet had been nice enough to heat up pre-made fettuccine alfredo for us, the kids and Jacque. Zoltan and I had temporarily overcome our distraction and faked pleasantries, then retired to my den, a move unusual enough for Jacque to give us a penetrating and quizzical look and for Janet to poke her head in and ask whether everything was okay.

"Yeah, long story," I had told her with a dismissive, no-big-deal wave of my hand. "Trying to figure out for Mark some logistics about our visit today."

"Hmmm ... Okay." Janet had replied. I suspected she did not believe a word I said but given that what we were doing was supposedly at Mark's behest, she would not pry further.

When the door closed, I said to Zoltan, "I hope to hell she doesn't give me the third degree later."

Zoltan shrugged. "You like you always do figure out what to say."

"Yeah."

From what we could see, Sammie had left Gertie's around a half hour ago. The thought that he probably was alone having struck out with the local ladies caused me to smile.

He was headed out into the country along local roads which wound their circuitous way west through the rolling terrain interspersed with a few farms and not much else.

Then halfway around a long, slow curve from west to south the icon slowed and took a sharp right onto an invisible road not featured on the map. It made its way slowly for perhaps a few hundred yards, then made a sharp left and moved even more slowly another hundred yards or so before stopping.

"There's his fucking hideout."

"Yes. Bastard."

"I'll switch to satellite and expand the picture."

An eagle's eye country scene appeared; the satellite picture taken in the spring of some year past.

I zeroed down another magnification and we could barely see through the new spring green tree growth the rutted, dirt driveway he had turned onto. In the distance the drive went to a farmhouse on a far hill surrounded by undulating fields of new corn, hay and pastures being grazed by black angus. From the road the drive first descended to a stream, crossed a small wooden bridge and then traveled uphill to the farmhouse. Just after the bridge was another smaller and more rutted drive to the left that followed the stream and then made its way uphill to a small house, probably originally a tenant farm, with a work shed beside it.

"There it is. God damn it. We've found him!"

"Yes ... What we do now?"

"Umm ... Time to take Sparky for a walk. Call Mark."

"Yes, good idea."

I went to my briefcase by my desk and pulled out an encrypted phone.

We left my office, put our drink glasses in the sink. At the hall closet I put on my winter coat and wool hat, while Zoltan pulled his coat from the hall chair. I took Sparky's leash from the hook on the inside of the door. All I had to do was say, "Walk!" loudly and she was there in a heartbeat, circling and making anxious noises.

We took our normal route across the street to a neighborhood cut-through while I placed our call and put it on speaker, turning the volume down, Sparky sniffing and squatting randomly as we walked in the frigid air, our collective breaths billowing out behind us.

"Howarya?" Mark's voice came through, flat and small.

"We've made some progress. Emily ID'ed him. It's Sammie all right. Unfortunately, she's super pissed at me. Knows I've been lying to her. I'm hoping there are no repercussions, but for now she's gone as a resource."

"Small price to pay. She doesn't know shit and that's what counts."

"Zoltan planted the tracking device. We came back to our place and picked up Sammie's departure from Gertie's and followed him a long way out in the country to a dirt road going to a farmhouse with a turnoff to what was probably at one point a tenant farm shack with a work shed. Perfect hideout."

"Damn, that's good work."

"What we do now?" Zoltan demanded.

"Look, I think you had the right idea about checking his hideout when he's gone, taking pictures as evidence that we can show the FBI. But Sammie's no dummy and he's probably paranoid, probably has the place set with motion detector cameras and all that other crap. Could even have the place booby trapped."

"Exactly what we were thinking."

"So, first, let's wait awhile, figure out his pattern of leaving and returning to his place.

"Second, you buy high-quality, daytime and night-vision cameras with a telescopic lens, go out there and see whether you can find a place in the woods to check out his shack. Maybe take pictures of Sammie when you know he normally leaves the place. The question is this: Is he so over-confident that he hasn't bothered with any security cameras, motion detectors, etc. I find that hard to believe, but it's a possibility. If the place is wired up for security, then we got a whole 'nother set of problems. We don't want him to vanish on us. If not, then, well, we'll see."

"He no dummy," Zoltan said flatly, "Could be too, like you say, he booby trapping place."

"Yeah, let me think about this."

"Yeah?"

"Look, we run billions of dollars of enterprises. You don't think we need the world's best security against illegal entry of different warehouses, offices buildings, getting hacked, etc.? So, who do we hire to do that?"

"I don't know. Security firms?"

"Hah! Fuck no. We have our own security firms. Blaylock's one of 'em. So, who do they hire? Mostly, former FBI agents. So, one of them's gonna know Pfaff. Not too hard to find that out. I let that guy or gal know what we're up to. They know me; they know I don't fuck around with conspiracy theories, etc. We go visit Pfaff and set him straight. Having some pictures would help. Let me think about it."

There was a pause while Berger considered the situation. Then he said, "Yah know, I'm always real hesitant to cross the line between my enterprises and Sessions, which is a personal cause, Blaylock being the exception because they were already on the case when we bought them. But this might be one time I make an exception."

"Sure."

"I'll get back to you. In the meantime, get me some damn evidence."

*

AN HOUR LATER, Zoltan already gone, as I was getting ready for bed, my phone buzzed on the nightstand. Berger. I picked it up, "Hey, wait a second," I said and walked out of our bedroom, Janet looking at me like I had lost my mind, and treaded lightly down the stairs to my den, closed the door.

"Okay, sorry. What's up?"

"Use your other phone."

"Sure."

I pulled the encrypted phone out of my briefcase and called Berger.

"Hey," he said when picked up, "I've had a better idea. Cuts through all the complications."

"Yeah? What?"

"If things turn out like I hope they will, you'll find out in a day or two. I'll probably be making a phantom visit to town. You don't know that. If I'm successful, you'll know shortly. If not, you'll hear from me."

"You couldn't just tell me what this is all about?"

"Nah. You'll know when you know."

"Oh thanks."

"Jus' suffer quietly my friend."

"You can be assured of that."

"Hah! Ciao."

We hung up.

"Fuck."

XXV

Pfaff

NEW YEAR'S CAME, cold, overcast, and wet. Sarah was at a party with Jacque. I was feeling ill at ease knowing that she and Jacque probably would not be seen until tomorrow sometime. Tommie was hunkered down with his computer in his upstairs bedroom. Janet and I watched TV celebrations around the world until about 10:30, looked at each other with The Hell With It expressions and went to bed. We lay there, listening to the popping and sizzling of small fireworks set off by neighborhood kids.

Wednesday the following week, 5:30 in the evening, driving home from the foundation in the dark and rain, stuck in traffic on the expressway, my phone buzzed in my overcoat pocket. I fished it out before it went to voicemail and answered.

A monotone, "Dr. Simpson?" For a second, I thought it might be a robocall, then I recognized the voice.

"Yes?"

"This is agent Pfaff," a voice flat as Nebraska.

"Oh ... um, what's up?"

"I'd like to meet with you and Zoltan."

"Ohhh-kay," I replied, puzzled.

"In about forty-five minutes at your village shopping center."

"What? How the hell are we supposed to do that?"

"I'm on my way there now with Zoltan, probably ahead of you. Picked him up at the medical center."

"Oh. Wow. Um, sure. What's this about?"

"I'll fill both of you in when we get there."

"Sure. Okay. See you there."

I hung up and called Zoltan.

He picked up, background noises of car tires on water-filled roadways, "Yes?"

"What the hell's going on?"

"No clue. He being mysterious." Zoltan laughed, "Maybe he arresting us?"

"Not funny."

"Yes funny. Anyway, he in front seat shaking his head. I in back seat because only place I fit."

"Awww ... hell. I'll see you there."

Finally in the wet, snarled traffic I came to the village center and pulled into the parking lot looking for an FBI fleet car.

The center was still decked out for Christmas, the awful weather having delayed any removal of its decorations. Wreaths and multi-colored strings of lights were everywhere, along with small plastic piles of fake snow and huge illuminated, plastic candy canes glistening in the downpour. Folks were scurrying about with umbrellas, hustling from their cars in and out of the grocery store and pharmacy, retrieving pizzas, hauling items from the hardware store to the curbside, items which were soaked by the time they drove up in their car to load them.

My phone buzzed again.

"We're over near the village square sign. Can't miss the sedan," Pfaff told me.

I looked out across the parking lot. Sure enough, under the village square sign with fake greenery bunting wrapped around it, a bright star of David suspended between its two poles, I could spot them, Pfaff in the front seat and Zoltan in the back. I could only see the outline of Zoltan's unmistakable torso, realized his head was pressing up against the headliner.

I parked nearby, loped over in the pounding rain, listening

momentarily to a tinny and static laden "Jingle Bell Rock" playing loudly from a large speaker attached to the closest sign pole, opened the passenger door and sat in the passenger's seat facing Pfaff.

"So, what's this all about?"

"I had a meeting with Mr. Berger yesterday. He's a very persuasive gentleman. He touched on a few things I might do to get an inkling that some other issues might have plagued the university over the last several years.

"He asked me whether I knew anyone who was with U.S. Special Operations, and it turns out I do. He said to give him or her a call and mention the university, which I did."

He paused.

"What was the reaction?"

"Stone cold silence. Okay, we know when not to cross lines and dig any further. What's of importance to us is solving this present case. So, I understand now that there's some deep background here that we shouldn't mess with but that it may have a material bearing on Sessions' situation. This adds some background credibility to your prior thoughts on the Drone Assassin's identity.

"So, of course, we also checked out Mr. Berger thoroughly. You know, some of these mega-rich guys, you dig into their way of doing business and it's a shell game where they really are not to be trusted, often playing fast and loose with their personal lives, their businesses, and the truth."

He paused again.

"That does not in any way describe Mr. Berger. He has decades of his word being his bond. He's built his enterprises the old-fashioned way through hard, shrewd, detailed work. Plus, he seems to have a sixth sense of when and how to make big moves. You know, he and his business successes are often studied in business schools."

"Yeah, he doesn't like to talk about things like that."

"I understand. So, here's what we're going to do. I've volunteered to work with you guys on this particular lead on my own time. The bureau is okay with my doing this. I've cleared it with them. If your lead pans out, then it becomes FBI business. If it's a bust, no one knows. That work for you guys?"

I looked into the back seat at Zoltan. His eyes were wide. He turned to Pfaff. "We be working with the FBI, with you?"

"Right."

He turned to me, "Thomas, this just what we need."

"Yeah!" I agreed, more enthusiastically than I had intended.

"What we do now?" Zoltan asked.

"If you guys got time for dinner, I need as full a debrief as you can give me."

"Okay, Christ, I gotta call home. There's a decent place to eat, The Hunters Inn, across the road from the other side of the center in the little strip there. Okay? I'll see you there."

I left the fleet car and loped back over to the Bimmer, thought for a moment about what to tell Janet. *Hell,* I thought, *"For once, why don't I tell the truth?"*

She answered on the first ring, "Hi, honey. Where are you?"

"You not going to believe this, but Zoltan and I are at the village center about to have dinner with an FBI agent."

"Really?"

"Yeah. Really. At the Hunters Inn. He just materialized with Zoltan in tow. Wants to question us about some aspects of the Drone Assassin case."

"My Lord, Thomas. The FBI?"

"Yeah, interesting, huh? Not sure how long we'll be."

"Okay, honey. You think they're getting any closer to solving this case?"

"I have no idea. In the meantime, probably best if you do not mention any of this to anyone?"

"Sure, I understand."

I thought with a satisfying reassurance, *One good thing about having a psychologist wife is her innate understanding of the importance of keeping confidences.*

"Great. Thanks!"

Our dinner in a back booth of the post-holiday, weather-eclipsed almost empty restaurant lasted two hours. Pfaff took notes on an iPad between bites of a bacon cheeseburger and fries and sips of a coke, Zoltan chowing down on a ribeye steak and beers, the number of which I lost count, with me having the Cobb salad and iced tea.

I started with Sammie's eulogy for his father and went through the meeting with Natalie and Joan the previous Christmas when I was cold-cocked by Sammie, then asked, "So, did Mark give you some indication about what we've found out about Sammie since?"

"He did. Very thorough."

"So, here we are." I filled him in on my visit to Chicago and what Walter Berenson had told me, what we discovered from the police about Sammie's ditching his RV, then Emily's chance meeting of him at Gertie's, our follow-up identification and our putting a tracking device on Sammie's truck and following it out into the country.

"So, we know where his hideout is and for sure, like clockwork, that he goes to Gertie's Place every Saturday at about 6:30 p.m."

Spaff absorbed all this with no reaction, then said, "Okay. Give me your tracking link and let me scope out the scene out there in the country.

"Once I've reviewed that, let's see whether we might be able to visit the site without detection to capture pictures of Sammie and if possible, get inside to prove he's the Drone Assassin. Gentlemen, clandestine breaking and entering and leaving no trace of having done so is in fact the FBI's forte. Is there some place we could meet in the evening? I can pick Zoltan up and we can review plans, equipment etc., say day after tomorrow, Friday. I'll be supplying our equipment by the way. No need for you guys to do anything."

"We can use the foundation offices downtown. No problem."

"Good. Let's meet there on Friday after work and plan our next moves."

I saw Pfaff and Zoltan off at The Hunters Inn and drove home along empty dark, rainswept roads, rain pounding off my convertible top, thankful for the short drive.

It was after 9 p.m. by the time I parked in the garage and made my way into the house, pleased to have Sparky's perpetually excited to see me greeting.

Janet was reading one of her book club novels in the family room, Sarah and Jacque hanging out around the kitchen table, focused on their iPhones, talking occasionally in low tones and sharing an iPhone glimpse with one another.

Janet put her book down as I approached her and bent to give her a peck on the cheek.

"You look exhausted."

"Yeah, no disguising that ... Hey, I've got to work out a to-do list for tomorrow. A lot going on. Be in the den. Okay?"

"Sure."

I turned on the lights in the den, shut the door, and sat in my lounge chair. My mind was racing with all the thoughts from our dinner, trying to come to terms that we were actually working with the FBI and that three days from now on Saturday we would be traipsing through the woods near Sammie's hideout in an attempt to capture photos of him and then explore his place.

There was a light rap at the den's door.

"Yes?"

The door opened a quarter and Jacque said, "May I come in for a moment?"

"Uh, sure ..." *Lord, don't let this be about you and Sarah. Please.*

Jacque entered, closed the door carefully and stood facing me, clearly feeling awkward.

"We could not help but overhear your earlier conversation with Mrs. Simpson. It seemed as if you are dealing with the FBI."

So much for confidentiality. Ker-rist.

"Yes," I told him, noting the peeved tone of my voice. "But please keep this to yourselves."

"I hope you do not mind my asking, but does this have to do with the Drone Assassin?"

I smiled a saccharine smile at him. It felt good to tell him, "I cannot say..."

He nodded.

"Please, Jacque, keep your thoughts about this to yourself. Okay?"

He gave me a puzzled look, but said, "Yes, I will do that. Thank you."

He paused as if he wanted to say something else, but then left the den, shutting the door behind him.

XXVI

The Plan

THE NEXT MORNING, at the foundation, having said hello to Jo Ann, I shut the door to my office and called Mark on an encrypted phone.

He picked up on the second ring, "Howarya?"

"Agent Pfaff had a surprise meeting with Zoltan and me last evening."

"Ah, good."

"He says you're a very persuasive man."

"Yeah," he paused, and I could picture a smirk. "Probably didn't hurt that I mentioned the number of retired, former FBI colleagues who we've hired for our security companies."

"Yeah."

"Or that I hoped his two kids, 15 and 16 who are doing well in school, apply for merit scholarships at Sessions."

"You devil."

"So they say."

I brought him up to speed on our meeting and plans.

"Good. Give me a call after the meeting on Friday and let me know what's up."

"Tell you what, I'll have you join us on the encrypted phone."

"Sure. Good idea ... Ciao."

We hung up.

Sighing, I turned in my chair to look out the window at the gray scenery of the city, the same low ceiling, overcast, forty-degree last day of the month. The forecast was for a cold front to be coming in this evening, bringing with it clear skies and freezing temperatures. As I looked out on the city I replayed in my mind yesterday's meeting with Pfaff, convincing myself that we were indeed doing the right thing.

Then, turning back to my desk, I began reviewing a pile of proposals Jo Ann had left in my inbox.

About fifteen minutes later faint elevator noises began to sound through my door.

I looked up, *Hmmm, who could this be?*

The elevator opened. Through my door's window glass, I saw Ursula step out.

Ohhh ... I thought.

I snatched the encrypted phone off my desk, dropped it into my briefcase beside my chair.

"Dr. Simpson is busy!" I heard Jo Ann as Ms. Bemis command her to stop.

"No, he is not," was Ursula's stern reply.

She breezed by Jo Ann, who jumped from her desk and was about to apprehend her, which I knew would not end well for Jo Ann.

I leapt to the door. "No, no, no!" I told Jo Ann, "She's an old, old friend, a friend."

Ursula looked at me seriously. "I am not that old."

"I, of course, meant we've known each a long time."

"Yes."

"Okay," I acknowledged, holding up both hands. "Jo Ann, it's okay. We're okay."

I held the door for Ursula, who walked in and sat in the chair fronting my desk. Shut the door carefully. Glanced back at Jo Ann who still had daggers in her eyes as she turned back toward her desk.

No love lost between those two, I thought.

I glanced at Ursula as I returned to my seat. She wore a black wool skirt, stockings, ice blue silk blouse, small gold chain necklace.

What fantastic legs. Why does she always have to look so good? I shook my head in one involuntary motion to rid myself of the thought.

She placed her elbows on the chair's arms, crossed her legs and looked at me. Serious. All business.

"How have you been, Thomas?"

"Okay, all things considered."

"And the family?"

"Good. As it turns out of all the crazy things Tommie is actually gifted in technology, so he and Sarah are now both taking courses in the Gifted and Talented Youth program. Tommie's also in a special school with other kids similar to him. You met Sarah's French boyfriend, Jacque, at the club the other day, one of Tommie's tutors. Begrudgingly, I'm beginning to actually like the young man. Very talented and a real gentleman if there is such a thing left in this world. Janet continues her counseling. No complaints."

"Ah, that is very good. I am happy for you."

"But you didn't come here to talk about my family, did you?"

"No."

"Perhaps we should rename you Ulterior instead of Ursula?"

She smiled at my comment. "That might be fitting. You are right, as usual."

She paused, then told me, "I heard from Special Operations that the FBI made an inquiry about Sessions."

"Yeah, I'm aware. They needed to understand that, without knowing what it is, there's a backstory at Sessions over the last three years. From the beginning, we've had an idea of who the Drone Assassin is and that his motive is vengeance on the administration, but the cops and the FBI discounted our thinking. At Mark's suggestion, the FBI called a contact in Special Ops and mentioned Sessions. Resounding silence. The FBI decided they really do not want to know any more, respecting the other agency's secrecy. But the stonewalling was enough to lend credibility to our and their suspicions about the identity of the Drone Assassin."

It was rare to see Ursula feeling awkward, but she was. "So, nothing was revealed?"

"Exactly."

"You're sure?"

"Yes."

She paused for a moment, considering. "You know, Thomas, you may be one of the few people in this world I actually trust."

"I'll take that as a compliment."

"You should."

She paused again.

"So, who is this assassin and what is the plan to capture him?"

"The plan?"

"Come now, Thomas, you know better than that."

"Ursula, you know better than to try pry from me what I absolutely cannot discuss. Besides, you and your colleagues have known about this person all along. You just never found out what the hell he was up to."

She smiled, "Ahhh."

Another pause. I just let it drift, while I watched her trying to decide whether she wanted to say whatever else was running through her Machiavellian mind.

Her expression changed slightly, became less ulterior, "I wish things had turned out differently with you and me. I am sorry circumstances prevented it."

I thought of her brilliant disappearance from Sessions as we became fully aware of the clandestine anonymous international wire transfers being received by the Sessions' capital campaign to further Fitz-Hugh's Global University ambitions in return for the placing of U.S. spies in the new international centers. We learned later of her departure with Jean Claude as he conducted his annual spring sail of *Calypso Too* to the Mediterranean. The news had come as a shock to me, galling and a great relief all at the same time.

"Christ, I'm not sorry. It's all for the best."

"Of course, you are right. In any case, I will report there is no cause for concern."

"Thank you." I said wholeheartedly.

She rose, walked around my desk and in a quick motion put her hand gently behind my head and gave me a much too passionate kiss, her tongue probing mine as it had done so many times before, then she straightened, turned, opened the door and walked to the elevator. Reflexively, I could not help noticing all of her in all the right places working so beautifully.

Lord, I am such a lucky man to no longer be involved.

*

ON FRIDAY, TOWARD the end of the workday, I sent Jo Ann home early, ostensibly as a reward for all her dedication and hard work. Needless to say, she was delighted by my generosity.

Once she was gone, the office was strangely quiet with only me being there. I tried to ignore that and readied the conference room for Zoltan and Pfaff. Pulled out the encrypted phone again to allow Mark to be part of our conversation.

Called Janet and told her I would be working late, more involvement with the FBI. She accepted my excuse grudgingly. Clearly, I was beginning to run out of goodwill at home.

As I turned on the lights to the conference room, the elevator doors opened, and Zoltan strolled in.

"Good evening. You have food?"

"No, I hadn't really thought about that to be honest."

"Hmm. I go eat downstairs when we finish."

"I'd invite you out for dinner, but Janet is kinda getting sketchy about our little adventure and my being away from home on vague pretenses."

"Yes. Make sense. Just tell her you love her so much," he said, pursing his lips and making Gourami kissing motions.

"Yuk. What the hell Christina sees in you, I'll never know."

"You want me to give you hint?"

"Hell, no!"

Zoltan actually chuckled.

The elevator doors opened, and Pfaff stepped out, carrying a laptop.

He came in, greeted us with a nod, went to the monitor at the head of the conference table and hooked up his computer. I called Mark on the encrypted phone, put in on speaker and placed it in the center of the conference table.

"Howarya?"

"I've got Agent Pfaff and Zoltan here. Pfaff has just synced his computer with the monitor."

"Okay."

"I'm bringing up a picture of Sammie's hideout and the surrounding countryside," Pfaff said to the phone.

I looked at the picture carefully. "Holy crap, when was this taken?"

"Yesterday," he intoned.

"Wow."

"We do our best."

Pfaff pulled a telescoping pointer from his suitcoat pocket and pulled it open.

"So, as you know, the state road here takes a slow turn. Halfway through is the drive to the farmhouse in the distance, owned by the Zwick family. From the drive's entrance down the hill and across the stream over a small wood bridge is a left onto a gullied drive that follows the stream and then turns right uphill to Sammie's place.

"But let's go back to the state road. You'll see here as it continues along the farm's property."

He placed the pointer on a spot at the border of the woods. "Here is a place we could pull off, between the road and the fence bordering the farm's property. Looks like maybe this was a planned driveway entrance to something that was never built, now almost completely overgrown but where we could pull in and be pretty well disguised, especially since it will be dark by then. I'll rent a small SUV for this assignment. Thomas your cars are routinely parked at the university with university parking stickers on them and my fleet car is readily identifiable, so we cannot use those.

"It looks like the woods are pretty clear of underbrush, maybe because of cattle being in there. In any case, we have to make our way through, so we can take a short hike through the woods and come to their edge on the pasture above Sammie's place. From there we can hang out, observing the site until he leaves. I'll have night vision goggles and binocs along with a video camera with night vision capability. As well, I've also got camouflage and bulletproof Kevlar vests for us. Zoltan, for camouflage because nothing will fit you, I've got a poncho. Luckily, I was able to locate a bulletproof vest that might fit. I'll have my standard issue Glock with me but, if we do this right, they'll be no need for it or the vests. Let's hope that's the case. While Kevlar vests will stop pistol fire, they really won't hold up to any heavy artillery, like an AR-15."

"Jesus," I heard myself remark.

"What we do when Sammie leave?" Zoltan asked.

"Zoom in and video his departure, then wait a bit to be sure he's truly gone, didn't forget his wallet or something. Then you guys will serve as lookouts while I'll go down there, case the place, deactivate any security, delete any video of me coming in, then I'll get inside and check the place out, take photographs, providing there's something worth taking pictures of.

"If the place is what you think it is, I'll alert you and you can come on down for a quick look-see and to corroborate, being very careful not to touch anything. At that point, Zoltan, you can video the place, then you guys scat and wait for me while I restage everything so Sammie won't have any idea we were there. If his place isn't what you think it is, then I'll take a few pictures and as quickly as I can restage the place and be gone."

I felt a momentary spasm of panic as it sunk in that we were really, actually going to be doing what he had just outlined. A strong anxiety lingered.

Mark's voice came up the phone, "Pfaff, it sounds like you've done a great job figuring out the right approach. Congrats."

"Save that for after we've been successful."

"Sure. Ciao, guys. I got my fingers, toes and eyes crossed for good luck on this one."

"Thanks!" The three of us chimed in.

I could hear the phone disconnect and retrieved it.

Pfaff said, "So, let's go down to the parking lot and I'll show you what I got."

XXVII

The Hideout

AS PREDICTED, A cold front came in Friday overnight, bringing with it temperatures in high 20's and low 30's, drying out the area except for large patches of ice.

At 5:30 p.m. Pfaff and Zoltan picked me up in the village center parking lot in a gray mid-sized SUV. The sun had already set, darkness spreading into every unlit corner.

I had left home dressed as if for the North Pole wearing two heavy sweaters and two pairs of winter corduroys, two pairs of socks stuffed into work boots, a scarf and my heaviest winter coat, gloves and hat. Janet giving me the silent treatment about this new 'meeting,' Sarah and Tommie looking at me strangely, like was I really their father? Not good.

I sat in the front seat, Zoltan squinched into the back row, all of us dressed similarly.

"How you doing?" he asked me.

"Okay, I guess. Got the 'alien in our midst' freeze-out at home about tonight."

"Consider yourself lucky," Pfaff told us in his monotone, "Think about what my home life is like, that is, on those few occasions when I'm actually there."

"Yeah, I can now relate."

"They're used to it by now. Actually, the kids now treat me with some respect, now that they're older."

"Good."

There was nothing we cared to talk about on the way out to the Zwick farm, lost in our own thoughts of the possible dangers ahead, the countryside and its few lights drifting by as we drove.

After following the turn past the Zwick driveway, along the property line Pfaff pulled into an almost invisible recess in the underbrush before the property line and its ancient hewn wood rail fence and took the SUV as far into the opening as he could.

Outside the car we donned our camo and tested out the equipment, Zoltan raving about the infrared video camera and night vision goggles, which we put on, our breaths steaming in the frigid air.

Pfaff motioned to the sky with his head. "Full moon helps matters. The temperatures have frozen the ground, which helps too. No mud to deal with. Follow me."

We made our way through roadside overgrowth and climbed the fence into the woods, shuffling through leaves between the trees and stepping over rocks, tree roots and fallen branches. I found the night vision of the woods as we moved through them to be very odd but also very helpful, seeing things that I could have easily tripped over in the dark.

After what seemed a long time but probably represented about a hundred yards of walking, we came to the edge of the woods where the cattle-roughened pasture in front of us sloped down to the same fencing as at the property line surrounding Sammie's hideout.

Damn it was cold. Now about 6:20, the field bright in the full light of a rising moon, lights on the ridge in the distance from the Zwick farmhouse and from around the barn and stables, Sammie's windows lit yellow orange.

Around 6:40 Pfaff said, "He's late."

"Yes," observed Zoltan. "He probably taking dump."

"As always, brilliant," I told him, between hasty, steam-laden breaths, wondering whether my teeth might begin to chatter.

Moments later the porch light came on. Zoltan came to attention, flipped off his goggles, brought up camera, turned it on infrared and began filming. As he zoomed in several lights in the house were turned off and Sammie in his farmer clothes and a large hunting jacket emerged. I felt my heart sink when I saw that he had an automatic rifle with an extended clip, its strap slung over his shoulder. At his truck he opened its creaking door, removed the rifle and carefully put it under the front seat, climbed in, slammed the creaking door shut, willed the reluctant engine to start, turned around and headed slowly, bouncing heavily, down the drive out of sight. We could hear his engine increase its speed as he made his way up the drive and then accelerate down the local road until its sound vanished.

An interminable fifteen-minute wait ensued until Pfaff said, "I'm going down. Text me if anything comes up."

"S-sure." I was now jumping up and down and shaking out my legs, walking in circles, anything to try to keep from freezing to death. Zoltan in his poncho with his protective layer of body weight and probably because of his Slavic ancestry simply watched stoically as Pfaff walked carefully, unhurried down to the house, climbed the fence and made his way around its perimeter. Suddenly all the lights in the house went off. Pfaff appeared around its far corner and went to the front door where he was occupied for a time, presumably picking the lock.

Another endless wait, probably no more than fifteen minutes but the cold and discomfort amplified the slowdown of time passing.

Finally, a text from Pfaff. "Come down. I'll let you in. Touch nothing. Unbelievable score here."

"Wow," I exclaimed.

I showed Zoltan the text. He grunted.

We made our way down to the house, carefully climbed the fence. I was pleased that Zoltan's bulk did not snap one of the fence rails. Pfaff opened the front door.

We stepped inside carefully into the infrared illuminated gloom of a small, low ceiling, rustic kitchen with antique appliances to the left, prefab maple cabinets and Formica counters probably reclaimed from a dump, broad beam wood floors. In front of us was a maple kitchen table with two rickety chairs against a white painted sheet-rock wall and a door to a small bedroom. The place had the feeling of being built by the Zwick family members and some farmhands.

"Come on out to the work shed," Pfaff told us, motioning toward a door on our right.

The door opened to a small den with a fireplace, throw rugs, a small desk and gun cabinets with rifles in them. At the end of the room was another door, leading to the shed.

Pfaff opened the ancient wood door.

We all stepped in.

"Holy shit," I heard myself say.

"Get your video camera going," Pfaff told Zoltan.

Zoltan began shooting a panorama of the room.

"Thomas," he said in awe as he filmed, "Look what he is working on here!"

There was a drone being built on a workbench. It was almost complete. Made of clear plastic, holding a miniature camera, its only other more visible parts were the small engines on each of four arms. In the corner was a large 3D printer.

Mounted in a vise on the workbench near the drone was a clear polymer plastic automatic pistol with a polymer cylinder mounted to the barrel. You could see its clip with bullets through the handle of the automatic and some of the works' electronics in the cylinder.

"He's building a stealth drone," Pfaff told us.

"Yeah," was the only response I could muster.

"What the hell is that?" I asked, pointing at the cylinder.

"It's a laser. He's setting it up so when the laser sights a target, he knows to shoot."

"Why? Why is he doing that? I mean, why would he need that when he can zoom in point blank? Why the stealth build?"

We all stared at it for a few moments, thinking.

Pfaff said, "Drone signals are difficult to pick up, get mixed in with other signals. If our teams can sight it, they can focus on it and pick up its signal. They don't sight it then it may be able to sneak through. Run close to ground for instance, weave in and out of places, around buildings for instance."

We stood there in the silence looking at the pistol.

"Oh my God, Thomas!" Zoltan exclaimed suddenly. He had just finished his panorama of the room after taking close ups of the drone, the automatic and the 3D printer.

"What?"

"I have vision. I see what he doing."

"WHAT?" Pfaff and I both said loudly.

More silence as Zoltan looked at the automatic and its laser.

"Why try to find people *outside* of building with FBI trying to jam drone and chase it when he can sneak in from lower level and shoot people IN building. He don't care if FBI destroy drone after that, he just need to get in strike first, then the hell with drone. Nothing about it to discover. It fucking kamikaze."

"Shit! He could kill Fitz-Hugh or even Mark or anyone else in the president's office or anyone else working in an office with a window, including me."

"Yes."

"FREEZE!" came a scream from behind us.

We turned simultaneously.

A rifle shot exploded and blew a smoking hole in the floor in front of us.

A furious Samuel Kravitz II stepped through the smoke from his rifle into the work shed from the den, took five steps toward us as he shouted, "HANDS UP! MAKE ANOTHER MOVE, I'LL KILL YOU! What the fuck do you think you fuckers are doing?"

All this happening in the odd light of my infrared goggles made it seem surreal.

Sammie. Bearded, now much heavier, in Farmer Brown overalls, flannel shirt, hunting jacket, but the same too intense black eyes, pointing his automatic rifle at us.

"OH, it's YOU!" he said to me. "I might have known. Who's this ugly giant fuck with you?"

"I Zoltan Vastag, cancer researcher at medical center."

"Lucky for me that Farmer Zwick spotted your two cars parked near the woods on his property."

Two cars?

"So, I knew right away I should double back here. Parked my truck down the drive, so you wouldn't hear me coming. Yeah, well, well, well, you guys are going to talk to me. Then I'll decide what to do with you, Laurel and Hardy, and who the fuck is this with you?"

"Agent Pfaff, FBI."

"Ohhhh ..."

"That's an AR-15 he's training on us," Pfaff told us.

Oh, God.

"This is a 300-plus-acre farm out here. Shouldn't be too hard to find a nice out-of-way burial plot for you guys to dig graves for yourselves. Even with the ground frozen a bit we can work something out. Then I can just continue to go about my business. And I've got all the time in the world.

"How'd you guys like it when you had to pay me a million-five in ransom, huh? I got a lotta resources at my disposal and I am going to use them very well."

"You are done, Sammie," Pfaff told him matter-of-factly.

A deeply cynical, "Oh, really?"

"The FBI always has backup. I guarantee you my colleagues are aware of us being here and another fifteen minutes goes by they will be here en masse. My best advice to you is to get your ass out of here."

"One more comment from you, dick head, and you're history," he told Pfaff and then turned to me.

"I want some answers. NOW. Why was my father murdered?"

I was thinking fast, panic setting in, my mind racing, "Because he was about through an independent audit to discover financial malfeasance at Sessions," I blurted.

Keep the Special Ops and all that other shit out of this. He wouldn't believe it anyway.

"Ah, now we're getting somewhere. So, Fitz-Hugh had this done, that bastard?"

"To be honest, we're not sure. But you're right, it was most likely not a suicide, more like a botched effort to talk him out of the audit is the general guess."

"Why hasn't this come out?" Sammie asked in a more rationale manner while he processed the information.

"No proof. I've got a family, Zoltan is making important progress with a possible cure for cancer. Blabbing some suspicions to the investigators or the authorities, particularly the press, could get us killed. We don't know what or who we're dealing with. Look, Sammie, it's not like we aren't all in the dark together here. I mean, Blaylock's findings were even inconclusive."

I could see a shadow of doubt forming.

Behind him through the door, to my utter shock, Ursula crept in slowly, wearing a form-fitting black thermal jump suit and black wool pullover hat, the same outfit she had worn the night Kravitz was murdered, when she told me she was going out for a 'jog' in 22-degree weather, pulled a small Glock from a hallway drawer and tucked it into a holster in the small of her back. Now in her right hand she held a pistol with a laser sight on it, aimed at Sammie. I tried mightily not to change my expression.

God damn she looks fabulous.

"DROP YOUR WEAPON!" she screeched at Sammie, her voice from Hades.

Sammie froze, shocked, surprised, a flash of panic ran across his features.

"Get down!" She commanded us. "You are in the line of fire!"

We dropped. Gravity did not seem fast enough to get my belly flat on the dirty wood plank floor.

Sammie stood still facing us, his AR-15 still pointed in our direction, uncertainty clouding his face.

"Sammie," Pfaff said as we lay there. "The young lady behind you has what looks like a laser-sighted Walther PK380 that I suspect is aimed at your head or heart, maybe your lower back. I'd suggest you do as she says."

"Sammie," I said, my voice quavering, raising my head slightly, "Her club sport at MIT was marksmanship." *What a fucking weenie thing to say! What the hell am I thinking!*

Both Pfaff and Zoltan gave me puzzled and irritated sidelong glances.

An angry, defiant look crossed Sammie's face and he wheeled.

Ursula moved her pistol. A shot rang out before he could fully turn, and the AR-15 clattered to the wood floor. Sammie yowled and grabbed his left hand which had been shattered by Ursula's hollow point round. Blood oozed from the wound, leaving small droplets on the floor.

With a roar he charged her. Another shot rang out and he went down hard in a heap, grunting in pain.

"She shot him though his kneecap," Pfaff observed.

Sammie lay there roaring.

"You must stay where you are," Ursula told Sammie loudly. "Do not move or you will lose your other knee. Your shoulder joints will be next."

Sammie, laying face down, went silent except for occasional groans.

"You on the floor, get up!" she ordered us.

We struggled to our feet.

I looked at her. "Ursula, thank God you're here but how?"

She smiled a tense smile at me, "You have a very lovely, caring future son-in-law. Very worried about you. I was sensing something going on ever since I saw you, Zoltan and Berger at the university club. I called him to ask him whether he thought you might be in danger. He did. Told me of you tracking someone. Told me of your working with the FBI. He had followed your tracking device. Hacked your phone I would imagine. So, I'm sorry," she shrugged, "but I too hacked your phone and bugged the conference room in your office several weeks ago, which gave me your plan. So, tonight I drove to the village center and followed you out here. Stopped well before you parked and after you went into the woods, parked behind you and followed. When he," she nodded toward Sammie, "came back, I knew you were in trouble, so I came down to help."

"Ker-rist," was all I could say, feeling both anger and gratitude simultaneously. The anger faded quickly, and the gratitude grew. "Well, you've saved our lives."

"Now what we do with him?" Zoltan asked.

Ursula turned to Pfaff. "I was never here. I leave this to the FBI to take all the credit for and I will be gone as soon as your team gets here."

"Who are you besides Fitz-Hugh's assistant?" Pfaff asked, as if inquiring about a paint color at Home Depot.

Ursula smiled, said simply, "A colleague and friend ... But also someone who does not exist. A phantom perhaps."

Pfaff shrugged and said, "I'll call in a team to work all this out, get Sammie some medical attention, incarcerate him, fabricate a report on his capture, clean up this site."

He turned to Zoltan and me. "You were not here either."

"Couldn't agree more. We'll leave with Ursula."

Pfaff called in his team who arrived in a half hour while we in the meantime watched Sammie lie there bleeding, not wanting to get near him. It seemed cruel but not worth the risk of getting tangled up with him.

An unmarked ambulance arrived making only road sounds, medics in gray jumpsuits put Sammie on a stretcher and removed him. The lights came on and a team of agents began cleaning the area while a photographer took pictures of everything as well as the whole house and work shed. We returned the night vision camera to Pfaff and did the same with our camo.

After the team arrived, I motioned to Pfaff to follow me into the house.

Once we were in the den, I asked him, "Was there a backup team like you said?"

He shook his head. "Usually there is but I was doing this on my own time. We're very lucky Wonder Woman in there showed up."

"I'll say ... Say, look, we never would have found Sammie except for a lead given to me by a reporter I know. Very trustworthy and capable source who on her own chose to share her information with me and not go public with it, which would have caused Sammie to vanish. Who knows if we ever would have found him or how many other lives would have been lost, possibly including some of your agents. So, do me one favor now that we are all still alive here thanks to our phantom. I want you to call this reporter, Emily Sayzak, once you have all your information about this case in order and let her break the story. We all owe it to her."

Pfaff thought about what I had just said for much longer than I felt comfortable, sifting, I imagined, through the FBI bureaucracy and reporting relationships, then he shrugged, "I think we can do that."

"Fantastic. And please, I wouldn't mind if you told her you were calling at my recommendation."

"Okay, but it won't be me. It'll be our communications office and what they'll do is give her a three-hour lead on our initial press release about our capture of the Drone Assassin."

"That would be fabulous!" I pulled out my phone. "Let me text you her contact information."

"Sure," he said as we turned to go back into the house.

As the clean-up wound its way to an end, Ursula turned to Zoltan and I and smiled, "You gentlemen need a lift?"

Under the full moon, we walked out of Sammie's place, climbed the fence and walked uphill. In the dark woods, without night vision we flummoxed our way to the cars. Ursula unlocked her grey Chevy rental.

Ursula dropped Zoltan and I off at my BMW at the village shopping center, got out and came around the car and gave me a long passionate kiss.

"We're going to have to stop this," I told her.

"That is too bad."

"Yeah."

She turned, gave Zoltan her hand. He bent and kissed it sloppily which made her laugh.

"Good evening, gentlemen."

We watched as she drove out of the parking lot and accelerated back towards the city.

"She dangerous lady. But good dangerous."

"Yep. Let's celebrate."

XXVIII

Elation

WELL, WHAT CAN I say about our celebration? As little as possible perhaps. As with any celebration of this sort where the weight of the world has been lifted from your shoulders, where all the angst, fear for your life, uncertainty and worry are suddenly, directly vanquished forever, our celebration at The Hunters Inn brought out our most inane, plebian, and wholly inebriated behavior. Not exactly a performance to be proud of.

High fiving at every new beer and slice of pizza, laughing uproariously at Zoltan's Slavic impersonation of Pfaff, the Oh Shit expression on Sammie's face when Ursula shouted at him to drop his weapon, the fact that for once we were ahead of everyone in our knowledge of what was about to transpire.

Toasting one another and Pfaff, Ursula, Berger, then Jacque and my family, we quaffed yet another beer and shoved yet another pizza slice into our mouths.

I had called Janet and told her that I had wonderful news I'd share with her should I ever come home, that I could tell her with great confidence that I would be having no future evening meetings.

Given the slurring of my voice, she simply hung up on me. *Damn,* I had thought, *They never understand,* only to remind myself that what the hell would I expect, when I never told them anything.

Then I had called Berger on my encrypted phone and had given him a blow-by-blow description of our experience at Sammie's hideout. He was stunned by what we found, shocked by Sammie's appearance and behavior, blown away by Ursula's surprise saving of the day and nodding, I imagined, appreciatively at all the FBI's plans going forward. It was a big, God-damned victory and I so wished he could have been there.

We made plans for him to fly down the next morning for an afternoon meeting so we, including Zoltan, could huddle with Fitz-Hugh and, it struck me as very amusing, Ursula. Obviously, we would, with her and Mark, be appropriately impressed by the FBI's stellar work in capturing Sammie.

Eventually, Zoltan and I made it to our house after midnight, Zoltan scrunched pretzel like into my reclined passenger seat. I managed to not hit anything as I very carefully and uncertainly pulled into the garage. Zoltan rolled onto the couch. Janet confronted me in our bedroom where I slurred that there would be great news tomorrow about the Drone Assassin as I crawled into bed still in my first layer of clothes, the top layer having been scattered along the stairs and into our bedroom. Janet, thankfully, saw that I was beyond redemption, not to mention that I immediately passed into a reeking coma.

The next morning, Zoltan and I watched the morning news, bleary eyed and dyspeptic, the family hovering away from us in the kitchen. At 9:30, the flash bulletin came on about Sammie's capture. News broken by our city newspaper under Emily Sayzak's byline, a news conference with the director of the FBI scheduled for noon.

We had shouted to the family to come watch as the news came on, with an interview clip of Emily reporting the highlights of the press release that no-damn-body in the world yet had. What a coup! Zoltan and I were high fiving while the family stared at us resentfully, like we were the idiots we are.

*

ZOLTAN AND I rallied with the help of cold cut sandwiches and more coffee, showers and shaving and drove to the university. The day was bright, cold and clear, as if the world had been cleansed of all our problems. We parked in the upper lot next to the administration building, breathed in fresh air deeply as we exited the car and rejoicing as we walked to the front entrance, spreading our arms and looking to the sky with thanks and laughing at one another. We, the university and world at large were free.

Our elation became considerably more subdued when we entered the overheated building and breathed in its urethane and burnt dust-tinged air. The reality of the permanence of the university bureaucracy and politics hit us. We had fought so hard and given up parts of our lives over the last four plus months for this?

In the elevator to the third floor, I looked over at Zoltan, grimaced and shrugged. I could see we were lockstep in our thinking.

"Yes," he said, lightly through his usual scowl, "Here we are in cluster fuck city again."

Our mood changed for the better as we entered the president's office where Berger in his *Calypso Too* jeans and a loose knit, pure wool sweater that looked to be from the Greek Isles, Fitz-Hugh in a tan corduroy sport coat with arm patches and Ursula in grey wool pants suit were waiting for us at the conference table all smiles, Ursula's with just a hint of deviousness to it.

We congratulated one another, shaking hands and gripping shoulders and arms and sat down with satisfied grins, looked at each other appreciatively, breathed deep sighs of relief.

Then, Mark said, "Okay, so much for celebration at least for now, we gotta lot to think about and even more to do. Let's go through things now that we're back in business. I'll start.

"The presidential search is now down to its final three candidates."

Fitz-Hugh nodded knowingly.

I looked at Mark inquisitively.

He smiled, "And yes, Greta Hauser is one of them."

As best I could, I tried not to change my neutral expression.

Zoltan, I could see, was doing the same.

"The finalists are coming in for interviews over the next two weeks and then our new president will be selected via the Search Committee's recommendation and the board approval." He paused. "So, that puts a whole lotta things in play.

"Bryan and Ursula, we need from you both an exit plan, a detailed orientation book covering the office of the presidency for our new president and, working with his or her office, a transition plan and calendar that melds with your exit and continuing counsel. Understood?"

"Sure," Bryan shrugged as Ursula took notes on her iPad. "We've been anticipating this."

"Once the announcement is made, I want a three-year goals and strategic plan report from each administration branch which will serve as a separate orientation report.

"One of the first assignments for the new president will be the appointment of a provost, so we need a set of recommendations from you regarding candidates, although we recognize the new president may have his or her ideas about who they wish to select. May be from outside."

"Sure," Bryan responded.

"Now that we're no longer totally distracted, let's get together with the Building Committee and try to accelerate their efforts to recommend our replacing this dinosaur," Berger said as he looked around at our space contemptuously.

"Um-hmmm."

"And do me a favor and send me a full interim update report on our foundation's funding initiatives with the university."

"Of course."

"Finally, let's push Blaylock on getting their technology assessment and recommendations to us. As for their investigation into who the hell hit us up for ransom, I think we know the answer to that question, thankfully, BUT it would be nice if they could figure out where Sammie stuffed my 1.5 million of Bitcoin and how he might've converted it thereafter. I wouldn't mind havin' it back.

Maybe I'll think about contributing it to Sessions to help build more robust systems."

"That would be fabulous, Mark," Fitz-Hugh said with a smile.

Mark turned to Zoltan, "For the record, I'll need a report from you on your research progress over the last months and get Ramis to sign off on it. Okay? I'll give Ramis a call and let him know."

"As you wish, *Commendatore*."

Bryan and Ursula looked at Zoltan, puzzled by his salutation.

I just smiled.

"And, Mr. Berger, sir," Zoltan said, "I think it time you visit my lab, so we can discuss what now seems many years ago."

"Great! Good idea."

Mark turned to me. "As part of this whole deal, in addition to your goals and three-year plan for marketing, communications, PR and branding, I'll need you to initiate with HR a search for a new Director of Communications."

I responded by smiling and said, "Fucking yes!"

Everyone smiled.

My spirits were lifted considerably.

"Anything else?"

"Yeah," I said, "Your interview with Emily Sayzak for a puff piece about your being chairman of Sessions board. Well-timed now."

"Oh yeah. Set it up."

I felt myself grimace, but I had to bring it up. "What do we do about the Kravitz's?"

A deep silence ensued as we looked at one another, and as I expected, all eyes came to rest on me.

"What do you wish to do, Thomas?" Fitz-Hugh asked respectfully.

"Yeah, I don't know, honestly ... Let me write a letter from you expressing our deepest sympathy and regret for Sammie's incarceration and that we stand by the family in continuing to honor Provost Kravitz's memory and offer our support. Empty words, but the best we can do. I'll call Natalie at some point. I'll see whether she'll even want to talk to me."

I did not want to go any further and say what I was thinking, *None of this, Samuel Kravitz's, Lusby's and Powers' deaths and Sammie's being in prison for likely the rest of his life would have happened if not for the disease of your ambition.*

"That sounds right," Fitz-Hugh said.

XXIX

Lunch at the Tribone

TWO WEEKS LATER, Zoltan and I sat in my car, stuck dead stop in a random traffic jam on I-95 under darkened skies and in a renewed onslaught of pouring rain, car exhausts steaming up into the air from those in front of us, all of us with no idea what had caused the stoppage and how long we would be there.

It was the day before the Foundation Association new members conference in Washington, DC and I was to meet for lunch with Berger, Alicia and her father, Gaylord, at Berger's Tribone Hotel where I would be staying.

Mark was flying in this morning. We were getting together in his suite before lunch to catch up with one another. Afterwards he had meetings with his lobbyists and then was flying back to Boston.

Alicia and her father had been working out of the McDonald Family Foundation satellite office for the last two days, visiting with non-profit cause organizations and associations, exploring funding interests for Chicago and possible future grants nationally. Her apartment being one bedroom, she had also put her father up at the Tribone. He was returning to Chicago later in the day, leaving Alicia and I to attend the conference together. *Sound logistical planning,* I thought and smiled.

Since Sammie's incarceration, the national press had had a field day discovering his background, his motivation for his assassination of Powers and his plans to murder other administrators, which had, of course, fanned new flames of conjecture about Provost Kravitz's death and encouraged a host of cockamamie conspiracy theories, the most ridiculous one identifying Sammie as an alien and his drones as mini-UFOs.

Of course, I had received a breathless and giddy call from Emily Sayzak thanking me so profusely for my role in getting her the scoop on Sammie's arrest that I had a terrible vision of finding her at the end of day splayed sensuously and enticingly on the hood of my Bimmer wearing nothing but a ratty, fake fur coat. It took several scotches that evening to get the image to retreat into the dustbin of my subconscious.

Now the media coverage was beginning to fade away with just occasional updates about the glacial progress of the judicial system dealing with Sammie's future trial and further incarceration. At the same time the press was reporting that numerous publishers were after Sammie for a tell-all book revealing the tale of the Drone Assassin, offering six- and seven-figure deals for his cooperation.

Jesus, I thought, *What could I make by going public with everything I know?* Then of course, I would think, *My life and our family are worth a whole lot more than that. Plus, who in the hell would believe me?*

I could only imagine what Natalie, Joan and the family were going through. I had written the letter of condolence from Fitz-Hugh, a letter that, as I had feared, no matter how well-crafted echoed emptiness.

Which of course brought me back to Natalie and Joan and my feeling deep sorrow for them. Yet I could not bring myself to call. What would it accomplish? So, I just regularly beat myself up about not responding to their tragedy but also admitted to myself that I had no intention of doing anything about it, at least for now. Maybe I could persuade Mark to call them.

As Fitz-Hugh and Ursula began to contemplate and plan their departure, Ursula had begun showing up at my office occasionally, unannounced, much to Jo Ann's chagrin, just to talk. Friendly.

About her adoptive family and being close to them again after her move to Washington, about Bryan's potential employment opportunities, all of them quite prominent and distinguished to either head a policy organization or become a senior fellow. We talked about world and national politics, the Sessions presidential search. I responded like I normally would on such occasions by simply listening, offering *pro forma* responses, and reflecting, *Who the hell else does she have to talk to?*

All was now right on the home front. Janet with her practice, Sarah and Jacque increasingly a couple, Tommie immersed with his robotics and our family planning a trip to France with three days in Paris and then a train trip and seven days in the Loire Valley visiting Jacque and his family at their farm and touring chateaus and wineries.

Zoltan turned to me from his semi-reclined position, his kneecaps up above the dashboard, the headrest under him probably between his shoulder blades. "So, tell me about what going on with you and someone else?"

He had hitched a ride so he could visit with Kristina during the conference, take in *Carmen* at the Kennedy Center and then we would return home together afterwards. Time off from his lab.

"Oh, hmmm ... You mean Alicia McDonald? You remember her?"

"Yes. She Blaylock agent. Interview me on Kravitz investigation."

"Well, a lot has changed since then."

I filled him in on Alicia and my relationship, how it had developed over the last year, my trip to Chicago and our new arrangement to see one another at these conferences. I was waiting for his condemnation and disapproval.

"I knew something going on."

"Yeah."

But after thinking about what I had told him, he smiled and shrugged, "How you feel about all this?"

"Well, that's the really odd thing. I keep feeling like I should be ashamed, feel guilty and anxious and I should I guess, but I'm frig-gin' exhilarated. I mean, Alicia, every time I deal with her, I feel my spirits lift and I'm excited and pleased. Does that make any sense or this just a prelude to my going to hell?"

"No. As I have said before, Americans very hung up by this kind of thing. To Europeans it not such a big deal. You think about it, what you have is very good, so much better than mistress who you would have to support, be worried about all the time that she blow your cover, plus because of that she have you by the balls. This deal free and easy and good. Like she tell you, see where it go."

"I can't believe I'm hearing this from you."

"When I not tell truth? You just be sure family number one pri-ority. They precious cargo."

"Yeah, it's funny. Not only does my relationship with Alicia help me cope with what's going on with our family, but it makes see the family in another whole perspective. So often I feel like a fifth wheel with them, just a taken-for-granted moneymaker. Nothing I can do affects Tommie wanting to tear down Tommie Town and build robots, Sarah and Jacque sleeping together, Janet and I kind of co-existing with less and less meaning to our relationship. But what's happening with Alicia somehow allows me to step outside and understand and appreciate our lives or at least have a more even-keeled perspective."

"Ummm ... Beware how much you bullshitting self."

"You think so?"

"Yes. What you say true enough but how much you rationalize infidelity?"

"Aw, shit. I figured you'd say something like that."

"Not just say."

"Yeah. Okay."

"Not that it change anything."

I chose not to respond.

After traffic finally cleared and we reached DC, I dropped Zoltan off at Kristina's near DuPont Circle and headed over to The

Tribone, an august, old-fashioned hotel of Romanesque Revival architecture, pulled up under its canopy. I happily let the valet park my car and the bell hop take my bag to my room in one of suites on the top floor, no more need to have to think about how to fabricate my Sessions trip reimbursement to cover up the valet parking like I had to in my university employment days. I loved my new job.

Mark's room was just down the hall, the President's Suite no less.

When I knocked at his door, there was a bit of a pause, then it swung open revealing a majestic suite, decorated in faux French style with sky blue walls, tapestry rugs, a chandelier over marble tile floors, even a fireplace.

"Howarya?"

"Livin' at the Tribone is easy, huh?"

"Yeah, if you like things overdone."

I walked in and we sat facing one another on blue damask couches with a coffee table in between on which were placed a silver tray and coffee pot, linen napkins, an assortment of pastries, croissants, butter, jams and jellies, which we ignored.

"So, I've done some more research on McDonald. The more I do, the more I like him. Rags to riches story. Hard knocks upbringing, father a fireman, mother a maid, public school education, brilliant, motivated kid, nonetheless. Got a full ride to Dahrtmouth where he was a star basketball center."

Mark smiled, "You know in those days you could be 6'5" and be the tallest guy around. McDonald was known for his sweeping hook shot where, while the ball rolled gracefully off his fingers toward the basket, his unnoticed outflung left arm not so gracefully clobberin' his defender. Hah!

"Originally Piper-Hale was a clothing goods manufacturing pahrtnership co-owned by a college classmate of McDonald's. Guy was an alcoholic, and his pahrtner wasn't much better. Business was about to fail so McDonald bought them out more than a half century ago and used the company as the platform to build what today is Piper-Hale, same name, now a conglomerate."

Given that I knew all this from Alicia, I simply replied, "Interesting."

"Imposing looking motherfucker."

"Yeah, Alicia once told me that his nickname at Piper-Hale, behind his back, is 'The Bird of Prey'."

"Yeah, I can see that."

"Hey, so how'd your interview with Emily Sayzak go?"

"My God, Thomas, what an agile little nubile nymph you hooked me up with. She's not only acrobatic but she's got stamina beyond belief. It was fantastic, my friend."

"I'm so glad I could be of help." *And that it was you banging her bones, not me.* "So, how'd the interview go?"

"Oh, we met in the foundation's office about six one evening – you guys had gone home – and the interview was okay, puff piece kinda questions, had a photographer there, the whole deal. I was impressed. She'd done her homework, knew about how I got started and the various phases of The Mark Berger Companies' development, actually asked some astute questions. With Sessions she focused on my objectives for the university and its global focus, touched lightly, thank God, on my current role during our crisis, the presidential search, etc. Standard stuff I could hit out of the park.

"So, as we're winding up, she admired the painting of *Calypso Too* behind my desk and I said, "Hey, you want to see the boat? I can order in some dinner from Chez Aimee. Oh, she was delighted by that. Called Jean Claude and he fixed up a nice electric candle-lit table and some Dom Perignon on ice and disappeared. We had a charming dinner before retiring to my berth and the fireworks began. Although there's one thing that's kinda weird."

"Yeah?"

"There's this funny, light smell coming from her clothes. Hard to place."

"Like someone barfed a martini mixed with a margarita and a Snickers bar?"

"Yeah, that's it. With maybe some olives thrown in."

"That's hilarious. I spared you her perfume. Told her you were allergic, and it would destroy the interview."

"Good man."

"So, you going to see her again?"

"Sure. When I'm in town. Will have to bulk up on supplements next time. But that's a sacrifice I'm willing to make!"

There was a pause as Mark gazed out his window which in the distance showed the top of the Treasury building.

"So, still unofficial, but Sessions has its new president."

"Oh ..." I felt myself lower my head, stare at the thick tapestry rug under us.

"Yeahhh ... as you thought all along, it's Madam Secretary. The board thinks it's the biggest coup in world history. Me, I won't mind working with her. She can make decisions and the faculty will be suitably respectful, i.e., intimidated," he began to chuckle, "If they wanna live."

"That's not very funny."

"Yeah, you're right."

"Jesus, and they'll put Fitz-Hugh on the board of trustees?"

"Yeah, in all likelihood."

"Man, I'm so glad I'm not working there anymore."

Mark smirked, "I think maybe I wish I could say that too. But here's my take. She's taking this presidency for a lotta reasons but the most ulterior one is to keep a distinguished, high public profile. Her real ambition is off there in the future, at least three years down the line or more."

"You think she wants to run for the United States presidency and Sessions is the perfect platform in the interim to lay the ground-work for that?"

"Egg-zactly. And if that doesn't pan out she can stay at Sessions

or become an ambassador or whatever, depending on the fickle political winds of fate."

"Yeah, makes perfect sense."

"So, in this scenario she has absolutely no interest in fucking
things up by engaging in any spy plan, plus, the new Secretary of
State obviously isn't going to have interest in that either. So, my
guess is, we don't have to worry about that. Bryan too is going to walk
the straight and narrow. It's in his interests to clean up his act in all
sorts of ways, although who knows whether he'll be able to keep it
zipped."

"Man, I don't know about that."

"Neither do I, but it ain't our problem."

"Yeah."

"So, look, go back to your room for about fifteen minutes while I
make a quick call or two, change, etc. Then meet me here and we'll
go to lunch together. I've arranged for a private, small dining room
off the second-floor restaurant."

"Sure."

When I met Mark fifteen minutes later, he had changed into a
well-tailored, obviously very expensive dark grey power suit, dark
red tie with a blue stripe, which made me smile. So Washington,
where everyone of so-called importance overdressed in direct pro-
portion to their insincerity and, in some cases, insecurity. I, of course,
had done the same as best I could via a cheap imitation.

The private dining room place settings were ornate silver and
linen, hotel staff at our beck and call. We were there first and took
our seats at the small, square table. Alicia and Gaylord McDonald
walked in moments later.

Alicia could not have looked more radiant and beautiful, Royal
blue pants suit, white blouse, pearl earrings. Mark turned to me and
whispered. "God damn, she's a knockout."

"I've noticed." I whispered back.

Mark gave me a glance.

Gaylord, as expected, was a friendly but imposing figure, tall, lanky in a heavy, chalk-striped dark blue suit, white-on-white shirt and red patterned tie, swept back thick, light-grey hair going white, large ears, pronounced jawline, a prominent hooked nose, bushy eyebrows and rapacious, penetrating stark blue eyes that looked right through you.

Holy shit, I thought, *The Bird of Prey.*

We stood.

"Gentlemen," he greeted us.

As we sat down and put our napkins on our laps, he spoke to Mark, "Alicia has told me admirably about your new foundation, and I have been following the university's travails over the last year. My God, man, I so admire you for your loyalty and dedication to Sessions, all the while running your multiple enterprises and creating a new foundation. Remarkable."

Mark gave him a nod, "Yeah, it's been a hell of a year. But let me also give you some praise. Your new foundation is off to a great start."

McDonald smiled, "You know, Mark, I spent all these years with a singular, I admit, obsessive focus on building our company. And now I am discovering not only how much I missed, but also that we," he nodded at Alicia, "Can through our philanthropy make an impact on helping our community at least for the present locally and perhaps in the future nationally or even internationally become a better place."

"I hear you," Mark said.

And with that we began a long conversation around our meal, outlining our missions, plans and operations to date, the good, the bad and the ugly, and then discussing ideas around different future interests such as sustainability, improving education, beginning with Chicago where schools had many students with zero proficiency in core subjects, more practical curriculums for higher education involving corporate and non-profit internships, fostering future entrepreneurs, programs Mark was and would be supporting at Sessions.

Before we knew it, the time approached 1:30, signaling that Gaylord and Mark needed to leave for other appointments.

"Hey, okay, we gotta go," Mark told us. "But look, Gaylord, here I am a multi-billionaire, still kinda young or at least I feel that way, but I got no heirs, and it doesn't look like I will have any. But I do have my foundation that could eventually do a lotta good, leave me a decent legacy thanks to Thomas's stewardship of whatever I leave to the foundation or however I fund it while I'm still here to fuck things up."

We chuckled.

"You, on the other hand," Mark continued, "Are more senior to me, but then again you also have your lovely and brilliant daughter to continue your family's legacy. So, to my way of thinking we are in much the same boat. So, I think we should meet say twice yearly and continue in the meantime through Thomas's and Alicia's research to develop our thinking for how to solve some of the bigger problems facing society, civilization even, as time goes on. You agreed?"

"I most certainly do. Let's go forward as you've suggested. I must tell you, I welcome an ally in all this new world to me of philanthropy. I would so much rather have Alicia crafting how our fortune can help others, than ruining her life via inheritance, although through various dynasty trusts and other instruments her mother and she will find themselves well taken care of."

Mark and Gaylord shook one another's hands enthusiastically. Alicia and I gave one another 'victory' glances and smiles.

As we walked back into the main dining room, I checked my phone and saw that Alicia had texted me, 'Check your side pocket. I'd like to show you my apartment, meet me at 6 for dinner. I'm cooking."

I smiled, thought of the many ways one could take that last word, hastily put my phone back in my suit jacket inside pocket, reached into my side pocket and found a slip of paper with her elevator code written on it. When the hell did she put that there? Must have been when we had a quick, collegial hug when we were greeting one another. A small reminder of her former skill set as a private investigator.

XXX

The Apartment

ALICIA'S TWELVE-STORY, modern building was on a side street near the top of Wisconsin Avenue as it rose toward the Washington National Cathedral. My first impression was that the building had a Mies van der Rohe Chicago look to it, which was mildly amusing. My second was that it was very secure: underground parking with a coded security gate, its entry in full view of an unusually capable looking doorman. Retired Marine, Navy Seal?

After I was cleared by the lobby receptionist, I took the elevator to Alicia's top floor apartment using the elevator code she had given me, thinking that in this day and age kidnapping was a real fear, even in the USA.

I was greeted as I stepped from the elevator with the luscious scents of good food being cooked, Alicia stirring a pan in the kitchen to my left.

"My Lord," I commented, "Something smells wonderful."

"Chicken cordon bleu," she told me as she finished stirring, turned the burner down and came out to greet me wearing a pair of tight, faded jeans, a simple white blouse with its tails tied in front, no makeup, her blonde hair in a long ponytail, bouncing as she moved. How was it that she looked as beautiful now in casual clothes as she did earlier in the day?

Her apartment was open, elegant, white walls, vaulted ceiling, straight ahead a long window and an informal living room/dining room, modern artwork, on my right a raised, gas-lit fireplace set in the wall, polished marble surrounding it and forming a bench extension at its base.

We embraced and kissed, her soft, pliable lips and the scent of her taking me away to the point where we it felt as if we could not get enough of each other.

"Whoa," she said, putting a hand gently on my chest and pulling back. "Everything will burn."

"Let it."

"No. There's a nice bottle of Pinot Noir airing there on the counter. Take a seat and have a glass while I finish up. Take a look at the view. It's why even long ago in my freshman year at Georgetown I had to have this place."

"You're not having any wine?"

"Well, not tonight," she smiled.

Hmph? I wondered about that momentarily and then thought no more of it.

I sat on a comfortable bar stool facing the marble counter between the kitchen and the rest of her apartment. Filled a goblet that had been set by the Pinot. Took a first sip. It was first class, went down very easily.

With my glass of wine, I walked over to her window and its view of the neighborhoods descending in the dusk to the university on the right and then to the Potomac River. Streetlights illuminated brick and occasional frame houses, bare trees, broken sidewalks and pavement. House windows lining the streets were yellow gold. The incandescent eerie glow of the university's security lights lit the skies above the campus.

"That is a hell of a view."

"I never get tired of it."

A dining table was set for us nearby, a new candle placed close to the window.

I returned to the kitchen area and sat again, watching Alicia continuing her preparations. I was struck by how much I liked just watching her elegant, athletic movements.

"So, how do you think things went today at our lunch?" I asked her.

"Oh, splendidly," she said, checking on the cordon bleu in the oven and then turning to me. "My father was all charged up. As you can probably tell, he does not do anything halfway. The foundation, I can see, is going to be his new obsession."

"You guys can get along working together?"

"Not in the past, but it won't be a problem now. He's really mellowed, and I feel like now we are becoming a team. Very gratifying. So, what was your impression about Mark's reaction?"

"Much the same. I think the conversation really expanded his horizons. Lord knows what the hell he might come up with beyond what we're doing, but for now we've still got to get Sessions straightened out. Then we'll see what he wants to do."

She turned back, opened a cabinet, and began pulling out a China serving platter and two bowls. "I have a distinct feeling that somewhere in the future we could be stewarding billions of dollars and hiring a bunch of staff to help us."

"The same," I told her. "That is, if Jo Ann can stand it."

She laughed, "Oh yes. You'll have to make her part of the interview process as Ms. Bemis."

"Hell no. No one will ever accept a job there."

"Oh, she would be a wonderful screening device. Anyone who could put up with Ms. Bemis would a worthy hire. Don't you think?'

"Maybe. I don't know. Could always test it out."

"Yes. Could be fun watching them run for the elevator... So, it'll be interesting to see what this conference has to teach us."

"Yeah."

I filled my goblet again and took it out to the table she had set, placed it, lit the candle from a nearby book of matches, then came back and helped her by transferring the scalloped potatoes and a mixed vegetable medley into bowls while she prepared the cordon bleu.

Once we had taken our seats, I held up my goblet and toasted, "To our future!"

We clicked my goblet with her water and began a relaxed and idle conversation. She had finally found an assistant, a very detailed and intelligent recent grad from Northwestern who seemed promising. I told her the backstory behind my hiring Jo Ann with whom she still spoke regularly. Told her about how our vacation plans for France were falling into place, which she was delighted by. And then we talked about the conference, evening plans for next three days. Time passed seamlessly. We finished dinner and cleaned up, leaving her kitchen spotless.

We relaxed for a time on the leather couch facing her fireplace. And began kissing, then made our way into her bedroom, as I expected, immaculate.

Our lovemaking this second time was so much more relaxed and familiar but perhaps its intensity and depth even surpassed our prior experience, which is to say impossibly, ridiculously ecstatic.

Afterwards, as I lay next to Alicia drifting in deep afterglow, she turned on her side and said, "I have some rather complex and joyful news to share with you."

All my alarm bells went off, overlaying my tranquility. "Yeah?"

"I'm pregnant."